"La... ...h's kidnapping wasn't the first on the ranch."

...wrung his hands on the steering wheel.

...'e talking about Cole Colton, Jethro's son?" ...sked.

...'s son," he repeated.

...asped, mortified. "I didn't mean anything by ...t's easy to forget that you're..."

... I'm his son, too? Don't worry. You're not ...nly one."

"I ... n't understand how any parent could choose to ... a child out of their life."

... shrugged. "By now, it wouldn't matter if ...d a change of heart. I'm not sure I could ...e him."

Bef... e she could think better of it, she'd reached acros... and set a hand on his arm. "Of course ...ould."

He c... st his eyes at the spot where they t... t... ocked his gaze with hers...

# COLTON BY BLOOD

BY
MELISSA CUTLER

First published in Great Britain 2013
by Mills & Boon, an imprint of Harlequin (UK) Limited,
Eton House, 18-24 Paradise Road, Richmond, Surrey TW9 1SR

Special thanks and acknowledgement to Melissa Cutler for her contribution to The Coltons of Wyoming miniseries.



ISBN: 978 0 263 90721 6
ebook ISBN: 978 1 472 01503 7

18-0813

Harlequin (UK) policy is to use papers that are natural, renewable and recyclable products and made from wood grown in sustainable forests. The logging and manufacturing processes conform to the legal environmental regulations of the country of origin.

Printed and bound in Spain
by Blackprint CPI, Barcelona

**Melissa Cutler** is a flip-flop-wearing Southern California native living with her husband, two rambunctious kids and two suspicious cats in beautiful San Diego. She divides her time between her dual passions for writing sexy, small-town contemporary romances and edge-of-your-seat romantic suspense. Find out more about Melissa and her books at www.melissacutler.net or drop her a line at cutlermail@yahoo.com.

The book would not have happened without my kids' six amazing grandparents, who opened their houses and their hearts to babysit so I would have time to work. Loutrisha and Don, Skip and Ann, Sue and Denny: thank you, thank you, thank you.

# *Chapter 1*

You can't make peace with a ghost. Kate McCord knew this as fact.

It was one of those secrets of life that no one would tell you and you had to uncover for yourself, like discovering Santa Claus wasn't real. It stuck in Kate's craw, all the truths that nobody saw fit to share. She'd found out the hard way, and not until it was too late, that bankruptcy would not solve your problems, not all men cared if a woman orgasmed and croissants—the real kind, not the ones sold in supermarkets—were nearly a third butter.

And the memories of the people you loved and lost? Well, all they did was haunt.

It was dark in the servant stairwell. A sprawling, fluid darkness that seeped into cracks and corners, and right into Kate's skin. A dessert tray, heavy and ungainly, was balanced on her right hand. Her left hand pressed to the wall, holding her steady as she stood rooted on a stair somewhere between the first and second floors, at least ten steps in either direction to the nearest door. Too great a distance for a woman who was afraid of the dark.

She had no idea how long she'd been waiting for the power to be restored, but it had to have been well over five minutes, perhaps ten if the rising heat and stuffiness were any indication. The watch she wore had a light, but activating it would require her to set the tray down. Not only was the tray too large to balance on a step, but she also wasn't sure she could convince her body to move.

Her pulse pounded all the way to the tips of her fingers and toes. Any second now, Horace or Jared or one of the other ranch hands would get the generator fired up and she'd be safe.

Any second now.

Every so often, distant voices cut through the unbearable silence that had replaced the hum of the air-conditioning system. Footsteps clomped away, fading off. Nobody ventured onto the stairs. All that mattered to the waitstaff was restoring the Colton family to the level of comfort to which they were accustomed. Locating a stranded cook's assistant probably didn't cross anyone's mind.

It would've crossed Faye's mind. She had been Kate's closest friend at Dead River Ranch. In all of Wyoming, really. But Faye was gone, and now the kind old woman was yet another person Kate loved who'd died before their time, only to haunt the shadows of her mind. Another ethereal face in the darkness.

She shivered.

The note she'd hastily stuffed in her pocket crackled. On the tray, the glass dish of bread pudding quivered.

*Steady, Kate. It's only a power outage.*

Maybe if she kept her focus on the pudding, she would survive this ordeal with her sanity intact. She'd spent hours on that dessert, baking the challah loaves, preparing the custard and whiskey sauce. It was a sumptuous creation topped by a pillow of fresh whipped cream. Mr. Colton's favorite sweet, if his frequent requests were any indication.

A boom of great force sounded from nearby. A door slamming or something hitting a wall. A tree falling, perhaps. Fierce windstorms were most likely to blame for the power outage. They'd plagued western Wyoming for more than a week, beating on the ranch house and surrounding wilderness, unrelenting. Sinister.

Another hard truth Kate had discovered for herself was that Mother Nature was the greatest devil of all, an unremorseful murderer. Every time the weather turned nasty, the faces of William and baby Olive—and now Faye—hovered in her mind.

She'd felt so safe at Dead River Ranch, where busy servants and the lazy, entitled family left the lights burning all day and night. The kitchen was her cocoon. A warm, bright, safe place to call home. Until last month.

Poor Faye.

Murdered by the devil's lackey, a hired gun who'd been caught and locked away, though the mastermind behind the murder was still at large. The writer of the note in Kate's pocket. Someone who, she dreaded, remained on the ranch. Maybe someone she spoke to every day or whom she'd helped prepare meals for. Without money or anywhere else to go, her only two choices were to carry on with her job, hoping that law enforcement levied justice onto the devil behind Faye's death before more harm was done, or take matters into her own hands and do what she could to help the investigation.

The note was a testament to her efforts, not that anything had come of the stolen evidence. She'd nearly been caught red-handed tonight in the pantry by Fiona and she could well imagine the repercussions of being caught with evidence she had no business possessing.

On one of the two floors above her, the stairwell door opened with a bang that made Kate gasp. The tray tilted perilously. She felt the shift of weight as the dish of pudding slid, the teacup, too.

Her gasp turned into a cry of panic as she bent her knees and crooked her elbows, willing the tray to level. No, no, no. Not the pudding.

But her correction was too severe, as she overcompensated for her first error. The tray lightened as the entirety of the contents crashed to the stairs in an explosion of shattering glass and clanging silver.

She squeezed her eyes closed and hugged the tray flat against her chest.

Agnes was going to be furious. Delivering dessert to Mr. Colton's sickbed was supposed to be the final task of her sixteen-hour workday. Fiona had asked the favor of her on the sly since they hadn't secured Agnes's permission. Kate wouldn't put it past the bitter-tempered head chef to demand Kate's dismissal, as she'd threatened to do almost daily since Kate took the assistant-cook job four years earlier.

The flicker of a moving flashlight accompanied hushed footsteps on the stairs above. Someone was moving through the dark in her direction. Wordlessly.

A savior or the devil?

Surrounded as she was by broken glass, she wouldn't have been able to move even if she could've convinced her feet to unstick from the ground. Even if she were able to decide if she should climb toward the person whose footsteps were getting louder and closer, or if she should run away.

"Hello?" she whispered.

No answer.

She shuffled her feet backward, unintentionally kicking glass shards with her heels. With a tinkling sound, they tumbled down a step.

Light, either from a candle or flashlight, came into view on the stairs above her. Another door opened, this time from the ground floor, and with the new arrival, more glowing light. The descending footsteps grew louder, the wobbling light brighter.

Kate held her breath, too terrified to move. Damn the darkness, and damn her crippling fear.

With a crack of surging electricity, the lights came on. Kate's relief was tempered by the sight on the landing above her of Mathilda holding a flashlight, her expression as severe as her black, high-collared dress. She held her lips in a pucker that drew attention to the numerous little wrinkles on her upper lip. "What on earth," she said with slow precision.

Strict but fair on the staff under her command, Mathilda had earned her position in the household through decades of devoted service. She ranked above every other member of the staff, yet the glass ceiling between her and the family was ever-present. Kate didn't envy her the loneliness of the position.

A rattle of dishes behind Kate preceded Agnes's grating voice. "Oh, Kate. What in the name of all things holy did you do, child?"

Kate bit her tongue against a retort. A child, she was not. A penniless widow, grieving mother and pastry chef, yes, but not a child. Not for a long time.

Twisting on the spot, she glanced at the dessert tray in Agnes's hands before fixing her gaze on the round woman's spiky, persimmon-red hair. "When the power went out, I slipped and the tray fell. There was nothing I could do."

A lie, but a necessary one. She had never dared confess her fear of the dark to anyone but dear, sweet Faye, and she certainly wasn't going to spill her soul for the Dragon Lady—the whispered nickname some of the staff used for Agnes. Kate didn't have much to call her own anymore, but she still had her pride.

Without a word, Kate knelt and loaded the wreckage onto her tray.

"Look what you've done," Agnes scolded. "What a disaster." With every word, Agnes's voice climbed in both decibel and register. "Careless, is what you are. And where is Fiona?"

Kate opened her mouth, but spotted the note near Mathilda's shoe. It must have fallen out of her pocket when the tray tipped. She reached for it but Mathilda was quicker.

Her heart dropped to her stomach at the sight of Mathilda unfolding the paper.

"Is this what I think it is?" Mathilda asked. Her eyes darted as she read. "How did you…?"

On pure instinct, Kate reached for the paper, but Mathilda lifted it out of arm's reach.

"She looks guilty. What is it?" Agnes asked.

Mathilda looked over Kate's head at Agnes. "It appears to be a copy of the kidnapping-for-hire note from when Mr. Garth's daughter was taken." Returning her focus to Kate, she added, "Where did you get this?"

There was no good answer that excused her misconduct, or at least Kate wasn't clever enough to come up with one on the spot.

The real answer was that she'd brought a tray of sticky buns to the Dead Police Department under the ruse that it was a thank-you from the Colton family. While the officers indulged, Kate rifled through the police file. Then while they washed the sticky syrup from their hands, she'd made a copy. She had no intention of revealing the truth, however. "I can't tell you that, but I swear I didn't mean any harm with it. I thought maybe I'd see something in the note to help the police. Faye was only trying to save a baby from a kidnapper and she died for it. She deserves justice for what happened to her."

"Of course she does, dear. She was a darling woman and we all miss her terribly. I'm sure the police are doing all they can. The Coltons are working closely with them, as am I. There is no need to put yourself at risk unnecessarily." She returned the letter to Kate. "My advice—destroy this before it gets you into trouble."

"Yes, ma'am." She folded the paper and returned it to her pocket.

"Why do you also have a tray, Agnes?" Mathilda's tone was placating.

"Mr. Colton buzzed. He hadn't received his dessert yet and was in quite a state. That Fiona is a lazy one. Makes us all look bad. She probably would've stolen away to eat the sweets herself. Takes advantage, that girl. And you—" She leveled a sneer at Kate. "I have half a mind to fire you both."

Kate set the last manageable shard on the tray and straightened. The remaining debris would require the use of a broom. There was no use defending herself during one of Agnes's tirades. The best course of action was to wait it out in stoic silence.

Mathilda's expression cracked into a smile that didn't quite reach her vibrant blue eyes. "Now, Agnes. It's not the poor girl's fault that the wind knocked a tree onto the power lines."

So she was a poor girl now, as if she was twelve instead of twenty-seven. Kate kicked a tiny shard of teacup with a bit too much oomph.

Glancing at the disturbance, Mathilda continued. "I'm certain there is a perfectly reasonable explanation as to why Kate is doing the task you specifically assigned to Fiona. Isn't that right, Kate?"

"Yes, ma'am. Fiona isn't feeling well tonight, with the new baby on the way, and I offered to help so she could get off her feet."

"That's kind of you."

"Oh, now, Mathilda, you're being too easy on her," Agnes objected. She wagged a finger at Kate. "You know good and well that we can't have the likes of you parading in front of the family in your stained chef smock and—" she flicked a grimace at Kate's neck, where Kate could feel the wisps of hair at her nape sticking to her perspiring skin "—common sweat."

There would be no use in pointing out that she was wearing a jacket, not a smock—and a pristine one at that—or that the air-conditioning unit had shut off along with the lights and Kate was perspiring because she'd been standing in an unventilated shaft for nearly ten minutes.

"And you decided, all on your own," Agnes continued, "that you're good enough to serve not just any Colton, but the head of the household?" She hunched her arms around the fresh tray she'd brought with her, holding it as if Kate's lowly station might taint the precious dish of bread pudding sitting atop it.

This new pudding was from the same batch as the ruined one, but without the whipped cream and whiskey sauce. Agnes had forgotten to add them. Kate squelched a sniff of shock.

From everything Kate knew about Jethro Colton's long list of sins, it was he who wasn't fit to lick her chef clogs, not the other way around. And anyhow, Agnes might think Kate too beneath Mr. Colton's station to serve him like a proper maid, but she would never, *ever,* present him with an incomplete dessert.

She summoned the remnants of her composure. "I thought, with it being so late and with the ranch short on staff, it wouldn't be so bad for me to step in."

Agnes threw an arm up in dramatic disgust. "Wouldn't be so bad? In the name of all things holy, she'll get us all canned."

"Agnes," Mathilda soothed, "of course Kate's face is flushed from working in the heat of the kitchen." She set a supportive hand on Kate's shoulder. "But am I noticing correctly that you changed into a clean smock, dear?"

"A clean jacket, yes, ma'am." Kate's face heated. She loathed being talked down to day in and day out by these women who controlled the flow of life and information at Dead River Ranch. But with no money or family she could turn to, this job was all she had. At least it came with a well-stocked kitchen to work in and a house of people hungry for sweets.

"As you so astutely pointed out, there's no time to waste," Mathilda said to Agnes. "If Mr. Colton doesn't get his dessert in short order, we'll all pay the price for the delay. There's no sense in you traipsing up two flights of stairs to Mr. Colton's quarters, not after the scrumptious meals you slaved all day to prepare." Agnes swelled up like a toad at the saccharine compliment. "Allow Kate to do the work."

*Well, gee. Thanks.* She mashed her lips together and thought about cheesecake. Plain, with a single fresh strawberry sliced on top.

"It would serve you right, Miss High and Mighty. You might as well take over serving Mr. Colton all his meals. If anyone can teach you a lesson about keeping to your rightful place in this house, it would be Jethro Colton."

Mathilda interrupted with a reproachful tsk. "Mind your tone. He's *Mr. Colton* to you."

Agnes's glare cut past Kate and narrowed on Mathilda. "As if you don't know what he's like."

A chorus of chimes, low but distinctive, came through the open ground-level door.

Mathilda gazed at the door, her lips pursed. "What

in the world would someone be thinking, intruding on the family at such a late hour?"

"You're not expecting anyone?" Agnes asked.

"Of course not. Mr. Colton needs his rest. I'm afraid our late-night visitor is going to be sorely disappointed. Excuse me." Holding her long, black skirt out of the way of the spill, Mathilda sidestepped around Agnes's ample form and strode with neat, stiff steps down the stairs and through the door.

"I think I'd like to see who it is myself." Agnes shoved the dessert tray into Kate's hands. "Go on, now, and hurry up. You think you're too good for kitchen work? Fine. From this point forward, Mr. Colton's meals are your responsibility. Maybe he'll have more mercy on you than he does on the rest of us."

Nothing had ever been handed to Levi Colton except his curse of a name.

Not love or prestige, and definitely not money.

In fact, it was a wonder his fingers retained the dexterity and sensitivity needed of a doctor given the succession of backbreaking jobs he'd toiled through to fight for the life he wanted.

For the hundredth time since he'd driven through the opulent gold-and-white entrance gate to Dead River Ranch, he asked himself the same impossible question he'd been asking the whole drive from Salt Lake City.

What the hell was he thinking, coming here?

The reason had seemed so solid that morning when he'd left his apartment. And it had nothing to do with sympathy for Gabriella, who'd burst into the hospital office he shared with the other first-year residents, with her high-end tailored clothes and porcelain features, begging him to return to Dead River Ranch, insisting that he was the key to her poor, dear father's survival.

Return. As if he'd ever been welcomed there before. As if he would've set a toe on Jethro Colton's property even if he'd been invited. He should've never said never because here he was, winding through the ranch land en route to the mansion he'd seen only in pictures.

What the hell was he thinking? Why would he go out of his way, jeopardize his standing at the hospital and place himself in Jethro's line of fire after he'd sworn to never do so again?

"This is my last chance to look into the old man's eyes before he dies," he muttered in reminder as he took a corner too fast.

It was the same answer—the only answer—he'd been able to come up with in the seven days since Gabriella ran from his office in tears, proclaiming, "You're a lot like Dad. Stubborn to the end."

The insult hit its mark. Levi had smarted for days at the comparison, stewing about all the many ways he wasn't like Jethro and cursing Gabriella because she'd made him feel something other than indifference for the Coltons, a state of mind Levi worked diligently to maintain.

But for seven straight nights the usual dreams that haunted him were absent, replaced by his mother's image standing beside Gabriella, both of them chanting that he was the spitting image of Jethro. As bad as him, they'd said, sneering. As corrupt and heartless. Time after time he woke drenched in sweat and breathing hard.

Last night, he'd reached his limit. Hating the way the

dreams and subsequent cold sweat made him feel vulnerable, he'd pushed from the bed and taken a shower without turning on the light. The bathroom fixture was too bright for 3:00 a.m., and besides, the darkness was exciting, as though he was bucking the rules. An explorer luxuriating in an underground waterfall.

The whimsy of it almost erased the vision of his mother from his head. But not quite. The knot in his stomach wouldn't completely ease. He braced his hands against the tile, picturing his mother, wondering how accurate his memory of her was, or if it had morphed over the years into someone more beautiful, less damaged by the world. He'd have to unearth the box of photographs from storage to know for sure.

Standing there in the dark shower, thinking about her and the unsettling dreams, the eeriest feeling crept through him, as if he sensed the presence of his mother and she was trying to tell him something important.

The problem was, Levi didn't believe in ghosts. He was a doctor, for pity's sake. He didn't buy for one second that his mother had returned from beyond the grave to give him a message that he was the spitting image of the man she'd obsessed over until her dying breath. She'd said that very thing repeatedly while he was growing up, and so the dreams shouldn't have gotten to him as profoundly as they had. Just random memories surfacing.

*Except...*

Except he couldn't shake the idea that he needed to prove the lack of resemblance once and for all. He needed to look Jethro in the eye one last time before he died.

Ludicrous because what did he think he'd see in

those eyes besides Jethro's typical arrogance and spite? He supposed regret would be too much to hope for from a man who didn't have a soul. Then again, maybe Levi had come back to Wyoming because he knew it would infuriate Jethro to lie there helpless in a sickbed while Levi took charge.

Hadn't that always been a fantasy of his as a little boy—that his father would need him?

Wincing with bitterness at the memory of the naive, hopeful child he'd been, he crested a ridge and the estate and surrounding pastures came into view. Illuminated by the moon, white fences spread in all directions over the rambling land, dividing it into sections for the livestock.

The house itself rose in the center of the spread in grand design, looming over the grounds in absolute darkness. Not a single light was on anywhere around or inside the main house, but only flickers of brightness behind the drawn curtains—candles or flashlights—as though a power line had been cut.

Given the violent wind, it wasn't an outlandish theory that a falling tree had taken out the ranch's power. In the beams of his headlights, leaves danced and skittered across the circular driveway.

He stepped from the car. A gust of warm, foul-smelling summer wind shoved against the side of his body, flipping up his shirt collar and pelting his cheek with bits of dirt. Those were two things he never missed about Wyoming—the relentless wind and the odor of livestock.

Folding his collar into place, he studied the house. Thick, beige stucco walls with rows of identical windows reached up to the sky like a fortress, impenetrable and impersonal. How could anyone find comfort living in such a monstrosity? A monstrosity for a monster, he supposed.

Gabriella hadn't said if she or either of her two sisters lived here still, but he'd bet they did. He'd bet Jethro kept his children on short leashes—the bastard son excluded, of course.

His old friend hatred crawled into his heart. He loathed that he was still quick to anger about how the old man had treated Levi and his mother. Because anger meant he cared. Why couldn't he go numb about the past like he wanted to? If not numbness, then he'd settle for peace.

Maybe peace would finally come to him when Jethro succumbed to leukemia.

As he watched from the driveway, the place snapped into brightness. Floodlights burst to life, illuminating the driveway in blinding light. Startled, Levi jumped and gripped the car door. His heart hammering, he squinted until his eyes adjusted. Faint cheers, women's voices, erupted on one of the upper floors.

He ducked into the car and popped the trunk, then hauled out his suitcase and medical bag. There weren't any hotels he could stomach staying at in the town of Dead—too many of those bitter memories he hated caring about—and so his only choice besides sleeping in his car was to stay at the ranch. That was, if Jethro allowed him to.

The door was as thick and unwelcoming as the walls. He pushed the doorbell but didn't hear a ring in response. After a few minutes of standing there, second-guessing his choice and asking himself over and over what the hell he was doing there, he raised his fist and knocked.

The door was opened by a severe-looking woman wearing a conservative black dress, her blond hair cut short, utilitarian. "May I help you, sir?"

Levi inhaled deeply. *Here we go....*

# *Chapter 2*

The expression of the woman who'd answered the door remained as unyielding as her posture. Levi cleared his throat. "I apologize for arriving at this hour. I'm here to see Jethro Colton."

She didn't miss a beat. "I'm terribly sorry for any inconvenience, but Mr. Colton is not receiving visitors tonight. Was he expecting you?"

Definitely not. Neither tonight or upon Levi's arrival into the world twenty-seven years ago. "Gabriella Colton, then. Is she here?"

"I'm sorry, sir. It's very late. Who shall I tell the family came calling?"

"I know it's late, ma'am. But you see, my name is Levi Colton, and I'm Jethro's—" He couldn't get the word out.

The woman's eyes widened. Her pale cheeks pinked.

"Oh, my," she whispered, stepping aside. "Do come in, Mr. Colton. Let me call someone to manage your luggage."

He didn't correct her that his title was actually that of Doctor, since he'd graduated from medical school the year before. No need to be a snob about it. He danced around her attempt to take the suitcase handle. "I can manage my own luggage, thanks." His focus skated past the gawking maid to the house beyond. The cavernous entryway dripped with wasteful privilege and smelled like oiled leather and fresh flowers. It was—like the rest of the Coltons were—everything Levi was not.

"You came." His gaze followed the direction of the breathless proclamation up the curve of the grand staircase to Gabriella, less put-together this time with her red hair in a careless ponytail and dressed in a T-shirt and jeans. Behind her stood his other two half sisters, Catherine and Amanda, all three daughters dearest as wide-eyed as the woman who'd answered the door.

Teeth clamped together, gut twisting, he crossed the threshold, moving far enough inside that the door could be closed behind him. "Yes, I came."

Gabriella dropped down a step, then another. "If you'd called, we would've had a room prepared."

He didn't want to admit he'd thrown out the business card she'd left in his office, and he had no other contact numbers. Regardless, not calling ahead had afforded him the opportunity to change his mind at any point during the drive with no one being the wiser. "Sorry to surprise you and make you and your sisters scramble to accommodate me." Too late, he realized the folly in those words. "Really, though, it's only your staff I'm putting out, right? They're the ones I should apologize to."

In the corners of the room and peeking from around the staircase, he glimpsed several people dressed in what he imagined were servant uniforms, watching him. Their faces were curious in the way that mice were curious.

Amanda stepped down until she was level with Gabriella. She was far less fragile-looking than her sister, with tanned coloring and straight, brown hair that curtained around her freckled, disapproving face. "You haven't changed a bit."

He was just like Jethro, he hadn't changed a bit—he was sensing a theme and had pretty much had enough of people slinging judgment at him. But sparring with the gilded Colton daughters was one complication too many for this already-loaded meeting.

Clearly, he'd have to work harder around the Coltons than he usually did to keep a tight noose around his gut-level reactions. No problem. It was his ability to compartmentalize that separated him from his contemporaries as a doctor because there was no place for emotions in medicine. Control of one's feelings was of paramount importance when dealing with patients and making treatment choices. He never wavered in his cool detachment.

He inhaled a sharp breath through his nose. Maybe that was the trick—to think of himself only as a doctor to Jethro, like Gabriella had begged him to be, rather than the unwanted son.

He gripped the handle of his medical bag and held it in front of him in a show of intent. "When was the last time Jethro was examined by a physician?"

"Two weeks ago," Gabriella said, worry clouding her expression. "He won't let a doctor anywhere near him. Not even Mia, the ranch's nurse."

Fantastic. Nonconsenting patients always made for a rollicking good time, especially those who were naturally churlish on their best of days. But he'd come all this way, and he was far too stubborn to quit now. He'd wanted to look into his father's eyes, and by God, he wasn't leaving until he did.

Releasing the handle of his suitcase to leave it for the maid hovering behind him, he let the medical bag swing to his side. "Lead the way. Let's get this over with."

Feeling all eyes in the place on him, from servants to the sisters, he mounted the stairs. On the second level, a trio of people he didn't recognize clustered at the edge of the hallway—a woman who looked to be in her early fifties with bottled-strawberry-blond hair and a body laden with chunky jewelry was flanked by two twenty-somethings sporting the look of overgrown, spoiled children with turned-up noses and permanent frowns. A new wife for Jethro? Were these Levi's stepsiblings?

Turning to ascend the next set of stairs behind the three sisters, he filed the questions away, not sure he cared about the answers. "Is Jethro on any medication?"

"No. He's refused all treatment," Gabriella said in a quavering voice.

With stage-four leukemia, that only gave him a matter of weeks or months to live. "In pain?"

"He'd never admit it."

With Gabriella still leading the way, they stepped onto the third-floor landing, which had been done up like the den of a hunting lodge, posh with overstuffed chairs and wood paneling.

Amanda gestured to the left. “This way.”

It was almost an out-of-body experience, walking over the plush carpet of the hallway. He couldn’t believe where he was or what he was about to do. Being in this house felt substantially less real than his dreams. He was about to see his father for the first time in… How long had it been?

Levi’s last recollection of Jethro was when he was twenty and on a holiday from college. He’d spied Jethro in front of the diner across a road from the supermarket he and his mother were leaving. To Levi’s mortification, his mother had waved and called to Jethro.

Jethro had looked their way—not at them, but through them.

He shook off the memory. “Does he have an appetite?”

Catherine flashed him a weary smile over her shoulder. “Only for junk food he shouldn’t be eating.”

He hated to break it to them, but if Jethro continued to refuse treatment, his diet was immaterial.

“There’s not much we can do for him outside of a hospital. He needs blood transfusions and a marrow transplant as soon as possible.”

“He doesn’t know this but we’ve been looking for a donor. We haven’t found any yet. No one in the family is a match. We’re hoping you—”

“I’ve already checked and I’m not a match, either.” He’d become a registered marrow donor during med school and after Gabriella’s visit had checked his tissue sample against the one Jethro’s physician had entered into the system. Wouldn’t that have been something if Levi could’ve swooped in and saved Jethro’s life?

Catherine nodded, wounded hope in her eyes. “Don’t

tell Dad but we've hired a private investigator to look for Cole. If he's alive—and we have to believe he's out there somewhere—he might be a match, and even if he's not, it would mean so much to Dad to see Cole before he..." Her cheeks hollowed as she fought the welling of despair in her throat.

Cole Colton. Jethro's real son. Unbelievable.

From the open door at the end of the hallway came a shout. "Damn you, a half hour late on dessert! How much time do you think I've got, you little twit?"

Jethro's unmistakable, gravelly voice had a cutting edge and a whole lot of life left in it. A good sign for a patient, even if Levi pitied the poor soul he was berating.

"I'm...I'm sorry," said a woman's meek voice. Another mousy servant, no doubt. Why in the world would all these people put up with Jethro's temper? Either the turnover of staff or their salaries had to be enormous.

Something breakable smashed against the wall inside the room. Bits of white porcelain tumbled onto the hall carpet.

Gabriella, Amanda and Catherine rushed ahead and disappeared through the door.

"Daddy, stop it. It's not her fault the power went out," one of them said, though Levi couldn't tell which.

"Damn it, girl, don't make excuses for the staff. It's unbecoming."

Levi remained in the hall, out of view, taking the opportunity to get a read on the situation he'd be walking into, girding himself to be shouted at. If the boar would snap at his own daughter dearest in front of the help, God only knew the volume he'd reach with Levi.

"She's an amazing cook." Levi recognized Gabriella's voice. "The best. You'd regret firing her, Daddy. Agnes's desserts aren't nearly as good."

"Don't 'Daddy' me. In fact, get out of my room, all three of you." A pause ensued, as though Jethro were catching his breath. "Coming in here, bossing me around, telling me how to treat my staff. The day you put me in the ground you can start pandering to the staff to your bleeding hearts' desire." Another pause and this time Levi could hear the labored breaths. "But I'm not dead yet and my word is still the law around this place. Now shoo!"

The old man kept shouting commands until Amanda, Catherine and Gabriella filed through the door, their cheeks tinged with indignity. Levi averted his gaze. Pretending he hadn't overheard the verbal smackdown seemed like the gentlemanly thing to do, even if he had distinct memories of the daughters dearest when their paths crossed growing up, gawking at him as if he was a circus sideshow freak.

The truth was, he was relieved they were leaving. He didn't think he could stand it for Jethro to berate him in front of the daughters dearest.

"He's not so bad. Please don't let him scare you away. He needs you. We need you," Amanda said. The desperation in her plea caught him off guard.

He looked her way, even more surprised to see the worry and hope in all three women's expressions. They looked like any of the other families he'd spoken to over the years who had sick loved ones, who were banking on him and the other doctors to save the day. The sisters' eyes were tired, their shoulders slumped. If Jethro wasn't allowing doctors or nurses to care for him, then that meant his daughters were shouldering the responsibility on their own.

Something that felt suspiciously like compassion took root inside him. How unnerving.

"Do you want us to stay?" Gabriella asked.

"No, I think it's best if I go in alone. Listen, I can't make any guarantees that he'll let me help him, but I promise not to leave without giving it a good fight."

The sisters crowded near each other, a mix of relief and apprehension in their expressions, looking unsure of what to do next. He was tempted to squeeze their shoulders or hands, do something comforting, like he might for a patient's family. Instead, annoyed at himself for having such a thought, he tightened his grip on the medical bag. "Go and rest. I've got this."

Nodding in resignation, they skulked away, their arms around each other. Levi had always wondered what it would be like to have the support and love of siblings, people to share burdens with, to bolster each other during hard times. It was yet another way the daughters dearest were spoiled.

He returned his attention to the bedroom. Jethro was back to yelling at the mousy girl, demanding an explanation.

"Sir, please." The girl's voice was stronger than before, more determined. "I had to return to the kitchen because the whipped cream and whiskey sauce had been left off."

"Do you think I care about that?" Jethro's shout boomed through the air.

"You should," she squeaked.

Levi cringed. *Bad move, mouse girl.* Even if he did admire her moxie.

"You've got some nerve, talking back to me."

"I'm sorry, sir. It's just that...well, the bread pudding doesn't taste half as good without the toppings."

Despite Levi's anxiety, despite the hate and bitterness swirling around his reunion with Jethro, he couldn't stop his lips from curving up at the edges at the serving girl's explanation. Of all the absurd reactions he could have while standing in the hallway of his dying, estranged father's sickroom, he was smiling.

This girl was no mouse, and for whatever reason, she had a serious passion for bread pudding. Levi liked dessert as much as the next guy, and bread pudding with whiskey sauce and whipped cream sounded pretty flippin' phenomenal, but to argue about it with a person feared by every man, woman and child in Dead, Wyoming? That took guts.

"Pilfering desserts from the kitchen?" Jethro yelled. "Exactly how many reasons do you think I need to fire you?"

"I made it, sir," the girl said. "I'm a pastry chef by trade and I make all the desserts for the ranch. That's how I know this is your favorite."

A pastry chef. That explained a lot. Except for the minor detail of why a chef was working as a serving girl in the middle of Wyoming ranch country. Not for the first time that night, Levi's instincts took over and he inched through the threshold. But he couldn't help himself—he had to know what she looked like.

Rather than a standard bedroom, as he'd been expecting, the door opened to the sitting room of a suite, with the noise and shouting coming from open double doors to his immediate left. Shattered porcelain and glass trailed from the hall door diagonally into the bedroom, where he could see the footboard of a massive dark wood-stained four-poster bed covered by a lush, moss-green quilt.

He crept closer, craning his neck until a careless bun of mocha-brown curls appeared on the far side of the bed. Below the mass of curls was a petite figure in a formfitting chef jacket and black leggings.

Looking at her, one thing became instantly clear. She was in no way a girl, as he'd originally assumed. Curves like those had to belong to a woman. A fit young woman. If only she would turn the slightest bit so he could glimpse her face.

"What's your name, girl?" Jethro asked.

Levi held his inhalation, shocked by how ardently he wanted to know and how grateful he was that the question had been asked.

"Kate, sir. Kate McCord."

Kate. It fit.

As though sensing Levi's eyes on her, she cocked her chin over her shoulder. Long dark lashes swept up and she met his gaze with brown eyes that widened, startled, presumably at the sight of an unexpected stranger lurking in the hall. He held his medical bag in front of him. "Doctor," he mouthed, feeling himself puff up with the kind of stupid, egotistical pride he sometimes lapsed into around attractive women.

She gave a little nod, not impressed. He liked that.

"Listen up, pastry girl," Jethro said, reclaiming her attention. "From now on, I want dessert at every meal, even breakfast. See that it's done."

"Yes, sir."

"And chicken-fried steak and mashed potatoes with extra butter at least once a week. Damn ungrateful daughters think they can force me to go on one of those hippie California rabbit-food diets. They think they run the place now."

"Yes, sir." She looked in Levi's direction again, this time her eyes lingering on his face and not his medical bag.

He held her gaze, unblinking, daring her to look away first. Her lower lip, pink and full and perfect, dropped away from her top lip, revealing a hint of teeth.

"Who are you looking at?" Jethro barked. "Are my daughters still hovering around?"

With no good reason to remain where he was, Levi decided to take a cue from the bold Kate McCord. He raised a foot to step forward and his heart rate picked up speed. He swallowed and reminded himself that the only thing in the room was a man in a bed. A very sick patient who needed his help.

And a pastry chef.

Kate McCord was in the room, too, and as much as Levi hadn't wanted the daughters dearest to sit in on his confrontation with Jethro, he doubly didn't want Kate to witness what was sure to be an ugly display.

Nevertheless, he gripped the bag and made his move, striding in with swift, confident steps the way he would into any other patient's room. This particular patient was sitting, propped with pillows, a tray across his lap, his spoon freezing midway to his mouth as he looked on Levi.

Ignoring Kate's intense scrutiny, Levi nodded. "Jethro."

He couldn't think of anything else to say. At least the word had sounded good, normal. It hadn't showed the adrenaline and apprehension roiling inside him.

The spoon clattered to the tray. Jethro leaned against the pillows. For several long seconds, he just stared.

Levi held steady.

Then Jethro did something wholly unexpected. A wide, hard smile stretched across his face. He picked up the spoon again and scooped a new bite of pudding, but paused before it hit his lips. "Well, well, well. If it isn't Levi Vessey."

And then he dissolved in fits of wheezy laughter.

The Vessey dig didn't sting. Not like it had the first time Jethro refused to acknowledge his paternity aloud, despite the monthly child-support checks he'd discreetly sent to Levi's mom since his birth. A lot of the reason Levi kept the surname after he came of age was as a big fat symbolic middle finger to the old man. "My last name's not Vessey. It's Colton, same as you...Dad." He said that last word like the filthy piece of truth it was, pouring twenty-seven years of hatred into it.

Kate took a sharp breath in through her nose.

Jethro's eyebrows flickered. He rolled the bite of pudding around his mouth behind his still-smiling lips. "I wondered if this day would ever come."

Levi adjusted his legs, squaring up, preparing for battle. "What day is that?"

Jethro stretched his chin up as he swallowed, his eyes glinting with grudging admiration. "You finally grew big enough balls to come after my money."

# Chapter 3

The experience of looking into Jethro's eyes for the first time in more than seven years was nothing like Levi had anticipated, despite having acted out a hundred different scenarios in his head during the drive from Utah to Wyoming.

He hadn't expected to see respect in the man's face. Certainly not respect for the perceived greed Jethro assumed had brought Levi to the ranch. In hindsight, it was a logical conclusion given that all Jethro cared about was money. So, of course he expected the same from those around him. But the only thing Levi had ever felt toward Jethro's fortune was unmitigated disgust.

That belief right there proved he was nothing like his father. Thirty seconds into the confrontation and he'd already achieved his goal of the trip—he'd looked into Jethro's eyes and proven once and for all he was nothing like the man. Mission accomplished. He could leave with a clear conscience and make it to Utah in time for Wednesday's shift at the hospital. And, with any luck, his brain would go back to playing his regularly scheduled nightmares, he thought wryly.

Yet, he recognized the signifiers on Jethro's body of treatable symptoms—sores at the sides of his lips that were a classic mark of anemia, bruising on his arms that blood transfusions would help, and shortness of breath that an oxygen supply and pain meds could regulate. Never mind his promise to Gabriella, Amanda and Catherine that he wouldn't leave without doing all he could for their father, he had a responsibility to himself as a doctor not to turn his back on a gravely ill patient.

And then there was Kate McCord, who'd stood up to Jethro even when his own daughters wouldn't. She didn't belong in this house any more than he did, and if he left Dead River Ranch without finding out her story, he'd always wonder. He moved to the side of the bed next to her. She stepped sideways, making room for him, watching with those big brown eyes that spoke of a keen intelligence. What would it take to get her to crack a smile?

And why did he care?

The foot of the bed afforded plenty of room for Levi's medical bag. He set it there and withdrew a pair of gloves, glancing sideways at Jethro. "You're not allergic to latex, are you?"

"Forget that," Jethro spat. "I want to know how much."

"What are you talking about?" He wanted to add, "Do you mean how much time do you have to live, or are you referring to how much I hate you and everything you stand for?" But he'd never say that in front of their audience of Kate, and never to a patient. It was cathartic enough to think it.

"Name your price for leaving me and my family in peace. That's why you're here, isn't it?"

Levi tugged on the second glove, wiggling his fingers to help with the fit. The latex edge snapped when he released it. "Your family came to me, begging for my help."

Kate's brows wrinkled. "But you said he was your fath—"

Levi cut in before she could say the rest. This wasn't her fight, even if she seemed hell-bent on butting heads with Jethro. "Would you happen to have any more of that bread pudding in the kitchen? It's been a long day and all that talk of whiskey sauce and whipped cream has given me a powerful craving."

As though sloughing off her shock and confusion, she gave her head an exaggerated, slow nod. "Yes, sir. There's plenty."

She started for the door but, acting on impulse, he snagged her sleeve as she passed. "It's not 'sir.' Levi, okay?"

Then it hit him what a foolish mistake he'd made and he yanked his hand away. He should've asked her to call him Dr. Colton, and not only her, but also the daughters dearest as well. The formality would have helped him keep his emotional distance from the ranch and everyone in it. What had gotten into him?

Something about Kate the pastry chef made him want to be Levi, just Levi. Without all the artifice and labels and volatile history. He wanted her to know him. What a disquieting thought.

She looked as though she wanted to protest his request until Jethro cut her off before she'd barely opened her mouth. "Well, go on, then. You're not getting paid to stand around."

With her lips pressed into a determined line, she headed for the door. Levi caught himself watching the swish of her hips as she picked her way over the broken glass, then jerked his gaze to Jethro. "Even though you're too stubborn to admit it, your daughters know you need a doctor. That's why they came to me."

"I'm dying, goddamn it. There ain't nothing a doctor can do to change that." Jethro's voice lacked any hint of sentimentality or fear. He was a man resigned to his fate, though he was flat wrong about what proper medical care could do for his odds of survival and comfort. "And I sure as hell don't need anything from you."

Levi didn't bother to answer yet. Giving Kate time to get out of earshot, he stayed busy digging his stethoscope out of his bag along with a blood-pressure cuff. Slinging the stethoscope around his neck, he strolled to the door. The glass shards crunched and tinkled under the door as he eased it closed. Time to talk to the man in a language he could understand. And he didn't want any witnesses.

With another snap of a glove he pivoted to face down Jethro, who jerked his face away as though he'd been watching Levi and didn't want him to know it. "You didn't answer my question before. Are you allergic to latex?"

Jethro's mouth crinkled in a sneer. "No."

"Good." With several long strides, he was over the old man. He grabbed a fistful of his flannel robe in one hand and punched his other into the pillow near Jethro's ear so he couldn't turn his head away. "Now you listen to me, you rotten excuse for a man, and you listen good. You're the last person in the world I want to help, and I know you don't want me here, either. Now that we've got that covered, you can stop whining about it like a damn child."

It felt good to growl, to let it all out, low and mean. If only it weren't just for show as a means of getting his point across. If only he lacked the conscience keeping him from really letting loose. When he was a boy, he fantasized about knocking out Jethro with a punch, kicking him in the ribs, making it hurt.

Then he grew up and realized that violence was Jethro's way, not his. Levi was a doctor, a healer. He'd never hurt anyone, least of all the cancer-crippled man his father was today, the dying patient with a gaunt face and a grizzled, graying beard who futilely shoved at Levi's arms, his movements weak and strained.

Levi's grip on his robe wasn't hard at all, since leukemia patients often suffered excruciating joint pain and skin tenderness, but even still, Jethro couldn't throw him off.

"Unhand me..." He stopped, overcome by several shallow breaths. "Before I call ranch security." He wrinkled his nose in a look that might have been intimidating if he hadn't been so sickly. The movement launched a trail of blood trickling from his right nostril.

A typical leukemia-related nosebleed. Jethro needed oxygen and a blood transfusion as soon as possible. Morphine would help, too, both with the pain and shortness of breath. Forcing himself to stay in character, Levi let out a hard grunt of disapproval. "Since when do you call on other people to save you? Jethro Colton doesn't need anybody's help, isn't that what you said?"

Jethro licked at the blood, smearing it over his upper lip. "Screw you. You've been nothing but a thorn in my side since the day that manipulative hussy told me she was pregnant."

Jethro paused to draw breath, and just like that, with the insult to Levi's mother, the show Levi was putting on became real. His mouth went dry, and his muscles tightened along with his jaw.

But Jethro wasn't done. "Only God knows how many men she spread her legs for so she could get at my money. You're lucky I couldn't be bothered to protest the paternity."

Rage exploded in Levi like a cloud of poison. How dare he.

How dare Jethro insult the woman who'd loved him her whole life—no, she'd worshipped him. Whatever love and caring she'd had left over she'd given to Levi, and while it hadn't been much, it had gotten him through until he could take care of himself. She'd died with a photograph of Jethro in a locket around her neck, and he repaid her loyalty by calling her, in so many words, a whore.

Levi twisted the flannel in his grip, his skin sweating in the gloves. The hand fisted in the pillow trembled with restrained aggression. "I want to hear you say it. Out loud. I want you to admit, for once in your life, that you're my father."

Jethro bared clenched teeth and growled, "What good would that do you?"

Hovering over the bed, Levi sucked in air through flared nostrils, more enraged than he'd ever been in his life. Even more than the night he'd stormed out of Dead after his mother's funeral, cursing the town of his birth and everyone in it, vowing never to return.

Then it hit him. Jethro was right.

What good would it do? Both men knew the truth, so why did he need to hear it aloud? Why couldn't he keep his emotions under control? He opened his hands and stumbled out of the bedroom and into the sitting room, looking anywhere and everywhere except at Jethro's cold eyes.

For the first time, he processed his surroundings. The suite was larger than Levi's entire apartment, and with more furniture, too, all outfitted in hues of rich greens and gold, as well as espresso-stained wood that lent a cozy, masculine feel to the space. Far less opulent than the rest of the house, it looked as if it belonged to a man of means, but one who appreciated simple comfort. Levi would've never guessed that side of Jethro's personality.

A massive stone fireplace, sitting cold and empty, formed the focal point of a sitting area buffered on both sides by crowded bookshelves. Levi walked to it. Books were like a magnet to him, his mom used to say, pride in her voice. In the wake of Jethro's insults, the memory sent a pulse of pain through his heart.

He scanned the books' spines, not reading the titles but simply taking comfort that they were there. He'd promised the daughters dearest that he wouldn't leave without a fight. Time to go one last round in the ring tonight. If it didn't work, he'd return in the morning and give it another shot.

Eyes fixed on the red and brown leather book spines, he made fists, stretching the latex gloves, then shook out his hands. "Your daughters are worried about you," he said loud enough for Jethro to hear in the adjacent room.

"They're like a bunch of hens." The words came out strained and were followed by a lengthy pause. "Clucking around a chicken yard." Another pause. "Making noise but not doing any good."

The labored breathing, which had gotten measurably worse in the past few minutes, helped Levi focus on what mattered. He was a doctor, and if he couldn't convince his patient to take immediate, drastic measures, his father would die. Painfully and soon.

Without meeting Jethro's stare, he returned to the room. From his medical bag, he withdrew a blunt-tipped oral syringe and morphine he'd picked up at the hospital pharmacy on his way out of town as a just-in-case addition to his medical supplies.

"Whatever that is—" breath "—I'm not taking it."

Levi measured a dosage, then walked to the bed and met Jethro's hard stare. "Open your mouth."

"Go to hell."

"Don't worry, this isn't going to add any time to your life. I realize how averse you are to that. This is for your pain and shortness of breath."

Jethro used the crumpled tissue he'd been clutching to dab at the blood still trickling from his nose. "I would've thought you'd want me to feel as much pain as possible."

For a lot of his life, yes. But not anymore. "I'm a doctor. We never want anybody to be in pain. It's in the job description." He swiped a fresh tissue from the box and blotted at the blood Jethro had missed.

Miracles of miracles, he let him.

"I'm not changing my will to include you...if that's

what you expect out of all of this." His eyes were still mean and hard, but he sat passively and allowed the blood to be mopped. "You're not getting a dime from me or my estate."

Levi narrowed his eyes, nodding. "You know what? I never thought you and I would agree on anything, but I guess I was wrong. You don't want me to have any of the Colton fortune and I don't want it, either. Forget about a dime—I wouldn't accept a cent of your money. The less I have to do with you, the better. If you so much as attempt to write me into your will, I'll make you rue the day." He held the syringe toward Jethro's mouth. "Stop acting a fool and open up."

Kate descended the stairs as fast as a rabbit, the memory of the blackout still fresh in her mind. Someone had been through to clean up the glass and spilled food between the first and second floors, leaving behind only a lingering dampness.

When she turned the corner for the final set of stairs, she saw a crowd gathered in the staff dining room. Most of the staff were watching the wall-mounted television intently. Some of the younger maids, as well as the other kitchen assistants, Jenny and Liz, gabbed over steaming mugs of tea. Mathilda sat at her desk in an alcove along the window, writing in a ledger.

Kate wasn't at an angle to see the TV screen, but the drone of a woman's stoic voice told her they were watching the news. She entered the room to see what news story had captured their interest. The screen showed a scene of darkness and fire. Under it, the headline Brush Fires Sweep Western Wyoming.

The same reporter Kate had heard on the stairs continued in a voice-over. "The brush fire, located in a remote wilderness area in the western region of the state, was reported earlier today and has burned at least 6,500 acres, with no containment in sight as wind gusts topping twenty miles per hour continue to fan the flames."

Kate's throat tightened. Was there a word for people who feared Mother Nature? *Weatherphobic,* perhaps? She couldn't possibly be the only one out there who saw what a cold-blooded killer the weather could be.

She touched the shoulder of Dylan Frick, the ranch's best wrangler. Faye was his mom and he'd taken her death harder than any of them, though he tried not to show it. "How close is the fire?"

Dylan angled his chin in her direction, but didn't take his eyes off the screen. "Seventy miles north of Dead, but the wind's pushing it away from us."

Thank goodness. She loosened her grip on the tray she was holding.

Misty—who'd been hired two weeks earlier and already held the dubious honor of being only slightly less grating on Kate's nerves than Agnes—leaped to her feet and rushed to Kate's side. "Forget about the fire," Misty said. "You're the one with the real news."

A few heads turned at the disturbance, and before she knew it, Kate was surrounded by people.

Jenny jumped to her feet, tossing her straight, brown hair. She was only a couple of years younger than Kate, but even though the two women had worked together for two years, Kate didn't like her any more than on Jenny's first day of work, when she'd shown up in a miniskirt and platform wedge sandals, letting everyone know loud and clear exactly which of her attributes convinced Mr. Colton to hire her. "Is it true? Is he here?"

Kate wasn't prepared to reduce Levi to gossip fodder. "What do you mean?"

Jenny scooped her index finger up through the air toward the stairs as though she was gesturing to the upper floors. "He who shall not be named. Mr. Colton's *other* son. Is he up there?"

Mathilda cleared her throat.

Kate sealed her lips. She couldn't afford to land herself into further trouble with Mathilda and, anyhow, she didn't have time for gossip, not with another bread pudding to deliver. She sidestepped the gaggle of people clamoring around her and made a beeline through the short hall to the kitchen. Rather than let her go about her business in peace, though, they followed her in.

Agnes looked up from the pot she was drying. "What is this, a party? Out of my kitchen, all of you."

"We're only trying to help Kate," Misty said in a cloying tone before her eyes turned cunning and she added, "And get the scoop on Levi Colton."

Silent, Agnes went back to work. Apparently she wanted the scoop on Levi, too.

Blowing a rogue curl of hair from her face, Kate marched to the prep counter, knowing it was no use to fight the inevitable. She was trapped.

"He's single, isn't he? You didn't see a ring, right?" Jenny asked with an enthusiasm that showed how eager she was to find a Prince Charming to whisk her off her feet and away from her life as a maid.

"I didn't see a ring, no." Protectiveness flared to life inside Kate. She didn't like the idea of Jenny pushing her ample charms on Levi, not when he was coping with his father's terminal illness—and his cruel words, for that matter.

"A young, hot, available Colton man doesn't come around but once in a generation. I think I'm in love," Misty said, fake swooning over the counter.

Clamping her mouth closed lest she say something regretful, Kate grabbed a dish towel and shined up the tray. Contrary to Misty's assessment, Levi wasn't the first available Colton male in recent history. Mr. Colton had been available more than once during his life—quite a few times, actually, for both new wives and new mistresses alike—but it would've been untoward to mention it. Misty's, Jenny's and Liz's glares bored holes into her back.

"I've never heard talk about any son of Mr. Colton's besides baby Cole," Kate said. "How did you three find out about him?"

"I heard Gabby and Amanda talking last week," Misty said.

"That's Miss Gabby and Miss Amanda to you," Agnes called from across the room.

Misty rolled her eyes. "While I was changing Miss Gabby's sheets, she said he was a doctor. Is it true?"

Kate bit the insides of her cheeks, realizing there was no graceful way to shield their new visitor from the staff's curiosity. Even if she didn't share what she knew, they'd find out soon enough from another source. "Yes, a doctor. That's what he said."

She pushed past the girls and opened the refrigerator, taking out the whiskey sauce, a carton of heavy cream and a serving of bread pudding. After a split-second deliberation, she snagged a second dish of pudding in case Mr. Colton wanted seconds.

Jenny hummed her appreciation, as if a doctor were a rarefied prize indeed. "What does he look like? I only saw the side of him, but…" She bit her bottom lip, her eyes glittering. "It was a fine side, if I do say so myself."

Misty bumped shoulders with Jenny. "Are you talking about his backside? Because that's what I was looking at while he climbed the stairs." She capped off the declaration with a catlike stretch of her spine.

Although Kate's frustration was mounting, in that Levi was being spoken of as if all that mattered were his looks, bank account and last name, she was no innocent angel. Oh, she'd noticed him, all right.

It had been impossible not to take note of his considerable attributes, what with the way he'd practically sucked the air from Jethro's bedroom with his presence and intensity of spirit. His body took up all the space, so much so that she'd found herself torn between wanting to flatten against the wall and drawing nearer to the magnetism emanating from those thick-lash-rimmed hazel eyes. The way he'd locked his gaze on her had left her as flustered as his unexpected declaration that Jethro was his father had.

After William's death, she'd come to grips with the hard truth that she had no more love to give, but she was still a woman in her prime, with all the hot-blooded desires of one, and so could forgive herself for admiring a fine-looking man when one crossed her path. The difference between her and Jenny or Misty was that Kate wasn't looking for a man to save her. Not anymore.

"I bet he's after Mr. Colton's money. That's what his mother always wanted," Agnes muttered as though she were talking to herself.

Misty, Jenny and Liz exchanged looks of intrigue. Even Kate's ears perked up, but she couldn't help it. She was hungry for details about Levi, what happened in his life that had made him such a force of intensity and how the bad blood between him and Mr. Colton began.

Misty scrambled around the center island and across the room to Agnes, with Jenny and Liz on her tail. "What do you know about his mother?"

"A trailer-trash druggie is what she was," Agnes said.

Kate's heart sank. If that were true, then no wonder Levi carried himself as though he had a cross to bear. She poured whipping cream in the mixing bowl. Once the loud motor of the mixer kicked in, she found herself scooting nearer to the gossipers to hear better.

"I remember when she came around the ranch—must have been near-abouts thirty years ago. Eileen Vessey was her name. A wisp of a woman, skin and bones." Agnes had abandoned her dish-drying to put on a full storytelling show for her rapt audience. She leaned against the counter, bracing her hands against it, as wind gusts rattled the window behind her and shook the old oak tree outside. It shivered under the moonlight, its branches scraping the windowpane.

"She stormed straight into the house," Agnes continued, "hollering for Mr. Colton to present himself like she was a wronged woman, and when security came to drag her away, she started crying about how Mr. Colton was the father of her baby."

"Was he?" Jenny breathed.

Agnes twisted the drying towel in her hands. Jenny, Misty and Liz leaned closer. In the doorway, a group had gathered. Everyone, it seemed, was eager to hear the salacious tale. "He was a skirt-chaser, no doubt, but to lower himself to the likes of Eileen Vessey would've been unheard of. He denied it, of course, but until her dying breath, that's what she swore."

Kate ached for Levi. The truth about whether or not Mr. Colton was Levi's father didn't matter because Kate had looked in Levi's eyes and could see he believed it with all his heart.

She turned from Agnes and her story to finish preparing the pudding. It was all she had to offer Levi for comfort tonight, but she knew that sometimes a sweet treat made with love could be enough to lighten a heavy heart, at least for a little while.

"What happened to Eileen Vessey?" Liz asked Agnes.

"That's right—you weren't working here yet when she passed to the other side. It must have been six or seven years ago. It was a big brouhaha." Agnes sounded all too cheery.

"A poor soul's death before her time isn't a brouhaha. It's a tragedy," Kate said.

"Who made you the morality police? Some say it was heartbreak that killed her because she never stopped loving Mr. Colton. But I say that's a pile of manure. There was no love in that woman's heart, never was. The drugs is all she cared about. When I went to town, I used to see her walking the roads or stumbling out of bars, and Levi, when he was a little boy, all alone, playing with leaves and sticks in the gutter like a filthy street rat. If he had Colton blood in him, there's no way Mr. Colton would've stood for it. Even if the boy was nothing but a bastard."

Kate startled at the ugly word, dropping the pan of whiskey sauce to the counter with a clang. Nobody challenged Agnes except Mathilda, but Kate had had enough. "Don't call him that."

The eyes of Agnes's audience all turned to Kate. Someone in the cluster by the door snickered.

Agnes's brows raised. She sauntered Kate's way like a school bully would approach a scrawny new kid. "What are you up to?" She banged the handle of her spoon on the mixing bowl. "Making yourself an end-of-the-day treat at the Coltons' expense? Wouldn't Mathilda love to hear that."

Kate cleared her throat. "No. I'm preparing a second helping for Mr. Colton and another for—" She nearly called Levi by his first name. The staff would have had a field day with that one. "For Dr. Colton." She drizzled whiskey sauce over the tops of the now-heated puddings.

"Feeling a bit big for your britches for being nothing but a cook's assistant, aren't you, girl? First the kidnapping letter and now this. You'd better watch your impertinence before you get yourself tossed out of this place."

"What about the kidnapping letter?" Jenny asked.

"Kate, here, fancies herself a detective," Agnes said. "She's trying to catch whoever sent the letter to Duke last month offering to pay him to kidnap the baby. She found a copy of the letter, God knows how."

Kate's cheeks burned. She looked inside herself, but couldn't muster a response, she was so infuriated. So much for her secret mission. She gripped the saucepan handle and drew herself up tall, then studied the faces of the people in the room. None of them would she take for the mastermind. They were her friends and colleagues. But it still sat uncomfortably with her that the information was out in the open.

She turned her back on Agnes and spooned pillows of cream over both dishes of pudding. If she'd been alone, she would've taken a moment to enjoy the beautiful sight of cream melting into the edges of the custard-saturated bread, but as it was, she couldn't wait to get out of the kitchen. After a few attempts, she finally found her voice. "I was only trying to help Faye. She didn't deserve to die."

Her gaze automatically went to Dylan, who stood behind the rest of the crowd, his hand gripping the elbow of the opposite arm and a stoic expression on his dark features. Over the past four years, he'd become like a brother to her, accepting her in a way her own brother couldn't. Dylan had shared his mom with Kate and she'd be forever grateful to him.

She hated the possibility that the mention of Faye now would feel to him like the ripping off of a freshly set scab. Yet she owed it to him, as much as to Faye, to do everything she could to help catch the mastermind behind her dear friend's death.

"It's okay, Kate," Liz said. "We all know how close you and Faye were. No one thinks worse of you for wanting to bring peace to her spirit."

Kate nodded, her heart heavy anew.

Agnes grunted, as if she had no patience for their grief. "And you're so full of yourself that you think you can identify the letter writer when the police haven't been able to do it? You barely ever leave the walls of this home, so now you expect me to believe you're going to go traipsing around town looking for a criminal?"

"Unless she thinks it's someone here on the ranch," Misty said.

A murmur rippled through the crowd. Kate smashed her lips together, wondering how the conversation had gotten out of control so fast.

"That's it, isn't it?" said Agnes. "You think one of us is guilty, don't you?"

With fingers that trembled with adrenaline and tension, Kate picked up the pace on the dessert prep. "I never said that."

"You didn't have to. But let me remind you that fools who stick their noses where they don't belong are likely to get them cut off."

"Oh, now, Agnes. Don't be so hard on Kate. If she wants to play like she's Sherlock Holmes, let her." Misty's snippy voice had a singsong quality that made Kate want to lob a spoonful of whipped cream in her direction. "We need her here to keep an eye on Dr. Colton and report back. I, for one, am dying to know what he's doing here and whether or not Mr. Colton is planning to make him one of his heirs—if he hasn't done so already. Maybe she'll solve both the Faye and Dr. Colton mysteries."

As if Kate would ever stoop so low as to spy and gossip on the family. She stuck the whipped-cream spoon in her mouth to keep from giving Misty and Agnes and the rest of them a piece of her mind. That hadn't gone so well the first time. She arranged the desserts and spoons on the tray, then sprinkled on the finishing touch of a cinnamon, sugar and nutmeg blend.

"I bet he wants to see for himself if the rumor's true that the SOB is dying," said one of the men gathered in the door.

"Or maybe revenge," said another. Uncomfortable laughter arose.

"That is enough." Mathilda's scolding voice preceded her appearance. She pushed through the crowd. "Have you all forgotten who's paying your salaries? Hmm?

You will not speak about the master of this house with anything other than deference. Now, you must all have something to do that is a better use of your time or I will be happy to assist you in discovering such a thing."

The crowd dispersed, heads down. Liz and Jenny tossed off a line about turning in for the night and disappeared up the stairs. Dylan wondered aloud about the wildfire and wandered toward the staff dining room. Only Agnes, Mathilda, Kate and Misty remained.

Kate set the spoon she'd sampled whipped cream with into the sink. Under Mathilda's questioning gaze, she gathered the tray in her arms. "Dr. Colton asked for dessert," she said by way of explanation.

Mathilda offered a brittle smile. "Then you'd better make haste."

"I'll wait up to show Dr. Colton to the guest suite when he's ready," Misty said with a swish of her skirt.

Eyes straight ahead, Kate breezed past Mathilda, aiming for the stairs and trying not to show any hint of emotion. Which was tough because it was far too easy to imagine the vigor with which Misty planned to throw herself at Levi once she had him trapped in the guest room. Being none of her business, the thought shouldn't have bothered Kate, except that it did.

It bothered her a great deal, actually. Because what if Levi responded to her advances? She'd wager he wasn't the kind of man to normally be so careless with his affections, but people did all sorts of things that were wrong for them when they were stressed or looking for escape.

Behind her, she heard Mathilda's response. "Thank you for the offer, Misty, but—" Kate froze, one foot on the bottom stair "—since Kate will already be in service, she can show him to his suite."

She sucked her lips, reining in her relief before answering, "Yes, ma'am."

But as she climbed loop after loop of stairs to the third floor, a new problem occurred to her. She'd been quite certain what Misty would do if left alone with Levi, but faced with the same situation, she had no idea how to act. It was exhilarating enough to think of seeing him again in a couple of minutes, and the thought of him savoring the dessert she'd created sent a thrill coursing through her.

But the idea of being alone with him? It wasn't excitement or fear that had her pulse racing, but the thought that maybe he'd want to be alone with her, too.

And that was a terrifying prospect indeed.

She rounded the top flight of stairs and caught movement out of the corner of her eye.

A figure emerged from the shadow near the third-level door. "Boo."

Kate startled, gasping, and stumbled, rattling her tray. "Jenny, you scared me half to death."

Jenny shrugged and descended the stairs to the landing where Kate was standing. "I want to see that kidnapping-for-hire note. Give it to me."

"It's none of your business, and, anyway, I don't have it on me."

"Yes, you do."

And before Kate knew what was happening, Jenny was frisking her. With the unwieldy tray and her back against the wall, there was little she could do to defend herself from the assault. "Hey!"

She attempted a kick at Jenny's shin, but she was already dancing out of range, waving the note.

"Aha." Jenny went silent, reading the note.

Kate set the tray down before she upended her second one of the night and scrambled up the stairs after Jenny.

Jenny jerked the paper out of her reach. "How did you get this?"

She lunged for the note again. "Like I would tell you."

Jenny danced around her, then bounded down the stairs, stopping just shy of Kate's tray. She slid the side of her shoe against the tray and scooted it a few inches over the edge of the landing.

Kate stopped her approach and waved her hands in front of her. "Not the tray. Please."

"Don't come any closer."

Kate stood still, jaw clenched. She'd always known Jenny was a manipulative wench, but had no idea how coldhearted she could be. "What do you want from me?"

Jenny folded the note, then stuck it in her bra. "Nothing anymore. Since you haven't been able to come up with any clues, I think I should give it a try. Maybe I'll find something in this note I can give to the police. Mr. Colton might even give me a reward."

Kate was so mad she could barely breathe. "I had no idea how greedy and shallow you were."

"This isn't greed, honey. This is self-preservation. I learned the hard way that nobody in this world is going to give you a damn thing. You've got to take it for yourself—and that's exactly what I aim to do." She patted her bra, then stepped around the tray and headed down the stairs. “You’d better get the good doctor his dessert before it gets cold. You wouldn’t want it to spoil.”

# Chapter 4

Levi stood in the second-floor suite that Kate had escorted him to four hours earlier. She'd hovered just inside the door, nervous, even after he'd praised her bread pudding all the way from Jethro's third-floor suite. Even after he'd invited her to sit because he had questions about the house and the people in it that he knew she'd answer without artifice.

After the first round of basic questions, Kate's shoulders had finally relaxed a smidgen and she'd no longer looked as if she were ready to bound away like a frightened gazelle. From her, Levi discovered that all three daughters dearest did indeed call the ranch home, that Gabriella was engaged to a man named Trevor, who was the head of ranch security, and that Amanda was the ranch veterinarian and the single mom of a four-month-old daughter. Jethro must have blown his top when he found out one of his precious, perfect children was having a baby out of wedlock.

While that news had sunk in, Levi had poured Kate a glass of water from a pitcher of paper-thin china and maneuvered her by the shoulders to the desk chair, a stiff-backed ergonomically incorrect design that was probably worth thousands.

According to Kate's answers during his second round of questions, the woman and young adults who'd watched him from the second-floor hall were Jethro's latest ex-wife, Darla, and her two kids, Trip and Tawny. What they were doing living in the house even though Darla and Jethro had divorced, Kate had no idea. She'd said that while flicking glances at the door, so Levi figured she was worried about being overheard and that there was far more to the story than she was at liberty to discuss.

He didn't want her to get in trouble for lingering in his room or talking out of turn, so he'd let her go after that. The problem was, when she'd left, she'd taken all the warmth in the suite with her. For a long time, Levi stood in the center of the sitting room listening to the whistle of wind gusts outside and the tick of the face clock above the mantel. Alone for the first time since arriving at Dead River Ranch, his brain decided it was time to process the events of the day, and despite the physical exhaustion of a long road trip and grueling night, he couldn't get his mind to quiet down.

The frustrating part was he hadn't reached any conclusions or settled any issues in his mind. He kept replaying the same moments over and over, like a car stuck in sand with its wheels revolving but not going anywhere.

The suite had the same setup as Jethro's but on a smaller scale, and without any of the larger room's touches of comfort. Showy was what it was. Showy and sterile. The ornately carved wooden four-poster bed was topped by a silk brocade spread that matched the drapes. The dark hardwood floor in both the bedroom and sitting room was shiny and cold. The fireplace was marble and, perhaps most disappointing of all, was not buffered by bookshelves but only a spindly-legged sofa and a matching spindly-legged table that looked as if it couldn't hold more weight than a glass of water.

No books, no personal touches, no imperfections. It smelled and looked as nondescript as an upscale hotel. About a million miles outside his comfort zone.

He hated it. The poshness, the lack of a comfortable mess, the fact that it all belonged to Jethro.

After a shower, he stole another glance at the bed then sank his hands into the silk bedspread, reaffirming his conviction that he'd never be relaxed enough to fall asleep in it. He didn't want to live like the Coltons of Dead River Ranch, not even temporarily.

How many servants had been roused from their evening rest to prepare the suite? Their night disrupted for a stranger who'd arrived unexpectedly. A pang of regret had him frowning. He'd have to be more attentive about respecting the staff. But though he was sorry for the obvious effort put into readying the suite, he needed a new room that was better suited to him.

Two a.m. was too late for that, but he could still go exploring. At this late hour, the house would be quiet enough that he could get his bearings in peace. He had a feeling that come the morning he'd be under the careful scrutiny of both the Colton family and the staff. Good thing he'd be gone most of the day filling Jethro's prescriptions and renting an oxygen tank.

Barefoot and dressed in nylon workout pants and a white T-shirt, he stuck his head into the hall to make sure the coast was clear. The space glowed with soft blue light from intermittent night-lights plugged into the outlets near the ground.

Most of the doors on the second-floor wing where his assigned suite was located were closed. He imagined they belonged to the daughters dearest or perhaps Jethro's ex and her kids.

There was one door that caught his interest, though. A strip of police tape was strung across it. A crime scene?

The best course of action would probably be to ignore that door in favor of exploring downstairs, but he couldn't stem his curiosity. He turned the knob, then pushed it open until he could stick his face in enough to tell it was vacant. Not in his wildest imagination did he think he was disturbing a real crime scene.

He opened the door the rest of the way. Enough light from the hall spilled in that he could see it wasn't a bedroom but a nursery, complete with an empty crib, changing table, rocking chair and plush baby toys. A nursery blocked off by police tape. A niggling unease crept up his spine. The only baby he knew of that lived in the house was Amanda's daughter, but Kate hadn't made mention of anything bad happening to her.

He pressed his belly into the police tape, inching forward and craning his neck. His toes curled over the lip of the hall carpet. Surprised, he lifted his foot and looked down. Bare plywood.

What the hell…

Reaching around, he groped for the light switch and flicked it on, staying in the hallway. If this was a crime scene, the last thing he wanted to do was compromise evidence. The carpet and padding underneath had been cut away in a wide, jagged circle from the center of the floor. Much of the exposed plywood was stained a dark brown. Blood-brown.

Whoever's blood it was, enough had been spilled to make the injury potentially fatal. Especially as far into the country as the ranch was. Blood spatter on the wall confirmed Levi's sinking suspicion—this nursery wasn't merely the site of a traumatic injury, but of a fast, gruesome death.

Something hard poked into his kidney. Surprise wrenched a noise like a yelp from Levi's throat. He tried to turn, but a hand on his shoulder pinned him straight.

"Don't move. You're on the business end of my gun and I'm not afraid to use it." It was a man's commanding voice.

Levi kept his hands in plain sight. His heart pounded in his ears, even though the voice sounded as if it belonged to the police rather than a killer returning to the scene of the crime. Been a while since he'd had a gun pulled on him. It'd happened a few times when he was a kid when his mom's dealers or friends got riled, then once in med school by a junkie looking for a fix. It never got easier to accept.

Maybe this was Gabriella's fiancé, the ranch security guy. He dug through his mental files in search of the name Kate had told him. "Trevor, is it? I'm Levi Colton. I got in tonight and was having a look around."

The hand on his shoulder loosened. The gun's muzzle left his back. Levi tried to relax.

A tall, dark-haired man came around to Levi's side, his gun lowered. "Strange time and place to be snooping around."

Levi turned to face him. "I couldn't sleep. And the police tape caught my attention." He held his hand out in offering. "Like I said, I'm Levi."

"Trevor Garth." He transferred the handgun to his pocket and shook Levi's hand. "Gabriella told me you were here, but we've had some problems on the ranch and there's no harm in being too careful. Sorry if I scared you."

Levi shrugged it off. "Doing your job, right? You're ranch security?"

"Yes, sir. And I've been busy lately."

Levi nodded toward the nursery. "What happened here? That's a lot of blood loss."

"Last month, my daughter was kidnapped—" At Levi's look of horror, Trevor held his palms out. "She's fine now. But when she was taken, the ranch's governess, Faye Frick, was shot and killed."

"Holy…"

"Yeah. Tell me about it."

"You caught the man responsible?"

"You better believe it. Caught and arrested him, and got my daughter home safe and sound. The culprit swore he'd been hired for the job. If that's true, then whoever it was, we haven't caught up with him yet. You can see why I can't afford to take any chances with the safety around here."

Levi nodded, processing the idea that a criminal might be nearby, threatening the people of the ranch. "You think someone on the ranch or in town was calling the shots on the kidnapping?"

"Hard to say. Except for a note with detailed kidnapping instructions that the hired gun had at his apartment, we haven't found any proof that someone else was involved, besides the maid who had provided the kidnapper with his alibi. Trust me, she's gone, too. This ranch is as safe as we can make it, so you don't worry about that. I wouldn't let my daughter, Gabby and the rest of them stay here if I didn't think it was."

"Relieved to hear it." Relieved, yes, but not completely at ease. The whole thing left a bad taste in his mouth. His gaze roved to the bloodstain on the floor.

"The police and FBI gave us the go-ahead to remodel yesterday, which is why the room still looks like this and the tape's still up. Gabby's had a lot to deal with—all three sisters have—and I know it's a relief to them that you're here taking care of Jethro."

Trevor seemed like a good guy. A blue-collar, hardworking type who knew what it meant to struggle. Never in a hundred years would Levi have guessed that one of the daughters dearest would end up marrying someone who wasn't a richie-rich like them. And lo and behold, Gabriella was doing just that. It was as shocking as Amanda having a baby on her own. It made him wonder what else he'd gotten wrong about Jethro's daughters.

"It's hard to see a parent that ill, refusing help." Something Levi knew from experience, if one acknowledged drug addiction as the illness it was. Not that he was jumping at the chance to equate what his mom had gone through with Jethro's privileged situation. Eager for a topic change, he hooked his thumb over his shoulder. "Just so you know, in case you hear more rattling around, I was thinking of going to the kitchen and getting myself a midnight snack."

The two men said good-night and Trevor headed off to a room farther down the hall. Levi made for the stairs, but though Trevor had insisted the house was safe, he kept one eye looking over his shoulder the whole way.

Where had Kate been during the kidnapping and murder? Had she been afraid? Had she seen the body? He hoped not. He hoped she hadn't even seen the bloodstains. A sight like that could stick in a person's mind permanently.

He knew the kitchen was going to be tucked off somewhere discrete. At least, that was what he figured in a place like this. In normal houses, the kitchen was the center of the home, a meeting place for families to gather. Not so for the wealthy, who'd rather pretend their meals were magically created before being delivered to their ornate dining tables.

That was another thing wrong with this house, now that he thought about it—no kitchen smells. Even when Levi and his mom were at their lowest and poorest, their living space still retained the scent of food, if only cups of ramen noodles or bags of chips.

Sure enough, Levi found a grotesquely formal dining room, illuminated by more night-lights. Chandelier, thick rugs, polished wood, the works. Even those fake place settings that were removed when the real meal was served. He would never eat in this room, of that he was certain. No servants were going to wait on him if he could help it.

On the far end of the hall was a door. Dollars to doughnuts it led to the kitchen. He walked through the room, temporarily distracted by a huge family portrait of Jethro and his daughters in the center of the wall, lording over the space. With a snicker of disgust and a shake of his head, he pushed through the swinging door and into a staging area that ended with an enormous kitchen.

He inhaled deeply. There it was, the right smell. His stomach growled. The burrito he'd picked up during his road trip had been a long time ago, and the bread pudding, while one of the most delicious dishes he'd ever eaten, was far too small to satisfy. If it hadn't have meant more work for Kate, he would've had second or third helpings.

The long, wide room glowed with dim lighting, like the rest of the house. He smoothed a hand over the stainless-steel island workstation that dominated the center of the space. It looked a lot like an operating table. The same way that there was a little magic in the science of medicine, he wondered if there were some science to Kate's dessert magic. He smiled, wondering what delectable sweet she'd prepare tomorrow. He could hardly wait.

The kitchen boasted two hulking, stainless-steel refrigerators. In the nearest one, he worked hard to tread lightly so as not to disturb the obviously meticulous organization. Behind a block of cheese, he found cartons of yogurt. Good enough.

He had his hand on a carton of strawberry flavor when a row of plastic-wrap-covered ramekins caught his eye. Custard. Vanilla, judging by the color. Kate would've made these. The big question was, were they available leftovers or earmarked for the next night's meal?

Deciding he didn't care, he nabbed two. It took him

another five minutes of opening every drawer in the room before he finally found spoons. Then, custards and spoons in hand, he decided to check out the darkened hallway to his left.

Through the hall was another dining room, but unlike the first one he'd encountered, this room looked and smelled lived-in. Other than Kate, this room was one of the few aspects of the mansion that felt authentic. The table was made of worn, scarred wood, with a newspaper holding down one corner and a caddy of salt, pepper and napkins in the middle, sitting on a lazy Susan. The caddy was so darn normal, he was drawn to it and gave the lazy Susan a push.

Watching the napkins revolve, he straddled the bench seat and dug in to the first custard. At that initial taste of vanilla, sugar and egg on his tongue, his eyes rolled up and he moaned. It took him only two minutes to dispatch the custard in both ramekins. Dropping the spoon in the second one with a clatter, he yawned and stretched, his hunger satisfied.

Near the hearth of a simple stone fireplace sat a sofa, rumpled and beige. And darn it all if it wasn't calling his name. He scratched his stomach and yawned again. This must've been how Goldilocks felt after she ate all that porridge and found the perfect bed.

He dropped onto the sofa with a contented sigh. It was even more comfortable than it looked, and smelled faintly of must and dust. He set the alarm on his watch for five-thirty, which would hopefully give him time to get up before anyone found him and still allow him a little under three hours of rest. Not really enough to stay healthy, but there had been many nights in med school and his first year of residency that he'd netted less sleep than that.

Bringing his feet up, he lay lengthwise on his back with his head on a shapeless, cream throw pillow, and crossed his arms over his chest.

Bleary-eyed and as cranky as she always was before her morning coffee, Kate pulled her chef jacket on as she clomped to the stairs from her second-floor room in the employee wing. She flipped lights on as she went, torn between being grateful for the alone time because she was the first person up every morning and ruing the fact that bread couldn't bake itself.

She punched the light switch to the dining room and frowned. Somebody had helped themselves to the crème brûlée, and rather than try to hide their crime, they had the gall to leave their dirty dishes sitting out. Not only that, but they'd also eaten the dessert incomplete, without the burnt sugar topping that balanced the taste of the custard. Un-freakin'-believable.

And definitely not something she was willing to deal with before coffee.

Thankfully, no other workers trickled downstairs until after five-thirty, so she could be as grumpy as she wanted in the morning and no one would be the wiser. Growling, she trudged to the kitchen and started a kettle of water heating, then measured coffee grounds into a French press. Bracing her hands on the counter, she sank into her arms and indulged in a full-fledged scowl as she stewed about the brazen custard thief.

The water reached a high simmer, and simply knowing she was minutes from tasting the elixir of life, she felt more human and less witchy. She poured the water into the press, checked the time and decided she might as well grab the dirty crème brûlée dishes before Agnes woke up and blamed her.

Fantasizing about fitting the refrigerator door with a lock, she plodded to the dining room again, but a snore coming from near the window stopped her short. From the hall, she peeked around the corner, looking first under the table, then farther into the room at the sofa. Her heart did a flip-flop.

# *Chapter 5*

Levi Colton was fast asleep on his back, one leg stretched on the floor and an arm slung over his forehead.

Morning grumpiness all but forgotten, she dimmed the overhead lights she'd turned on and tiptoed across the room to him, though she probably was being overly careful since he hadn't woken during her clomping and grumbling. Why had he slept on this sofa instead of in the guest suite on a bed as comfortable as money could buy? If Kate had a bed like that, she might never get out of it in the morning. Fresh bread—and her job—be damned.

Perching on the edge of the bench, she propped her elbows on her knees and studied the devastatingly handsome face of her custard thief. His dark blond hair stuck up at odd angles, and without the intense soulfulness of his hazel eyes, his face looked boyish and carefree. Adding to that illusion was that he slept slack-jawed and his long, muscled arms and legs stretched haphazardly in all directions—the total opposite of the self-containment he exuded while awake.

His T-shirt had pulled up, revealing a strip of hairy skin above the elastic waist of his pants. And beneath the pants, an absolutely impossible-to-ignore erection.

Eyes widening, she gave it her full focus.

The sight got her blood moving south and her heart beating faster, probably because it'd been a while since she'd last seen one of those. At least a year.

She'd been determined after William's death not to let her sexuality die with him, at least what was left of it given the tepidness of her married bedroom life. After a couple years, she'd been brave enough to give intimacy a try. The opportunity had come in the form of a rodeo cowboy traveling with the circuit. A perfect, no-strings-attached guy to test the waters with.

The experience had been okay, better than she'd expected, actually. Not shout-from-the-rooftops good, but satisfying nevertheless. Every year or so since then, she'd stepped out of her comfort zone and into some man's bed, refusing to feel guilty about giving in to her basest needs. Men did that all the time, so why shouldn't she?

In a lot of ways, going solo was more consistently successful than her dalliances were—it'd been that way when she was married, too—but the problem was that taking care of her own business didn't satisfy the need nearly as much as being with an actual man. She reveled in the feel of strong, rough hands and manly smells and being squished under a broad, muscular body. Plus, fanaticizing about erections was nowhere near as good as the real thing. Not even close.

Levi was impressive. She couldn't tear her eyes away or stop wondering exactly what he looked like or how he would feel sliding into her body. Did he make love like he slept, with abandon, or with that same steely control he had while awake? What would it be like to sleep with a man who had a doctor's knowledge of the human body and an intensity of personality so sharp he stole the air from every room he entered?

He'd stirred something to life inside her last night. A part of her she worked hard to keep under control. The part of her that craved more. More attention, more excitement, more sex.

The trouble with that way of thinking was that life didn't work that way. Once upon a time, she'd gone after more. She'd let dreams and love and cravings rule her, and it'd left her in financial and emotional ruin. The past six years had been so rough on her, she wasn't certain she could handle what she thought she craved. Like a child who begged for extra sweets then got sick to his stomach.

The longer she stared and wondered, the heavier she sank into arousal and the more aware she became that it was totally inappropriate for her to ogle him in that way. He was a guest in this house, and a Colton at that. Desiring him was a complication she couldn't afford. Literally. She was only now beginning to crawl out of the hole of debt she'd sunk into after William's death. Losing this job was not an option, not if she wanted a roof over her head and food to eat.

With a sharp inhalation, she wrenched her gaze away.

From the kitchen, her coffee timer beeped. She stood,

sweeping her gaze from Levi's tousled hair all the way along his lean, long body to his bare feet, and an entirely new feeling took root in her—not replacing the arousal, but merging with it. She wanted to take care of him. He needed somebody and part of her wished that somebody was her.

With a shake of her head at the notion, she strode from the room, snagging the empty crème brûlée ramekins as she went. If anything had the capacity to sneak past her defenses it was a person with a weakness for sweets. Although she'd have to be vigilant with her heart, she could still take care of him in that small way and offer him the only part of herself she shared freely.

In the kitchen, she assembled for Levi a tray of coffee fixings and added a new cup of custard, sugar and a brûlée blowtorch.

Tray in hand, she turned toward the hall and paused midstep. Levi had his shoulder propped against the threshold, his hands in his pockets. His hair was still in complete disarray and in direct odds with the quiet gravity of his eyes. Her face grew hot as she considered the possibility that he'd been faking sleep so she could study him, but she shoved the idea aside. No one could act out a snore that convincingly.

She held the tray up. "I was bringing you coffee."

"Thank you." Holding her entranced with those disarming eyes, he pushed away from the wall, took the tray and set it on the prep island. Brows up in a sheepish look of apology, he lifted the custard ramekin. "I guess you found the evidence of my midnight snack on the table. I couldn't help myself. Sorry if I messed up your plans for them."

The apology was so sincere that she smiled. "No,

you didn't. Not at all," she lied. "But it does bother me that you were eating an unfinished product."

"I was?" He frowned at the custard. "It tasted finished to me. It was the best custard I've ever eaten."

Inwardly, she beamed at his compliment, though his opinion on the point was meaningless since he hadn't even eaten it correctly. She took the ramekin from him and set it on the counter, then poured them both coffee. "That's no ordinary custard. That's crème brûlée, except you missed out on the brûlée part, and I'm afraid I must insist you try it again the way it's meant to be eaten."

Leaning his hip against the island, he picked up his mug of coffee without adding any sugar or cream. "Right now?"

Kate dropped two sugar cubes in her mug. "We have to rectify the wrong."

He brought the mug to his lips for a slow sip. Over the rim of the mug, his eyes lightened with amusement.

The effect on his whole face was electrifying. Like eating a crumb of dark chocolate, the taste hinted at splendor but only left her wanting more. What would it be like to see him really smile? To watch him let go and laugh?

When he finished the sip, he lowered the mug and the lightness remained on his face. "You like things done the proper way."

He was teasing her. Well, two could play at that game. She waited until he had another mouthful of coffee, then said, "Only with desserts. With everything else, I'm shamelessly improper."

He spluttered the coffee, as she thought he might. And then the extraordinary happened. The cough turned into a laugh. Her heart gave a squeeze. Now that was a sound she could get addicted to fast.

"Shamelessly improper, hmm?" His smile lingered. "I hate to break it to you, but no one who is actually shamelessly improper would ever phrase it like that."

She sprinkled brown granules of turbinado sugar over the custard, racking her brain for a response that would feed into his turn of mood and keep the conversation buoyant. "Quibbles."

Much to her delight, his smile broadened to show a hint of teeth. "And a shamelessly improper person would never use the word *quibbles.*"

Who would've guessed that an intensely serious man like Levi would have such a cheeky sense of humor? Kate was transfixed. She couldn't remember the last time she had so much fun chatting with someone, much less a man, of all the preposterous things.

She brought the flame of the blowtorch to life. "What are you, some kind of expert on shamelessness and impropriety?"

"Big-time. It's an arduous certification process." He watched with rapt attention as she moved the flame over the sugar. "A bit early in the day for blowtorches, isn't it?"

"Don't worry. I'm a trained professional."

"And a very proper one at that."

She waggled a brow at him. "So the rumors say." She wanted to linger near him indefinitely, but the bread couldn't wait any longer if she was going to serve it to the family for breakfast. "I've got to get busy on the bread. Let the burnt sugar sit for a few minutes to harden. And don't let me catch you sneaking a bite."

He placed a hand over his heart. "I wouldn't dare cross you on that."

She could feel his eyes following her as she moved between the pantry and the island, gathering ingredients and mixing tools. There was no other word for the way he made her feel but *infatuation.* When was the last time she had a bona fide crush on a guy? It had to be William when she was in high school. She barely recognized the feel of it anymore—the light-headed, pulse-quickening high of attraction that knew no reason or consequence. Levi Colton was witty and gorgeous and… Oh, boy, was she in trouble if she didn't get a grip immediately.

As she mixed yeast into warm water, she forced herself to conjure an image of her bank account's measly balance. If she ever wanted to break free of working at Dead River Ranch and strike out on her own, she'd need at least another year to pay off the last of the creditors and sock away a little savings as a cushion. A fling with her employer's estranged son was out of the question. And she refused to contemplate the possibility that the Colton daughters would shut down the ranch after their father passed on.

"Can I try it now?" he asked.

She glanced his way to see him holding a spoon over the crème brûlée, waiting for her to give him the green light. "Dig in."

A satisfying crunch filled the air as he broke the spoon through the burnt sugar shell. Her hands paused in the flour she was measuring, her breath held in anticipation of his response. It was pathetic to be so hungry for a compliment when she already knew it was one of the best batches she'd ever made, but his opinion mattered to her.

He gave a thumbs-up as he chewed. "That's amazing. You were right about the brûlée part."

"I tried to tell you." She set the oven to warm, then checked on her yeast.

"I'll never doubt you again. May I make a request?" Levi added.

"Name it."

"You know how last night Jethro ordered dessert at every meal?"

She combined the dough ingredients and got busy mixing. "Mmm-hmm."

"You'd better double that order."

Elation flooded through her. "You've got yourself a deal. Anything else?"

"Yeah, on a related topic. Please tell me this ranch has a gym."

Her grin was so wide, it hurt. When was the last time she'd smiled so much? "It does. Around the corner from the infirmary I told you about last night."

"Good." He shoveled a heaping spoonful of crème brûlée into his mouth.

She turned the dough out onto her kneading board. "Do you live in Wyoming?"

"No, Salt Lake City. I went to med school there and it made the most sense to stay for my residency."

Good to know. She could crush on him all she wanted because he didn't even live in the same state as her. All she had to do was keep her desires to herself until he left. She pushed a lock of hair away from her face with the back of one floury, doughy hand. "You had quite a drive yesterday."

"You're telling me. I did my undergraduate work at the University of Colorado, and I made the drive from there to Dead to visit my mom every chance I got. I'd forgotten how tiring it is to drive distances like that." He walked across the room to the sink and grabbed a paper towel, then wet it. "You didn't grow up in Dead, did you?"

"No. Cheyenne."

"Didn't think so. I would've noticed you." Then he was in her space, reaching the paper towel to her forehead. "You have flour in your hair. Hold still."

Keeping her head steady, she looked sideways at him.

His brows furrowed in concentration as he wiped the paper towel over her hair, yet a hint of amusement remained. "You need a scrub cap."

"Like doctors wear?" At his nod, she added, "I usually wear something but I forgot today." That wasn't true, precisely. Kate's hair was so impossibly unruly that she normally wore a bandanna while she baked, but it made her look like a chubby-faced pirate wannabe. With Levi as company this morning, vanity won out over practicality.

"I think the water from the paper towel turned the flour into glue. Oops." He held the afflicted lock of hair out and wrapped the paper towel around it, then pulled.

"It's been a long time since a boy put glue in my hair. This is like kindergarten all over again."

He tucked the damp hair behind her ear. "Blowtorch notwithstanding."

"You know what I say to that?"

"Quibbles," they said in unison.

Their matching smiles were short-lived. Judging by the way Levi huffed an exhalation that turned off his smile and then practically jogged to the end of the island where his coffee awaited him, he was freaking out the same way Kate was at the discovery of their compatibility. Damn it all, she wished she'd never found out how much she enjoyed his company, because now that voice inside her yearning for more out of life was louder than ever—and that scared the snot out of her. Tense and irritated by her foolish battle of emotions, she turned her concentration to the dough prep.

Levi cleared his throat. "What brought you all the way out here to the middle of nowhere?"

No one had ever asked her that except Faye. To Faye, she'd eventually told the truth, but it wasn't something she shared lightly. "I needed a job."

"Do you still have family in Cheyenne?"

"Yes. My parents and my brother and his family."

"Do you see them often?"

"No." Enough with the hard questions. Time for her to turn the tables. "Why were you sleeping down here?"

"Like I said, I got hungry for a midnight snack. Then I wasn't sure I could find the guest suite again."

It sounded like a pat excuse, but that's all she'd offered him in return for his questions, so she could hardly fault him for it. Besides, she wasn't in a position to press him for details. She probably shouldn't have asked such a prying question in the first place.

Come to think of it, any minute Agnes would arrive, and shortly thereafter the rest of the waitstaff, to prepare for another day of service to the Colton family. The thought had her wishing Levi would return upstairs to the family area of the house. She wanted to protect him from the staff's prying eyes and greedy, gossipy hearts. He deserved better than their overcurious attention. She set the dough in a greased bowl and covered it with a towel, contemplating the best way to get him out of the room.

After an extended, awkward silence, Levi strummed his fingers on the island. "I do have something else I wanted to ask you. Last night, after you left the guest suite, I went out to have a look around, and Gabriella's fiancé, Trevor, found me looking at the nursery." Kate's heart dropped. "He told me about the kidnapping and mur—"

"This weather is turning my bones brittle, is what it's doing." Agnes stormed into the room like a tornado, Liz on her heels. "I swear, I'm going to turn to dust before this dry spell's over. If I ever scrounge up enough money to retire, I'm moving to Florida." She saw Levi and ground to a halt. "Oh! Dr. Colton. What an honor."

He stretched his hand out in greeting. "I haven't had the pleasure of making your acquaintance."

Agnes stared at his hand for a beat, then curtsied as if Levi were the king of England. "My name is Agnes and I'm the head chef here at the ranch. And I— Oh, dear, did that worthless girl serve you coffee in a common mug? She's aiming to get herself fired."

Kate clamped her molars together and marched the flour back into the pantry.

"Agnes, on the contrary, I applaud you for employing such a brilliant talent as Ms. McCord." Levi's voice had the rich timbre of a person who was used to soothing cranky old women, and Kate wondered if that was innate to him or if he'd learned it as a doctor. "I barged in here and she's taken excellent care of me. Besides that, I find her bread-making process captivating."

Captivating? Kate emerged from the pantry and

searched his expression for a hint of condescension but found none. His gaze found hers and one corner of his lips hitched up briefly.

Agnes, for once in her life, held her tongue as she set a china teacup and saucer on the island in front of Levi and poured it full of coffee. Levi narrowed his gaze at it and Kate could tell he wasn't keen on making the switch. Mr. Colton hated using the china, too, grousing about getting his fingers stuck in the handle, or the danger of accidentally crushing it if he sneezed.

In a clamor of voices, Liz, Jenny and Misty poured into the room. When they caught sight of Levi, their demeanor instantly shifted. Smiling coquettishly, their hands shot up to pet their hair and stroke their skirts.

"Good morning, Dr. Colton," Jenny said through her bright smile.

He wiggled fingers in their direction, then turned his concentration to his mug of coffee as though he suddenly found it fascinating beyond belief.

"Go on now and get to work, you three," Agnes barked. "This isn't a modeling agency where you get paid to stand around posing."

The girls dispersed but kept their eyes on Levi, who looked to be working hard not to acknowledge the attention.

Agnes took the mug from his hand and traded it out for the china. "The girl must not have told you that family breakfast is at eight, and we put coffee and pastries in the dining hall beginning at six each day. This morning, I'm making a special breakfast to celebrate your arrival. Bacon, a nice frittata and a fruit salad."

Kate mopped the prep counter with a rag. "And my French bread."

Agnes shot her a scolding look. "That's enough out of you for one morning."

"You're so kind to want to welcome me like that, Agnes, but..." Levi set the teacup down and rubbed his neck, looking as uncomfortable as he had the night before when Kate showed him into the guest suite. "What time does the staff eat? Seeing as how I'm here to work, and not as a guest, I thought I'd keep it simple."

Everyone in the kitchen froze. Liz, Jenny and Misty turned as if their heads were on swivels to gape at him.

Agnes wrung her hands, looking disturbed. "You want to eat with the staff?"

His look of discomfort gave way to a poker face as Levi looked past Agnes to the other women in the room. Kate offered a supportive smile that he did not return. Never had she seen such an old soul on a face that handsome; there was no trace of the smile or devilish gleam in his eyes she'd glimpsed when they were alone, only an iron wall of an expression.

"You know, the real problem is that I'm not hungry. Thank you for your good intentions, Agnes. The breakfast sounds wonderful. But, um..." He shook his head. "I have to go into Laramie today for medical supplies, so I don't have a whole lot of time this morning. I'll check in on Jethro, then hit the road."

"Whatever you say, Dr. Colton."

At the door leading to the dining hall, he stopped and turned. "Ms. McCord? What dessert are you bringing Jethro this morning?"

"You'll have to wait and see. It's a surprise," she blurted before stopping to think that maybe it wasn't the right call to evade direct questions from the family, or to seem overly familiar with Levi in front of the keenly observant eyes of Agnes, Jenny, Liz and Misty.

Sure enough, Agnes gasped. "Answer Dr. Colton, or you're going to find yourself out on the street before the day is done."

"No, she's right, Agnes," Levi said. "I'd rather be surprised."

With a final grim look around the room he was gone. Behind her, Jenny, Liz and Misty sighed. "I'd like to be his dessert," Misty said.

"If by dessert, you mean tart, then I think you're well suited for the job," Agnes snapped.

Kate paid them no mind, too busy planning her baking schedule. She had two men with sweet tooths counting on her for three fantastic desserts today, and she planned to exceed their every expectation.

Levi could tell something was amiss the moment his shoe hit the third-floor landing. The double doors of Jethro's suite were wide-open and a cacophony of womanly chatter drifted through the hall.

He was nearly to the door when he collided with the same young, bouncy brunette who'd been batting her eyelashes at him in the kitchen earlier that morning, the one that looked like Trouble with a capital *T*.

"Dr. Colton," she purred as she brushed her hands over his chest. He released her elbows, wedged his medical bag between them and backed out of arm's reach. "We can't keep running into each other without proper introductions." Her hand fluttered to her neckline. "I'm Jenny. If there's anything you need around here, anything at all, then I'm your girl."

"Thank you."

"Has anyone taken you on a tour of the estate yet? Because it would be my pleasure." She puckered her lips at the end of that last word and Levi supposed she meant the pout to be sexy.

"I did take a tour, thank you. This morning Mia, the ranch nurse, showed me around." Mia had impressed him with her professionalism. She'd sought him out shortly after he'd left the kitchen and during their tour hadn't seemed the least bit offended by his sudden presence. He'd been worried about that, worried about her feeling as if he was sweeping in and taking over her job. But she seemed genuinely relieved that Jethro was finally accepting help.

As far as his impression of the ranch, Levi had to admit, grudgingly, that the setup was outstanding. The infirmary was well stocked, the fitness room state-of-the-art and the stable filled with beautiful, healthy horses and shiny, new tack.

Jenny flipped her hair at his refusal of her offer after having frowned peevishly at the mention of Mia's name. "Well, I suppose if you like that kind of girl."

Yep, this one was nothing but trouble. "You mean the competent, friendly kind?"

She looked taken aback by his snark, but she was saved from answering when Kate bustled down the hall from the opposite direction, where Levi imagined the employee stairwell was located.

A shock of nerves jolted him, like it had every time he saw her, as if someone so pretty and full of life had no business in this dismal, artificial place.

Stopping short, she hefted the heavy tray in her arms to one hip and took in the sight of Jenny and Levi standing together with a hard expression and eyes that shifted back and forth between the two. "Jenny, Agnes has another tray ready in the kitchen. Would you mind grabbing it for me?"

Rather than answer, Jenny sidestepped so that she bumped Levi with her hip, then pretended to catch herself, throwing an arm around Levi's waist. He made fast work of removing it, but Jenny was unfazed. With a simpering gaze, she tossed her straight, brown hair and grinned. "Remember, I'm your girl." Then she sashayed past Kate and through a door at the end of the hall.

Only after Jenny was out of sight did a hint of Kate's usual warmth return to her features. "Hi," she said with a guarded smile.

Levi bridged the distance to her, far too riveted by her flushing cheeks to glance into the suite as he passed the open door. "Let me take that tray for you. It looks heavy."

She reversed a step, shaking her head. "I can't let you do that. But thank you."

"I'm here as a doctor, not a guest. A worker like you. You all pitch in to help each other and it's no different with me."

"Not to your way of thinking, but I answer to Agnes, Mathilda and Mr. Colton. And I'm certain they'd disagree."

"I don't think Jethro would, actually."

She pressed her lips into a straight line as though she desperately wanted to comment. Their stilted interaction was a stark contrast to the fun, easy connection they'd had that morning, which was for the best.

While in Jethro's house, it was critical that Levi remained impartial and unemotional—a doctor and nothing more. He refused to allow Jethro or the daughters dearest the satisfaction of seeing him weak or vulnerable, which meant that Kate and the feelings she stirred inside him were dangerous in every way.

This morning, he and Kate had laughed and joked. She was so easy to be with. He could've stood like that with her for hours, drinking coffee and eating dessert and chatting as he watched her work. When they'd jokingly said the same word at the same time, a powerful yearning had cut through him with the force of an alarm bell. He'd let his guard down. He'd gotten comfortable and forgotten how painful the consequences of being overrun with feelings could be.

For the rest of his stay at Dead River Ranch, he needed to ignore Kate and suppress all the instincts in him drawing him into her orbit. If only she weren't carrying a tray of picture-perfect cookies.

She swished around him. "Excuse me. I've got to get this tray set up before I get in trouble."

Before he could think better of it, his arm shot out and he snagged her around the waist. "Are those for me and Jethro?"

She offered him an anxious smile. "Yes. You have as big a sweet tooth as him, you know."

Normally, Levi bristled at any comparison of him to Jethro, but if the two of them had to have something in common, a love of dessert was a rather benign one. Besides, he couldn't fault the old man for having the good sense to appreciate Kate's cooking. He released her waist to snag a cookie and popped the whole thing in his mouth. He was rewarded by a flavor explosion—molasses, cloves, cinnamon and sugar and probably a whole bunch of other spices he couldn't name—and did a little hum and eye roll to let her know how good it was.

He fully expected her to dash off, but she watched him chew. When he'd finished, he nodded toward the suite. "Do you know what's going on in there?"

"Mr. Colton's feeling better and asked to have breakfast with his family."

Amazing what a little morphine could do for a leukemia patient. When Levi got him on oxygen, Jethro was going to feel like a new man. It might be enough to convince him to receive blood transfusions and a marrow transplant. "It's good to know he's feeling better."

"It seems that way, yes." She took a step toward the door. "We're setting up a table in his sitting room so he doesn't have to walk too far. Agnes told Mathilda you wouldn't be joining them, but if you've changed your mind another place setting can easily be brought up."

"No, thank you." He took a second cookie. "When are you going to stop to eat?"

She looked flustered by the question. "Oh, I don't really stop until the day is done. I'll grab a bite while I clean."

Kate shifted her weight and hoisted the tray higher, reminding Levi of how heavy it looked. He gestured toward the suite door. "After you."

He wasn't sure he'd ever fully understand what made him do it, but as she passed, he stroked a hand along her spine down to the flare of her tailbone. She paused and swayed into his touch before walking on.

He bit the inside of his lip, annoyed with himself. *Way to keep it impartial, man. Nice job.*

He looked up too late and saw Gabriella watching him, smiling.

He dropped his hand and wiped it on his pants. What a fool. He'd been at the ranch less than twenty-four hours and he couldn't stop making judgment errors. Good thing he'd be out on the road for much of the day. Jethro needed oxygen, a proper prescription of morphine and some iron pills. The iron pills he could get in Dead, but the local health clinic wouldn't store enough oxygen to rent out, which was why he was headed to Laramie, the nearest city.

Indeed, a table had been erected in the suite's sitting room. Kate had set her tray down on the far edge of the table and was transferring the contents. Everyone in the room was ignoring her. Levi bristled. Kate deserved to be the one waited on, not the other way around. He hoped someday, for her sake, she got a better job.

She'd evaded his prying questions that morning about how she came to work at the ranch. He doubted he'd allow himself to be alone with her long enough to ask again, and though it irked him that he'd never know more about her, he knew it was for the best—for both of them.

Catherine was seated at the table and chatting with Jethro and Amanda, who was holding a baby girl. Amanda was listening in on their conversation, but when she noticed Levi, she smiled and stood. "Good morning."

He waved his hello as she approached him.

"This is Cheyenne. Your niece."

"Hi, Cheyenne. Nice to meet you." He shook her foot like a handshake and pulled a silly face. She laughed around the fist she had crammed in her mouth. He didn't consider himself a silly-face kind of guy, but found it impossible not to turn into a clown around little babies. His gaze darted to Kate, who had her eyes on her work and a sweet smile dancing on her lips, as if she'd noticed his baby face and found it charming.

"Mathilda told us you're not staying for breakfast," Catherine said.

"No. I'm here for a morning checkup. I promise not to delay your meal too much." He plunked his medical bag on the sofa behind Jethro's seat at the table. While he adjusted a blood-pressure cuff over Jethro's arm, he said, "I met Mia the ranch nurse this morning."

"What about her?"

"She's good and seems to have the ranch's medical needs under control. I'm mentioning her because I have to drive to Laramie today to pick up oxygen tanks and—"

"I'm not using any damn oxygen tanks. What do you take me for, a decrepit old geezer?"

Levi ignored the man's balking. No sense getting into an argument now. They might as well save their battle until Levi was actually standing over Jethro with an oxygen tube in hand. He went quiet as he listened to Jethro's pulse through his stethoscope. After jotting his blood pressure down on the file he'd started yesterday, he said, "As I was saying, I'll be gone most of the day for supplies, so I'm leaving orders for Mia to administer your midday morphine and check your vitals in six hours. Don't give her any hassle."

"I can give hassle to anyone I want and it's none of your damn business."

He could see that every day was going to be a battle of wills between them. Unlike Jethro and his blessed life of luxury, Levi had been battling against one thing or another his whole life and he had the tough-as-nails will to prove it. Jethro's surliness bounced off him like tiny pebbles.

Gabriella sat next to Jethro and squeezed his forearm. "Dad, let Mia help you."

Behind Jethro, out of view, Levi measured a dosage of morphine. "I wouldn't use the *h* word with him if I were you. It seems to be the one four-letter word he's not real fond of."

His demeanor matter-of-fact, and without asking permission, Levi walked to Jethro's side, pushed the oral syringe into the corner of his closed lips and depressed the plunger. "All right. No Nurse Mia today. Have it your way. Just so you know, I probably won't be back until dinnertime." Levi had a hunch that after eighteen hours of being relatively pain-free and breathing easily, Jethro would be in for quite a shock when his current dose of morphine wore off.

Jethro's scowl deepened. "I already told you—I'm not using oxygen, and whatever other supplies you're going to pick up, I bet I'm not going to like them, either."

Levi closed his medical bag. "Were you expecting there to be some part of having leukemia that you'd like?"

He was rewarded by a wheezy laugh. "There is that."

With a wink to Kate that he instantly regretted, Levi grabbed a handful of cookies.

Jethro reached forward and snatched the plate, hugging it close. "Are you stealing my cookies? The pastry girl brought them for me."

"She brought enough for both of us," Levi said. "And her name is Kate."

"What's that now?"

"I said she has a name and it's not 'pastry girl.'"

On the far side of the table, Kate gave a small shake of her head in warning. Her cheeks were stained pink and so pretty that he stared a few heartbeats too long.

"I'm paying her salary, so I can call her whatever I want." He set the plate in front of him and shoved a cookie in his mouth.

Levi was ready with a dressing-down for Jethro's imperial attitude, but Gabriella spoke up first. "Just because you're employing somebody doesn't give you the right to treat them poorly." She removed the plate from Jethro's reach. "And, Daddy, you can't have dessert for breakfast. It's not good for you."

Jethro pushed his palms against the table and stood. "It's only eight o'clock in the morning and I've got a room full of people trying to tell me what to do. If you don't like the way I'm living my life, then get out of my room. That goes for all of you."

Amanda and Catherine pressed their lips together, and Levi could tell Jethro's words stung. How they loved such a nasty human being was beyond him.

Behind the daughters, Kate inched toward the door holding her empty tray in front of her like a shield. Levi nearly asked her to wait for him so they could walk downstairs together. What a stupid thing to think.

He swallowed hard and returned his focus to Catherine, Amanda and Gabriella. "It's not going to do any harm for him to eat what he likes. If you're going to pick battles to fight, this shouldn't be one of them. Not at this point, anyway."

Jethro took the cookie plate and set it down hard in front of him. "You might be handy to have around after all, Vessey. Hey, pastry girl, you know the peach ice cream we ate last month?"

Kate paused near the door. Her eyes were wide and mousy. "Yes, sir."

Levi frowned and finished packing his bag. He hated that servant look on her face and the dutiful way she said "yes, sir." He wanted bold Kate back. Shamelessly improper Kate with her quibbles and blowtorch.

"Did you make that ice cream?" Jethro asked.

"Yes, I did."

"I want that again. Immediately." He jammed another cookie in his mouth.

Kate bent her knees as though in curtsy. "I'll ask Agnes to pick up the ingredients when she goes to do the grocery shopping this week."

"Not good enough. How much time do you think I have left to waste? Go today. Buy the market out of peaches. And lemons. Lemon pie would hit the spot, too."

"Yes, sir. I'll talk to Mathilda about borrowing one of the ranch's trucks."

"Or Levi could take you," Gabriella said. To Levi, she added, "You said you were going into town today."

Kate's expression remained unreadable.

Cringing inwardly at the proof that Gabriella had seen him touch Kate's back in a manner that gave his feelings away, Levi cleared his throat and made sure his expression was blank. "I am but I'm also going to Laramie. I'm sure Kate has more important things to do than go on an all-day road trip."

"It's a good idea, Miss Gabby, but I can't be away from the ranch that long."

"Sure you can." Gabriella walked nearer, snagging

Cheyenne from Amanda to bounce in her arms. "You never take days off, even the ones you're supposed to according to your contract. Getting away from the ranch for the day would be good for you, especially with Levi as your escort."

A thrill shimmered through Levi at the idea of spending the day with Kate alone, away from the ranch. That thrill, along with Gabriella's insight, was reason enough to make the road trip a horrible idea. The trouble was, he didn't want to hurt Kate's feelings by protesting too vehemently. "I think Kate knows what's good for her. She doesn't need us telling her what to do." He picked up his medical bag and walked toward the door. To Kate, he said, "If you give me your grocery list, I'll pick up whatever you need."

"Nonsense." Gabriella pressed between them. "I insist you both go."

Kate took a deep breath, her focus solely on Gabriella. "Yes, ma'am."

Levi's pulse sped up in anticipation. All right, then. This was really happening. "I'll meet you out front in an hour."

# *Chapter 6*

"I have questions."

Kate turned from staring out the side window of Levi's car, watching the passing trees along the half-hour journey to the highway, to smile at him. When he'd shown up at the door the night before, he knew next to nothing about the ranch or the people who lived there, as evidenced by the myriad of questions he'd peppered her with after he coaxed her into his suite. "I figured you'd have more. What do you want to know?"

"I started to tell you this morning that I saw Cheyenne's nursery last night. Trevor told me what happened there, about the kidnapping and murder. That must have been horrible."

She folded her hands in her lap, girding herself to talk about the painful subject. "It was. Faye, the woman who was murdered, was my closest friend at the ranch. It's been a tough loss."

"I'm sorry. I had no idea."

"Her son, Dylan, works here, too. He's taking it the hardest, understandably. She was his only family."

Levi's lips flattened into a grim line. "I know what that's like. It was the same for me when my mom died. Where were you when all of that went down last month?"

"At the rodeo, along with most everyone else on the ranch that day."

"And it's thought that the timing was intentional?" he asked.

"If you believe the letter that the kidnapper, Duke, who was a worker on the ranch, handed over to the police. Whoever wrote that letter offering money in exchange for Cheyenne knew what he was doing."

"But the kidnapper didn't get Cheyenne. He got Trevor's daughter."

She drew circles on her leggings, remembering back to that terrible time. "Exactly. Everyone thinks the motive behind the kidnapping was to demand a ransom but that didn't happen because whoever wrote that letter realized that the wrong baby had been taken."

"Who found Faye? It wasn't you, was it?"

"No, thank goodness." If she had, she may never have recovered her nerves. An image of William's limp body flashed through her mind and she shuddered. "Trevor and Gabby did."

"The person who wrote the kidnapping letter, he hasn't been caught yet?"

"No. The police claim they're doing all they can, but they don't have any leads as far as we know."

"But it has to be someone close to the family, doesn't it? How else would they know that the kidnapped baby wasn't Cheyenne?"

"Exactly what I was thinking. I hope the police are thinking along those same lines, too."

He wrung his hands on the steering wheel as though engaged in a tense mental debate. Finally he said, "Last month's kidnapping wasn't the first on the ranch."

"You're talking about Cole Colton, Mr. Colton's son?"

"Mr. Colton's son," he repeated.

She gasped, mortification dropping in her stomach like a rock. "I didn't mean anything by that. I'm sorry. It's just that I'd never heard of you before yesterday and it's easy to forget that you're…you're…"

"That I'm his son, too? Don't worry. You're not the only one. I mainly knew about Cole's kidnapping because my mom never got over her grudge about how Jethro and the rest of the town cared so much about Cole in a way that nobody in town, Jethro included, cared what happened to me."

"I don't understand how any parent could choose to cut a child out of their life." She curled her hand around her middle and narrowed her gaze at the black smoke on the horizon. The affinity she'd felt between herself and Mr. Colton for each having lost a child didn't seem so accurate anymore. It still saddened her to think of baby Cole's fate, but she found it incomprehensible that Mr. Colton could care so much about some of his children and not even be willing to call Levi family.

The car slowed to a stop at the traffic light that marked the juncture of the road that led to town and the highway to Laramie.

"It's okay," Levi said with a shrug. "I mean, it's not okay, but that's the way life goes. Anyway, I wouldn't have wanted to grow up in that house with him lording over me like he does everybody else. And now, it wouldn't matter if he had a change of heart. I'm not sure I could forgive him."

Before she could think better of it, she reached across the seat and set a hand on his arm. "Of course you could."

He turned and cast his eyes at the spot where they touched, then lifted those long lashes and locked his gaze with hers. "You don't even know me yet."

*Yet.* That word, those eyes. Her insides fluttered. Then he leaned her way, his lips on a straight path to hers, and the flutter turned into a full-out body tingle. She wanted to kiss him, taste him. More than she'd wanted anything or anyone in a long, long time.

The roar of an engine snapped them to reality.

Kate flopped against her seat, blinking and breathing hard as a shiny, loud motorcycle swerved into the empty oncoming-traffic lane to go around them because the stoplight had turned green.

She glanced at Levi, who stared out the driver-side window, not seeming to have noticed the light change.

Her instinct that morning about it being a terrible idea to spend the entire day alone with him had been spot-on. "How about you drop me off in Dead right now and you can pick me up on your way back from Laramie?"

He gave a slow nod. "It'd be three or four hours."

"Don't worry about me keeping busy. It's been a while since I've had time to myself, and there's plenty to keep me entertained around town."

Instead of turning onto the highway, he went straight through the intersection toward Main Street. "How am I going to find you when I get back here?"

"My friend Grace works at the Dead River Diner. You can give me your cell phone number and I'll give you the diner's number. If you're running late or need to get ahold of me, Grace will be able to find me easily enough. Otherwise, I can meet you at the supermarket."

Cell phones, cars, expensive hair salons and fancy shoes were some of the many money-suckers Kate had learned to live without since William died and her business went under. She was a relentless penny-pincher because the faster she saved money, the sooner she could finish repaying her debts and build herself a new life.

Thinking about her goal reminded her of the other reason she didn't want to go to Laramie with Levi. She hated driving over the very spot where William and Olive had perished.

It wasn't as though she never drove that road. Laramie was the closest big town, so avoiding the route altogether was impossible. Over the years, her coping strategies with the drive had evolved, though not in a straightforward progression. She'd learned from experience that the stages of grief weren't tidy, but unpredictable and loopy. One road trip she'd be at peace with her losses and then the next, something would trigger a fresh wave of fury or tears—or worse, hollowness, as if the hole inside her was so vast, her body was more emptiness than substance. Who she was ceased to matter and all that existed of her were edges surrounding a vast, vacant space.

She was infinitely relieved that she'd managed to avoid the confrontation with her grief today. In front of Levi, especially.

Ten minutes later, they stood in front of the Dead River Diner. The streets were crowded for a weekday during a heat wave. The wildfires northwest of the town seemed to have drawn people out of their houses to discuss the latest news with their neighbors or gather emergency supplies, and judging by the trucks loaded with belongings, the voluntary backcountry evacuations to the north had brought some of the displaced people through Dead.

Levi rattled the key ring in his hand and shuffled his feet. "This place hasn't changed at all. Is their soda mix still flat?"

He was so ill at ease at the ranch, so out of place, that it was hard to think of him as a local. A barrage of questions popped into her head about his life there—where he'd lived, how he'd spent his time, if he still kept in touch with schoolmates in the area. Maybe Grace remembered him. Then again, his past, his life, shouldn't matter to her.

"It is. Safer to stick with iced tea."

After an awkward silence punctuated by more key rattling, Levi puffed his cheeks. "Okay. I'd better hit the road again. I'll meet you at the supermarket around two. If something changes, I'll call the diner or the supermarket and have them get the message to you."

"Sounds good. Have a safe drive." The common pleasantry gave her chills. There was no volatile weather today to speak of, not counting the gusty winds, but she send up a silent prayer for Levi anyway. If there was one thing in life that could be counted on, it was that Mother Nature loved to exercise her violent, unpredictable prerogative.

Levi turned onto the street leading from Laramie to Dead, shaking off the disquiet that always settled over him during that particular drive. He didn't know exactly where along that stretch of road the accident had occurred, because the last thing he remembered that night was getting in his car after his mother's funeral, so instead, the whole length of the highway haunted him.

That was the trouble with the kind of trauma-induced amnesia he'd experienced. The whole night was a black spot in his memory, only coming out in his dreams to torment him. Years later, he'd requested a police report on it, trying to find the answers to the questions that plagued him, but the report didn't seem to exist.

In the absence of anything concrete to hang on to other than the feeling that he'd done something horrible that he couldn't remember, he'd chosen to look at the accident as a sign, a push by the hand of God to become a doctor, as he'd been debating. To help patients like the doctors had helped him. It turned out to be the perfect job for him, giving his life a purpose where none had existed before, allowing him to connect with people without getting emotionally involved.

The town of Dead wasn't much different than Levi remembered. Run-down, with some intermittent businesses that had been spruced up with face-lifts. The arcade had gone under, as had the shoe-repair store. Orville the barber still had his shop on the corner, but now it sat next to a tech-gadget depot.

The Roundup Motel was still standing. Levi had entertained a wild fantasy that it had been torn down, that he wouldn't be forced to face it, but there it was, as it ever had been, across the street from the supermarket.

He pulled into the supermarket parking lot at one-forty-five. Kate was nowhere to be seen, perhaps already grocery shopping. He picked a spot near the rear of the lot, his ribs squeezing so tight that he couldn't get air. Dark thoughts felt like a hammer pounding down on his heart. Thank goodness Kate wasn't around to witness it.

He stretched his legs out of the car, tucked his sunglasses in his shirt pocket and gave the Roundup Motel his full attention.

It hadn't changed much. A two-story box sandwiched between a field of weeds and a bar called Fuzzy Bear's. Maybe the brown trim had been given a fresh coat in the past few years, and maybe it sagged in the middle more than when he'd lived there, but the feel of it was exactly the same.

Brown-orange rust lines trickled from every hinge of the place, marring the painted stucco and making it look as if the building were bleeding at its joints. Every few windows, the glass was cracked. One window had been covered in foil and duct tape.

The roof was little more than shreds of shingles and felt. On rainy days, he and his mom passed the time racing between the patio and their room, emptying the buckets that were catching the water coming in from the ceiling. She'd laugh her wheezy, sickly laugh and say at least they knew this place would never be haunted. Plenty of holes in the roof for souls to escape. How ironic her words had been, now that he thought about it. Made him wonder how many other people had suffered their last days there, besides his mom.

He hadn't been the one to find her. Her best friend, Luella, had. She'd told the motel manager, who called Levi as well as the police. Every lifeless body Levi saw in med school and his residency, he couldn't help but think about his mom, about what she might've looked like in her bed, or laid out on the medical examiner's table.

His throat closed. He sucked in as deep a breath as he could manage until it felt as if his lungs might crack his ribs. He missed his mom. He missed her telling him she loved him. It didn't matter how drunk or high she was, she'd told him she loved him every day of his life for eighteen years—until he left for college and she'd taken a turn for the worse.

In the winter, she'd give him their blanket, doubling it up on the bed they shared so he would be warm. He hated to think about how many nights she'd shivered from the cold until he grew up enough to know what she was sacrificing and insist they share.

Wasn't fair, the way love worked. It wasn't fair or kind or easy. Mostly, the question that came to mind when he thought about his mom and the drug use and her obsession with Jethro was *how?* How could a heart be so full of love and demons at the same time? How could she let herself turn into nothing when she had so much to live for—when she had Levi to live for?

He thought about his mom a lot, nearly every week, but standing there in the weed-riddled parking lot, it was the first time he'd wanted to cry since she died. The tears were coming on strong behind his eyes, welling up along with a terrible ache in his throat and pressure in his sinuses. The sorrow was so tremendous a sensation it was as if it'd been waiting inside him all these years like a prisoner.

He sniffed but his nose was growing impossibly stuffy. This wasn't the time. And it wasn't who he was anymore—the forlorn, serious child who cried a lot and escaped into books. He was supposed to be at the grocery store, buying dessert ingredients with one very pretty, sweet, sassy pastry chef. He didn't want to feel, especially this, especially since staying in Jethro's house already had him feeling raw.

"What does it mean to you, this place?"

He jumped at the sound of Kate's voice, then quickly got out his sunglasses and shoved them on his face. Not certain he could find his voice, he flattened his tongue against the roof of his mouth and shook his head.

"This has to do with your mom?"

"Yeah," he croaked.

"Did she live here?"

His left cheek twitched, pulling his lips sideways. After a few hard swallows, he felt safe in answering. "We both did."

She slid her arm around his, hugging it, and rested her cheek on his shoulder. "She'd be proud of you."

"She already was." He didn't ever have to do anything to earn it. She was proud of him just for being alive and being hers, and she'd told him so often.

They were quiet for a while, looking, thinking. Kate felt good there, tucked up next to him. She was solid and warm and full of life. He wanted to rest his cheek on the fluff of her curly hair and lean into her goodness. But that wasn't who he wanted to be. He wanted to be a man who didn't lean on others but found his strength from within. He didn't want to be the type of person who dissolved into an emotional mess over a building in front of a pretty girl, but a man who controlled when and what he felt.

There was no higher state of being than having a disciplined mind and a disciplined heart.

Yet even knowing that, he couldn't find it in himself to pull away from Kate's embrace or look away from the Roundup Motel. He couldn't stop remembering.

"I was married once." Kate's tone was wistful. Pensive in a way that wasn't burdened with unresolved emotion.

He looked down at the top of her head, a fresh hit of turbulent feelings smacking him in the gut. Curiosity, jealousy, sadness for her that her life hadn't gone as she'd planned and—most disconcerting—inappropriate, unabashed relief that she wasn't married any longer. It was a villainous way to react, beneath him in every way. Choking back his self-disgust, he asked, "What happened?"

She cocked her head to meet his gaze. "He died. Unexpectedly. It took me a long time to find any semblance of peace, and when I did, I never expected a relapse. But grief comes back, sometimes only a little, but sometimes so strong it feels like…"

"Like a ghost," Levi finished.

She nodded slowly, studying him. "You know what I'm talking about."

Did he ever. "I'm sorry for your loss."

She slid her arm down his and took his hand. "I'm sorry for yours."

Her hand in his felt good. Exactly what he wished he didn't need. He gripped it tight. "Why do you work at

Dead River Ranch? They don't treat you well enough there. You deserve better."

Her face softened into a melancholy smile. "Something tells me you know as well as I do that life isn't about getting what you deserve."

True, that.

"Why did you come here?" she asked.

"To prove once and for all that I'm nothing like Jethro."

"You doubted that?"

Her response filled him with a warmth that chased away the bitterness from his grief. The sting of tears in his eyes subsided; the ache in his chest eased. When he was working, he never felt this messed up, like damaged goods. As a doctor, he was strong and confident in his abilities. The one healing rather than the one needing to be healed. But the ghosts he hoped to silence by facing Jethro were pressing on him harder than ever.

A woman stepped outside from a door on the second floor of the motel. She met Levi's stare and raised her hand. Levi recognized her sandy-gray hair and gaunt body immediately.

"Do you know her?" Kate asked.

"Yes. That's Luella. She was my mom's only real friend."

She'd been around all Levi's life. He'd hated her as soon as he got old enough to decide his mom's behavior was Luella's fault. Talk about projecting. Looking at her now as she shuffled their way, a brown box in her hands, he had nothing but pity in his heart.

He and Kate watched her pick her way across the street. Walking to meet her would've been the gentlemanly thing to do, but Levi couldn't fathom stepping a single foot closer to the motel.

"Hello, Luella."

Her body was twitchy, her eyes unable to focus on any one thing for long. Hard to tell if she was presently on something, or if her lifetime of drug abuse had saturated her system so that she was never not on anything.

"This is Kate. Kate, Luella."

Kate offered Luella a kind smile and her hand to shake, and even then Luella wouldn't make eye contact. She pushed the box into Kate's arms, then shifted her focus to Levi. "That's the last of Eileen's stuff. I seen you standing there and I said to myself, 'That's Eileen's boy. I can finally get this box out of my way.' Don't have the space for it no more."

Levi took a good look at the box, which had a stamped blue-and-yellow picture of a soup can on the side, as though it had been pilfered from a Dumpster behind the supermarket. He was torn between wanting to drop it in the nearest trash can and wanting to rip the flaps of the lid open right there on the spot.

He fisted his hands. The box didn't look heavy and Kate hadn't made a move to transfer it to him, so he decided to let her hold it until he got a grip on his haywire emotions. "Thank you."

Luella sniffed, stroking her bony hand over her other arm. "I was the one who cleaned out her room afterward. Took me more than a day. I never got paid for it, neither. Just did it 'cause she was a friend. How about something for my trouble?"

Luckily, Levi was fluent in junkie-speak. He reached for his wallet as Luella dissolved into a string of phlegmy coughs. He withdrew two twenty-dollar bills and held them her way. With the speed and smoothness of a pickpocket, and without breaking pace in her coughing fit,

Luella snatched them fast and tucked them away in her pants pocket.

When the fit passed, she cleared her throat. "Well, okay, then. Guess I'll be seeing you."

She shuffled past them, not toward the supermarket, but the liquor mart. Levi watched her go, wondering if his mom had been that bad off without him realizing it through the blindness that came with his love and distance and denial.

"Give me your keys."

At Kate's command, he tore his gaze from Luella and looked at Kate, bracing for the pity he was sure he'd see on her face. But all Kate exuded was solace and strength. Everything he wished he embodied. He stuffed his wallet in his pocket and fished out his keys.

She locked the box in the trunk, as though she understood its volatility. All he could do was stand there, mute, while she helped him. She returned to his side and took his hand. That was when it hit him about what a gift she'd given him by hiding the box. She'd given him permission and opportunity to put his pain and his past out of mind, at least for the moment.

The truth was he didn't want to dwell on the past any longer. Not today, with Kate holding his hand. They were going grocery shopping together. When was the last time he'd done that with a woman? It took him a fair bit of thinking to dig out the memory. Med school, to pick up late-night snacks and beer with Trudy Wong for their study group.

This, with Kate, was different. Intimate. Loaded with potential. And not only because she was sexy as hell and he was lucky enough to be holding her hand. Around her, he felt lighter, more even-keeled and able to cope with whatever came his way.

He'd never thought too deeply about dessert, and didn't consider himself a stress eater, but rather than dwelling any longer on his grief for his mother or anger toward Jethro, all he wanted to do was think about Kate and her desserts. He couldn't wait to taste her peach ice cream and lemon pie. "What's your favorite dessert to make?"

She grinned, clearly welcoming the topic change. "Dessert or pastry in general?"

He rubbed his chin. "Hmm. In general, I guess."

"Croissants." She said it with a French accent. Absolutely adorable.

"Say that again."

A bashful smile curved her lips. "Are you teasing me?"

"A little. Go on and say it."

She pressed her lips together and made a show of debating whether to grant his request. "Croissants."

Now he was smiling, too. "That accent of yours makes them sound sophisticated, but aren't croissants just French doughnuts? I would've thought your favorite pastry to make would be something challenging."

She scoffed good-naturedly. "Says someone who's never tried to make them."

Her moxie was back in force and it pushed the last of the heavy fog from his soul. "Maybe you can teach me. I have absolutely zero experience in the kitchen, but, being a doctor, I do have one skill going for me."

"What's that?"

"I'm really good with my hands."

Her cheeks pinked.

The comment hadn't been intended as an innuendo. He'd honestly decided that having deft fingers would be a handy kitchen skill. But it seemed his pastry chef had a dirty mind. How decadent. He should've guessed that nobody could care so passionately about whiskey sauce and whipped cream and not be full of passion themselves.

If he wasn't such a gentleman, he would've pointed out that, yes, he thought his hands were pretty damn skilled in that respect, too. He let go of her hand, draped an arm across her shoulders and turned them away from the motel. He could say his goodbyes to it when they were finished shopping.

She didn't pull away from his hold, and for that he was grateful, but he let her go as soon as they got to walking. He didn't want her to get uncomfortable, thinking he was coming on to her, especially since he was in the mood to tease her a little more. "If talking about my capable hands makes you blush, then you'd better pick out the peaches on your own. I can be in charge of getting the other ingredients."

"What's wrong with peaches?"

Quirking a brow, he gave her a sidelong look. "Peaches give me dirty thoughts."

She folded her arms in a show of fake incredulity. "Really, peaches?"

He nodded sagely. "Oh, yes. Peaches are downright wicked. Don't ever let me see you eat a peach or I'll lose all composure, guaranteed."

And then he held his breath, worried that he'd come on too strong anyway, praying that she didn't freak out.

She touched a finger to her chin, looking nonplussed except for eyes that flashed keen wit. Thank goodness.

"I always thought bananas were the most wicked produce."

He released the air he'd been holding in a sharp peal of laughter, loving that she shared his sense of humor. "Well, you'd better never let me see you eating one of those, either."

As they crossed through the sliding door of the supermarket, she took the cart Levi had snagged and handed him a basket. "To be on the safe side, I'll take care of all the produce. You get the butter. If I'm going to teach you how to make croissants, we're going to need a lot of it."

# *Chapter 7*

Jenny stuffed a pillow from Mr. Colton's bed into a freshly laundered case while admiring the huge diamond ring on her left hand. It hadn't been there that morning, as far as Kate recalled, and she highly doubted the stone was a real diamond, even if Jenny was flaunting it as though it were.

The worst part was that Jenny was acting as if they were back to being friends. As if she hadn't assaulted Kate yesterday in the stairwell and stolen Kate's best hope for tracking down the person responsible for Faye's murder.

Kate would've never volunteered to help Jenny with her chores except that Mathilda had assigned her to because Fiona was still experiencing morning sickness and the regular maids were busy waiting on the family. Under Levi's care, Mr. Colton's cantankerous energy had returned in force. For the first time in weeks, he felt well enough to join the family at dinner, so Mathilda had jumped at the opportunity to give his room a thorough cleaning.

"I haven't had the chance to ask you how your trip to Laramie with Dr. Colton was."

Kate stripped the fitted sheet from the bed and added it to the growing pile of soiled linens on the floor. "Fruitful."

"I'll bet it was. Next time, I'm going to see if I can ride along with him. Betcha I can think of some better ways than you to keep him happy while he drives."

Jenny had waved her ring in Kate's face so much since they'd started cleaning that Kate had begun to worry that she might inadvertently get smacked with it sooner or later. So it didn't add up why Jenny was still pining over Levi. "What about that shiny ring you're wearing? I figured it meant you already had yourself a man."

"Oh, you noticed after all, did you? I thought you were going blind." Jenny wiggled the fingers of her left hand. "I got it today from my secret admirer."

The two of them pulled a fresh top sheet over the new fitted one. "Secret admirer? Looks to me like an engagement ring."

Moving in synchronicity to the foot of the bed, they tucked the corners. "Well, he wants me to marry him and I told him I'd think about it," Jenny said. "And he said I could go ahead and take the ring for a test drive."

"Who is this mystery man?"

"That's for me to know and you to find out if I let him take me away from here like he's promising." Jenny walked to Kate's side of the bed and groaned. "That's not a hospital corner. Haven't you ever made a bed before?" Scowling, she pulled the sheet out, then folded and tucked with a proficiency that Kate had to begrudgingly admit was impressive.

"I still don't understand why you're going on about Levi if you're accepting diamond rings from secret admirers."

Jenny stood, hands on hips, and rolled her shoulders. "It's *Levi* now, is it? Maybe you did do a worthy job entertaining the good doctor on your little outing today."

Kate's cheeks grew warm. Of all the people to slip a juicy detail to. Then again, the more she thought about it, the more aghast she was at the invitation she'd issued to Levi about baking croissants. Cozying up to him in the kitchen would be a mistake of epic proportion. Waitstaffs were experts at reading nuance—their jobs often depended on it—and they'd waste no time in drawing conclusions about her friendship with Levi. Especially with the palpable undercurrent of attraction she felt buzzing between them every time they were in the same room.

She might as well French-kiss him at the top of the grand staircase.

Thinking about kissing Levi was enough to send a sizzle of awareness through Kate's body. Who was she fooling by calling what she and Levi had a friendship? Friends didn't flirt about how skilled their hands were or the naughtiness of eating bananas. Friends didn't ogle each other's bodies while the other was sleeping, or contemplate what the other's lips would feel like, or daydream about how incendiary their compatibility would be in the bedroom.

Yeah, that wasn't friendship. That was a whole heap of trouble she couldn't afford.

Not with her heart or her bank account. Staff members didn't go around seducing the boss's son, despite Jenny and Misty working overtime toward that end. Levi and Mr. Colton might not consider each other to be family but Mathilda, Agnes and the Ms. Coltons did…and they had the power to fire Kate.

"You have so much to learn," Jenny continued. "A girl can never have too many backup plans, and being the wife of a rich, powerful Colton doctor would suit me fine, thank you very much."

Not that Levi had come right out and said it, but Kate had gotten the distinct impression that he didn't have an overabundance of money, and he certainly didn't consider himself part of the powerful Colton family. "You know as well as I do that we're forbidden from dallying with anyone else at the ranch."

"That didn't stop Trevor from getting with Miss Gabby. True love finds a way."

Kate snorted. She highly doubted Jenny understood the concept of love. "If you hate this place so much, why don't you leave on your own and get a job somewhere else?"

"Because the point isn't to work the rest of my life as a servant. The point is to meet my Prince Charming and let him take care of me in the manner I deserve. You see, unlike you, I know how to use the gifts God gave me."

Nothing like mixing in an insult with her delusions of grandeur. "You mean your looks?"

"That's one of them, of course. But looks don't do a girl any good without the ability to plan ahead."

"Ah." Apparently there wasn't much difference between planning and scheming. Jenny was right about one thing, though—Kate was no good at planning out her future. If she was, then her bakery wouldn't have gone under and she wouldn't be working off her debts as an assistant cook. She might even have a few dollars in savings.

"That's why my conscience is clear about taking that kidnapper note off your hands."

"How in the world do you figure that?"

"I'll prove it to you. What were your plans for the note?"

"I wanted to see if there was anything I could do to help catch the culprit."

Jenny snickered as they pulled a dark green blanket onto the bed. "I rest my case. There's got to be something in that note that I can use as leverage."

"I've looked at that thing so much I've memorized it. If there was something in there to help solve the case, I would've found it already." She didn't mention the paltry details the note had yielded—the underline with the swirl at the end and a misplaced apostrophe that indicated a lack of basic grammar schooling.

Jenny shrugged. "Maybe a fresh set of eyes will do the trick. If I help put the man responsible behind bars, then maybe Mr. Colton will even give me a reward. Or maybe I'll sell the information to the police. The possibilities are endless."

"You're not worried about the person who wrote it finding out you're looking into the case?"

"I'm not stupid. I haven't told anyone I've got the letter, and if someone does find out, I'll know it's you who's guilty of telling them. This is what I'm talking about, Kate. Making plans for the future. There's a lot of power to be had by being a woman who has a few secrets up her sleeve. You wait and see."

How was Kate ever going to help Faye now? She'd have to steal the note back from Jenny or find another way.

"Don't feel bad, Kate. At least you know how to use one of your talents." Kate cringed inwardly, wondering what talent Jenny was referring to, until Jenny added, "You can bake better than anyone I know."

She hated to concede a single point to Jenny, but she was right. Kate might not have much else going for her but she'd always have her passion for desserts. The lemon pies she'd baked that afternoon had turned out great. She fully expected rave reviews. She couldn't wait to hear if Levi had enjoyed it as much as she hoped he would.

"Let me check your hospital corners before we get the quilt on," Jenny said.

A deep sigh told Kate she'd failed at the task yet again.

"You tucked the whole side in. How's he supposed to climb in bed?" Jenny lifted the corner of the mattress and yanked the blanket out. With it came something hard and heavy that clattered onto Kate's foot.

"Ouch!" She pulled her foot away and saw a wooden picture frame. Quickly, so Jenny wouldn't beat her to it, she dived down and picked it up.

"What is it?" Jenny asked. "A picture? What is he doing with that under his mattress?"

Jenny and Kate stood shoulder-to-shoulder and studied the picture inside the frame. A young woman dressed in what was probably high fashion in Wyoming thirty years ago. She was holding an infant.

"Do you think that's Jethro's first wife and baby Cole?" Jenny asked.

"Probably." But what if it wasn't? What if it was Levi and his mom? What if Mr. Colton really did care about him but didn't know how to show it? Jenny didn't need to be privy to those questions, though. She'd probably snatch the photograph and barrel straight to Levi's room.

Jenny ran her palm over the glass. "Wait until Misty sees this."

The only way that was going to happen was over Kate's dead body. After Jenny shared her plan to exploit the kidnapping note, there was no telling how she'd use a picture like this. "Misty isn't going to see this. And we shouldn't be looking at it, either, because it's none of our business. We could lose our jobs."

Jenny's eyes remained riveted to the photograph as she shrugged. "I'm leaving anyhow, one way or another. As soon as I get the money together or catch a guy with money to burn, I'm out of here. Maybe I'll sell this ring and go off on my own if I decide my secret admirer is too much trouble to keep around. It's a real diamond, you know."

And unicorns flew through the sky on waves of rainbows. "Maybe you don't care, but I have to. I can't afford to lose this job, and I don't have a knight in shining armor to come riding in on his horse and sweep me off my feet." She didn't want one, even if they did exist.

Why, then, did Levi's face pop into her head?

Frustrated that he'd sneaked into her heart so fast and made her feel what she most certainly had no business feeling, she returned her focus to the photograph. She'd never seen a picture of baby Cole. No one had.

The word around the house was that after the kidnapping, once the case went cold, Mr. Colton destroyed every reminder of the son he'd lost because he was so heartbroken.

Levi had a right to be furious with his father. Kate couldn't blame him one bit because she didn't understand it, either, how a man could be heartbroken over the loss of one son but never so much as breathe a word about the other, who was living in poverty right under his nose.

If this was a photograph of Levi and his mother, then maybe it meant Mr. Colton secretly did care about Levi all those years. It was a long shot but one worth taking nonetheless.

"Do you think the kidnappings are connected?" Jenny asked.

"No idea."

"Trevor and Dylan think last month's kidnapping was a copycat crime." Jenny picked at a cluster of dust that had collected in the corner of the frame. "Not a very good copycat, if that's the case. When baby Avery was kidnapped, nothing else from the house went missing and there was no evidence of breaking in or robbery, like they say happened when Cole was snatched."

"How long after Mrs. Colton's funeral was baby Cole kidnapped?"

Jenny's mouth screwed up. "I can't remember. A month or two, maybe? Do you think Cole Colton died?"

"I like to think that he's alive somewhere, happy, with a good life. It's too sad to imagine otherwise." Though the realist in her figured differently, the part of her that still dreamed of a good, fair world wanted to believe in miracles—even if they never happened to her.

Images of William and Faye crowded her mind. She closed her eyes and imagined the weight of a baby in her arms.

The picture frame was tugged on. Kate clamped her hands more firmly around it and opened her eyes. "Back off, Jenny. This photograph is staying where we found it, and I don't want to hear another word about it."

Jenny shot her an "oh, please" look. "Bossy much? I wanted a closer look is all."

"Ladies. Busy snooping, I see."

Whirling to face the door, Kate flattened the picture behind her back. Trip was leaning against the door-frame, his stylishly shaggy hair hanging over his eyes and his usual smirk mucking up what might otherwise have been a handsome face.

Kate bristled. Trip Lowden, Mr. Colton's ex-stepson, was one of her least favorite people in the world, but—lucky her—he was Jenny and Misty's favorite and therefore a frequent topic of discussion in the staff quarters. If he wasn't such a freeloading, good-for-nothing slacker, she would've pegged him as Jenny's supposed secret admirer. But unless he was getting paid to watch television and grope the maids, she couldn't fathom how he would've afforded a diamond ring—even a fake one. And he definitely wasn't the type to give up his life of leisure to run off with Jenny and provide for himself and a wife.

"Not snooping, cleaning," Kate said. To demonstrate, she gathered a handful of the linens to be washed.

"Trip, darling." Jenny walked his way, throwing each hip up as she moved. With a fake pout that was probably supposed to look sexy, she added, "What a devil you are, sneaking up on us like that. You scared me."

It was the diversion Kate needed. While Jenny and Trip made googly eyes at each other near the door, Kate slipped the picture into the wad of sheets and stuffed the whole pile into the laundry bag she'd brought.

Heart pounding, she took inventory of what she still needed to clean so she could get the heck out of there before Jenny realized what she'd done. All that remained was putting the bedspread on. "Come on, Jenny. Let's finish this up. Agnes is probably looking for me in the kitchen, and you know she's always angling for an excuse to get me in trouble."

Jenny drew a pattern over Trip's chest with her fingertip, then sashayed to the bed. Not sensing any of Kate's urgency, she gave Trip a great view of her backside as she bent over and took up a corner of the bedspread. Oh, brother.

Once they got the bedspread smoothed out and were fluffing the pillows, Jenny whispered, "Where is it?"

Kate gestured to the mattress. Jenny would probably look for it as soon as Kate was out of the room, but she planned to have it well hidden before Jenny caught up with her. Once the room was in order, Kate slung the laundry bag over her shoulder and took up her tray of dirty water glasses and other dishes she'd collected from the room. "I might as well take this laundry to the basement for you since I'm already headed to the kitchen."

Jenny managed a "thanks" even though she was distracted again, making use of her feather duster like Kate imagined a stripper might during her French maid routine.

Trip was blocking the door, and despite Kate standing there with her arms full, all he did was offer her a sneering grin.

"Excuse me." She attempted to scoot past him without touching him or dropping the tray but he wouldn't budge. Jerk.

"Don't work too hard, now, Katie." And he looked straight down the neckline of her chef jacket.

Screw it, she thought. Hooking her foot around his ankle, she faked a stumble that tipped the tray just enough that one of the water glasses sloshed onto the back of Trip's linen pants. "Oops."

With a curse, Trip twisted to get a look at the spill. "You little—"

Jenny rushed forward, a napkin in hand, clucking and soothing. She was probably thrilled by Kate's spill so she could get up close and personal with Trip's backside.

"So sorry. I don't know how that happened," Kate deadpanned.

"What is this commotion?" It was Mathilda, striding down the hallway toward Kate.

"I tripped over Trip," Kate said. Too late, she realized how unapologetic the explanation had sounded.

Mathilda looked predictably horrified.

Kate made a show of how precariously balanced she was with the tray and laundry. "I'm on my way to the basement with the laundry, then the kitchen to help with the dinner dishes."

"Slight change of plans for you. Mr. Colton is on his way up. Dinner left him feeling fatigued, and he'll be taking his dessert in his room. Jenny can take the laundry."

Mathilda reached for the laundry bag. Kate danced toward the staff stairwell, light-headed with panic. Nobody disobeyed a direct order from Mathilda.

Indignation flared in Mathilda's eyes. "Set that bag down at once and do as you're told. Mr. Colton is expecting dessert shortly after he arrives in his quarters. I suggest you make haste so as not to keep him waiting."

Kate was already at the stairwell door. "Yes, ma'am. And don't worry about the laundry. I'm already on my way and Jenny will have her hands full with cleaning supplies." She adjusted her tone of voice, hoping to make it sound as if she was doing Mathilda a favor. "I'll leave the bag on the first-floor landing and she can take it the rest of the way to the basement when she has time. It's no trouble at all."

Before Mathilda could disagree, Kate was through the door, dashing down the stairs.

"Tell me you're not calling in sick tomorrow. I'm already short of people." Chris Ortega, Levi's chief resident at the hospital, seemed even more strung out with nerves than usual, which meant he sounded a lot like Kate's kettle right before the water hit the boiling point.

Since Levi hadn't known he was driving to Dead River Ranch until minutes before he hopped in his car, he'd neglected to call in to the hospital until now. He'd never bothered to find out the hospital's policy on family medical leave, but he sure hoped his choice wasn't going to set his career back too far. Chris was a standup guy and he'd lost a parent recently, so Levi was confident Chris would do all he could to give Levi the time he needed.

"I'm not sick, but, uh, I had a family emergency. My fath—" He swallowed the lump in his throat. This wasn't supposed to be difficult to say. A formality. A discussion of a patient's status and nothing more. He shook his head and stared at the sunset from the window in his suite's sitting room. "My father's dying. Acute lymphocytic leukemia."

Chris was silent for a beat, absorbing the news, then offered all the usual words of sympathy one might to someone losing a loved one.

Levi accepted the sentiments, not seeing a need to explain the lack of love between him and Jethro or the complicated nature of their relationship. "I just found out and, uh, didn't give it much thought before I packed up and drove to his house in Wyoming."

"Wyoming, huh? That's quite a haul from Utah. I take it you're going to need some time off work?"

"Yeah. Look, I'm sorry I didn't call you about it sooner. I didn't understand how bad he was." And he definitely hadn't anticipated to be overcome with the need to remain at the ranch and take over Jethro's care.

"It's okay," Chris said. "I've been there myself. I'll take care of the paperwork on this end, and you keep me in the loop on when you think you'll be back."

"Thank you."

"Do you have other family—brothers or sisters, your mom?"

He almost said no. But that wasn't true. Besides the daughters dearest, who knew how many illegitimate half siblings Levi had floating around? Or if Cole Colton was alive somewhere? "My three half sisters are here, too."

"So you're not dealing with this alone. Good."

The conclusion had Levi smiling through his bitterness. The only person at Dead River Ranch preventing Levi from feeling utterly, irredeemably alone was Kate McCord.

When the call ended, Levi stayed at the window. All that talk with Chris about family and loved ones had dredged up Levi's old familiar longings. And despite what he'd told himself to get through the conversation with Chris about Jethro being just another patient, now that he'd said it aloud, it was starting to sink in that his father was dying.

After Jethro died, the state of their relationship would be trapped in amber. There would be no more chance that Jethro would one day express his regret for the way he treated Levi or acknowledge Levi as his son. The epiphany felt like a hard slap to his back, knocking the wind from him. He folded forward, bracing his hands on the desk next to the window.

My God, he was still holding out that ridiculous, juvenile hope. That was the real reason he was staying at the ranch until the end—giving Jethro all the chances left in his life to say what Levi needed to hear. How pathetic.

He sank into his arms, letting his head hang. Why couldn't he stop caring? Why couldn't he let go of the things that were out of his control? One would think he'd have perfected the art of tuning out unpleasantness after the childhood he'd endured. By the time he'd graduated from high school, he'd thought himself numb enough to handle anything life threw his way. But he'd proved that assumption wrong on the day of his mother's funeral and had been battling the same damn demons ever since.

It wasn't until his forehead hit cardboard that he realized he was curling over the box of his mother's possessions. He clamped his eyes closed, gritting his teeth to fight the rush of grief.

*Damn it, Mom. Why did everything have to turn out so screwed up?*

He flattened his palms on the box lid. The element of the unknown infused the box with a kind of toxic cloud, eating up the air and stability of the room. Levi's heart was already crowded with darkness, so perhaps it was as good a time as any to open the box and dispel the mystery before it ate away at him any further.

He'd timed his call to Chris to avoid dinner with the Coltons, planning instead to raid the refrigerator later, and he owed Jethro one last check-in for the night, but all of that could wait. With any luck, he wouldn't find anything worth keeping and could then walk the whole thing out to the trash. Like amputating an infection, he could wipe his hands and heart clean and retake control over his emotions. And move on.

Box in hand, he strode to the carpet in front of the fireplace, set it on the sofa and tore off the lid. The box was half-full of broken odds and ends, old makeup, saggy candles and papers. A pair of white plastic sunglasses sat atop a newspaper clipping. When he read the words scrawled over the clipping in sloppy blue ballpoint-pen ink, his gut twisted.

Maybe this wasn't going to be so simple an exercise after all. He flicked the sunglasses out of the way, snatched up the paper and sank to the ground.

# *Chapter 8*

Kate stared at the closed door, debating how big of an error in judgment it was that she'd volunteered to bring dinner to the private room of a man she found irresistible in every way.

Her heart hammered with anxious exhilaration at the idea that as soon as she knocked, she'd be face-to-face with him again, or rather her face at eye level with the vee of skin framed by his shirt collar that hinted at the tight, muscled chest she'd created a perfect visual of in her imagination.

He'd eye the tray, homing in immediately on the massive wedge of lemon pie she'd brought. She loved the way her desserts changed the landscape of his features, lightening everything. If he was her man, she'd probably carry cookies in her purse to ply him with when he got too serious.

Yeah. Coming to his room wasn't the smartest plan she'd ever dreamed up. Too late now.

Shifting the weight of the tray to her left side, she knocked.

After what felt like an eternity, he opened the door no wider than his body, his expression wary. When he realized it was her, he opened the door all the way and offered a smile that didn't reach his eyes. "Hey."

She pushed the tray out in front of her, ridiculously nervous, waiting for him to notice the pie, but his gaze never strayed from her face.

"I heard you weren't at dinner, so I made you a plate," she said. "Agnes plated the dinner, actually, because it's shrimp and I'm allergic to shellfish, but I offered to bring it to you."

And now she was babbling. Nice going. She bit the inside of her cheek and waited.

He took the tray and leaned against the doorframe, a pose that would've been casual had his face not been tight with repressed emotion. Something was wrong. She sure hoped she wouldn't make it worse by sharing with him the framed photograph she'd smuggled from Mr. Colton's room, presently hidden below the napkins and silverware.

"You don't have to wait on me," he said. "I can take care of myself."

"I know that's one of the reasons why you weren't at dinner, seeing as how you don't like to be waited on, but I brought you a slice of lemon pie, so I also know you won't turn me away."

His focus shifted to the tray and, just like that, his smile turned genuine. "Is this because you're afraid I'm going to wipe out the rest of your crème brûlée when I raid the fridge tonight—which I still plan on doing, by the way? I might even try out that blowtorch of yours so I don't run the risk of eating an incomplete dessert."

Eager to keep his smile in place, she planted her hands on her hips, faking annoyance. "I swear, every man on this ranch wants to get their hands on my blowtorch. One time I walked in on Trevor using it to light birthday candles."

"Nice."

She rolled her eyes. "You're such a guy."

"You noticed."

Her gaze flickered to the vee of skin above his collar while her imagination kicked to life, conjuring an image of him sleeping on the sofa. She wrenched her focus to the tray of food. "Kind of hard to miss."

He tipped his head toward the interior of the room. "Come on in."

She hesitated. This was her last chance to scram before his charm obliterated her already-shredded willpower. Then she recalled the haunted look on his face when he'd first opened the door. Whatever he was going through, maybe he needed a friend. That, she could handle.

She strolled into the room, feigning casual coolness though her heart was hammering like mad. He'd settled cross-legged on the carpet near the fireplace, the tray to one side and in front of him a box she recognized as the one Luella had handed them. Forgoing the covered plate of shrimp and pasta, he picked up the pie.

"You're going to eat the dessert first?"

"Absolutely." He sliced off a bite so huge he had to angle the fork to fit it into his mouth.

"Aren't you worried about the rest of the meal getting cold?"

He swallowed, rolling his eyes back in his head in a demonstration of bliss. "It's no use eating the dinner first while a slice of homemade pie is waiting. With every bite, I'd grow to resent the main course for not being the pie, and by the end of the meal I'd have transformed into a bitter, passive-aggressive diner. It won't do."

She sat across from him, with the box between them, grinning widely as she took in his chatter as though she was starved for it, starved for wit and humor with someone whose worldview matched her own. "That's logic a pastry chef can appreciate."

"Why didn't you bring a piece of pie for yourself?"

She shrugged. "Because the staff doesn't eat with the family."

His face wrinkled into a pained look of incredulity. "Is the staff also trained to only give evasive, B.S. answers?"

In a way, they were. The opinions of employees, especially those as low in the pecking order as Kate, weren't valued or sought. Opinions could, in fact, get you fired. "Sorry. It's habit."

He nodded, thoughtful. "Do you know I have yet to see you eat dessert?" He speared his fork in her direction, waggling a brow. "It's pretty suspicious when a chef's never seen eating her own creations. For all I know, you don't like sweets."

She indulged often, but it usually took the form of sampling as she worked. Rarely did she find the time to sit and eat a proper meal, or even a proper dessert. "Trust me, I eat plenty. But if it makes you feel better..." She swiped the spoon from the tray, carved off half of the remaining pie and popped it in her mouth.

"It does, actually." He polished off the last of his pie with a flourish. "You know what that tasted like? More."

"I'll make it easy to find in the refrigerator at midnight-snack time."

He set the empty plate on the tray. "I'm not like them. I'm serious, Kate. I don't want you to feel like you're a servant around me."

"I know you're not like them, but you might be surprised to discover that the Coltons are good people."

He shot her an "I smell horse pucky" look.

"I'm serious. The Colton women are kindhearted to their cores. I'm happy here. This ranch is a great place to call home." *Until...* Grief washed over her. Poor Faye.

As if reading her mind, he said, "If you don't count the kidnapping and murder last month. Or Cole Colton's kidnapping thirty years ago."

She chewed her lower lip, deliberating. "I brought something to show you." She pushed the napkins out of the way and held out the photograph. "I found it in Mr. Colton's room, under his mattress. I thought it might be you and your mom. Maybe he cares about you more than he lets on."

Levi held the photograph by the wood frame and stared at it, his face turning stoic. When he finally looked up at her, his eyes were mournful. "I don't know what I looked like as a baby because my mom never took any pictures, but that's not my mom. I bet it's Cole and Jethro's first wife, Brittany. Thank you for thinking of me, though." He handed it back to her and she tucked it under the napkins again. "Would you like to see a picture of my mom? I think there's one or two in here."

He rummaged through the box and pulled out a sepia-tinted square photograph. Kate scooted close and took a long look at the smiling face of the frail-looking woman in orange bell-bottoms and a crocheted blouse. "You inherited your eyes and hair from her."

He studied the picture. "I suppose you're right. She was prettier than this picture shows."

Kate took a second look at the picture. "I can tell how pretty she was just from this."

He huffed. "It's weird, going through this box of her stuff. I thought I knew everything about her life, but there are a couple things in here that threw me for a loop." He cringed and scratched his neck. "I don't know why I'm telling you that personal stuff. I'm sorry to dump that on you. You're a really good listener." He shook his head as if to clear it.

Men could be so dense. Trying to be tough and stoic. Of course he didn't like to talk about topics that brought his grief to the surface. Then again, maybe it was short-sighted of her to think it was only men who tried to bottle it. Kate hadn't wanted to talk about William's and Olive's deaths, either.

She couldn't talk to her parents or brother, or any of her friends. But Faye helped her see the value in opening up. Under Faye's gentle coaxing, Kate began to heal. Didn't mean she was over her losses. She never wanted to be okay with what had happened to William and Olive, but she now knew better than to let such things sit like poison in her soul.

She inched closer until their shoulders touched. "You're not dumping—you're getting it off your chest. Big difference." She tapped the rim of the box. "Walk me through it."

* * *

He wasn't sure he could talk about his past. He never, ever did. There wasn't a point to it except to get dragged back into the grief and the guilt that had consumed too much of his life already. But if he refused her gentle persuasion to open to her, then she'd probably leave. She'd take her softness with her and that full, thick head of hair that was brushing against his arm. She'd take those big brown eyes away, and her warmth, too, and he'd be alone in this sterile, uncomfortable room again. With nothing but a box of pain as company.

And that was unacceptable, even if it meant giving voice to parts of his life he wanted nothing more than to bury.

From the box he picked up the sunglasses. He didn't remember his mom wearing them, but they looked like the kind of cheap, gaudy accessory she favored. He flipped the ear pieces out, let his mind get temporarily distracted wondering what those ear sticks were called, then shook his head to clear it. "I always thought Jethro's affair with my mom was brief. Like, a few weeks. Just long enough for her to get pregnant with me."

"Anything specific make you think that?"

Sighing, he thought back. "No…not really, I guess. She never said it exactly, but it was obvious when I got older that she'd gotten pregnant with me because she thought it might make Jethro love her and invite her to live on the ranch. She never let up about how I needed to be ready to live here because someday we were going to be called home."

"Sounds like how some people talk about the 'end of days.'"

The comparison was so perfect that he released a

hard, silent laugh, then tossed the sunglasses in the box. "Pretty much. You could definitely describe my mom as evangelical about Jethro."

"That must have been hard to hear."

"I didn't know any better until I started school. All I cared about was making Mom happy and that meant the two of us daydreaming about when we'd move to the big mansion on the hill, as she called it. I have a very specific memory from first grade of telling my friends about it and getting laughed at. It took a cold shoulder from Jethro when we saw him in town for me to figure out that maybe Mom wasn't the best authority on where she and I would be living in the future."

"Mr. Colton ignored you?"

"For the most part, yeah. That time I mentioned, my mom saw him coming out of a church after a wedding ceremony with his daughters. She started waving and hollering. I must've only been six or seven because I was still a believer, so to speak. I ran right up to Jethro and grabbed onto his leg. He shook me off like I was a stray dog and told my mom to control her child."

There was a lot of shame floating around in that particular memory. He could summon it still, the shame and confusion of that day, of looking up from the ground to find Amanda, Catherine and Gabriella watching him from over their shoulders as Jethro hustled them away.

He flinched at the unexpectedness of Kate's hand touching his skin, smoothing over his arm. Man, he liked the feel of her hand, those slender fingers and smooth, soft palm. He crossed his right hand over and captured hers, then transferred it decisively into his left.

"Anyway, look what I found in the box." He pulled out the newspaper clipping that had rocked him off his axis before Kate had arrived with the food tray and set it on his bent knees for her to see. "Do you know how Brittany Colton died?"

"Yes. Faye told me she died in a car accident when Cole was an infant."

Levi's gut clenched. After all this time, the mere mention of car accidents shouldn't have affected him so acutely. He blamed the recurring nightmares of his own accident for keeping the wound raw.

The black-and-white photograph had been roughly cut away from the article that it had most likely accompanied. It depicted a line of people standing outside a church where, according to the caption, Brittany Colton's funeral was taking place. One woman's face had been circled at least a dozen times with the sloppy loops of a ballpoint pen. *Whore* was written next to it, over the face of a young, strapping Jethro. The word had been written with such force that little tears had been made in the paper.

"Who is she?" Kate asked as her focus shifted to the photograph's caption.

"Desiree Beal," he replied, having already performed the name search. "Does that name ring a bell to you?"

Her mouth screwed up as though she was thinking hard. "It does, but I can't remember where I've heard it. I've only lived in Dead for five years, and there's a lot of history I don't know. If her identity doesn't come to me, then Agnes and Mathilda would know. They were around back then."

"My instinct is telling me that this Beal woman was Jethro's mistress. Why else would my mom feel so strongly about her? I mean, doesn't that look like the work of a jealous woman? But a mistress at his wife's funeral…even Jethro wouldn't stoop that low."

"Agreed. How old are you? Were you born around this time?"

"Over two years later. I'm twenty-seven."

"I'm going to come right out and ask you—please don't be offended. Are you sure about your age?"

"Yes. I mean, why wouldn't I be? I have a birth certificate." He didn't have any other proof than that, not really. But what would've been the purpose of faking his age, especially in a small town like Dead, where something like that would be nearly impossible to get away with?

Then it hit him what Kate might be getting at. "I'm not Cole Colton."

"I don't think so, either, but it's at least worth considering. Your mom didn't have much money and she was obsessed with Mr. Colton."

Damn it, she was right.

"Mathilda would know who Desiree Beal is. Agnes, too, but I would never ask her. Both of them worked here since before Jethro's first marriage, and I know Mathilda would never betray your confidences if you asked. She's a strict boss but also kind and fair. And unlike Agnes, she doesn't gossip."

"But she might not know why my mom hated Desiree. The person I really need to talk to is Luella, fingers crossed that her memory isn't too fried from the drugs. It's the best place I can think of to start."

"Agreed." She picked up his dinner plate. "Time to eat before it gets cold."

He accepted it and dug in enthusiastically. "You said

you've lived in Dead for five years. How long have you worked here?"

"Four years."

"And before that?"

"I worked at the Dead River Diner for a few months. Before that I owned a bakery in Laramie."

"Wow. You were young to own a business."

"True. Too young, I think, looking back. It'd been my dream since I was a little girl to open my own bakery. William supported my dream, financially and emotionally. He was my neighbor growing up, older than me by ten years and a successful structural engineer. We opened the bakery in Laramie the year we got married. I was nineteen."

"What happened to it?"

"Life."

"Your husband died."

She nodded. "I tried to hold on to the business on my own, but…" She shrugged, her expression taking on the dull weight of defeat. "When the money ran out and my bakery went under, I had nothing. Less than nothing, according to the creditors. Faye—the woman who died last month—helped me secure this job. I'm grateful for it because at least I get to make dessert while I regroup and figure out what to do with my life next."

"What is your new dream?"

"*Dream* isn't a word I throw around anymore."

"Why not?"

She fiddled with a button on her jacket, her expression pained. "I had everything I cared about taken away, my one dream destroyed. And it's not like my spirit is some kind of magic well that will refill whenever I want. It doesn't work that way. My goal is to someday soon get back on my own two feet and survive."

He knew all about having a soul marred with holes and cracks and irreparable damage, but it frustrated him that she'd let it destroy her hope. He set the plate down and brushed a lock of hair away from her face. "I want more for you than that. I want you to want more for yourself than that."

"You don't even know me."

She'd thrown his words from that morning back at him, which was fitting, he supposed. And she was right, as far as details of her life or past went. But he knew her. In the ways that really mattered, they were two of a kind. "I might not know you, but I get you."

Of its own volition, his focus dropped to her lips. He'd fantasized about kissing her since he'd overheard her arguing with Jethro about bread pudding. Tonight, she'd taste of lemon pie and sweet skin and womanly softness. He could hardly stand to sit there next to her, he wanted her so badly.

She squirmed, putting a few inches of space between them. "You should stop looking at me like that."

"Why?"

"Because it makes me want to kiss you."

A thrill lit through him. It was uncanny how similarly their minds worked. She wanted to kiss him, too. Pulse pounding with anticipation, he touched his thumb to her chin. "And the problem with that is?"

She shook his hand away and launched to her feet. "Assistant cooks don't go around kissing Coltons. And I can't afford to lose this job."

He stood, preparing to chase after her when she fled, but she walked to the window.

He followed. "There's no one here but the two of us, and I would never tell. You're going to have to get more creative in your excuses if you expect me not to kiss you now, knowing that you're thinking about it like I am."

Determination settled over her features. "How about if I tell you it's because I like to take things slow?"

He braced a hand against the windowpane behind her. "No, you don't."

Her hands were by her sides, and she gripped the drapery behind her. "How would you know?"

Because he just did. Because although they'd only known each other for a span of days, he felt as if she'd been a part of him for an eternity. She'd call him crazy if he said so, though. "With as much passion as you put into your baking, there's no way you like to take things slow. Try again."

"Fine." She sucked in a sharp inhalation. "It's because you scare me."

Oh. He froze, processing, then stepped back, giving her space. "Seriously? Why?"

She shook her head.

"Kate, please. I need to know why."

"Because I want you too much. I can't stop thinking about you, and I can't—"

The words shattered his control. She wanted him. He snagged her around the waist and took her head in his hands. The thought that he was about to kiss her made him light-headed and hyperaware of every shift of her body, every breath she released, the delicate floral scent of her hair.

Eyes searching, she touched his chest. "Levi," she said on an exhalation. "You scare me so badly."

"You know what experts say is the best way to get over your fear, right?"

The question earned him the slightest hint of a smile. "To face it head-on."

He lowered his lips to hers. "Exactly."

Then he kissed her. And it was everything he'd imagined. Sweet and lemony and soft…and Kate, in his arms and all around him, kissing him back, flooding his senses with the power of her passion. It was better than crème brûlée, more wicked than peaches.

He pressed her against the window and kissed her deeper. She purred her pleasure and threaded her fingers in his hair. Bliss, pure and simple. Like coming home. Locked against him, she was everything he never knew he needed, and he had no idea how he'd ever get through another day without this, without Kate.

The thought was enough to shock him to reality. He tore away from her mouth. Breathing hard, he stalked to the far end of the room and scrubbed a hand over his face, as if it were possible to erase the memory of the feel and taste of her. As if he could ever forget something so powerful.

This wasn't how it was supposed to be. He was a rock—an island. He, alone, was in charge of his destiny. No one else. At this stage of his life and career, he sure as hell didn't need someone swooping in and making him dependent, making him crave more out of life than he could control. What had gotten into him? What was it about Dead River Ranch that stripped him so completely of his carefully crafted composure?

"I can't do this," Kate said.

He jerked his gaze up to look at her. She remained pressed flat against the window, a battle warring in her expression that told him she was as freaked out as he was.

Maybe they could agree to forget the kiss had happened. Okay, maybe not, because that kiss was the most mind-blowing he'd ever experienced, but at least they could agree not to do it again. "I can't, either."

She twisted the drapes. "It took me six years, but I'm almost out of debt, and I may not have any dreams, but I have a plan for myself. Since William died, I've gone without this, and until you showed up on the ranch, it hadn't bothered me. I didn't want it. But you..." She shook her head. "You're too..." Her head-shaking grew more vehement, as if whatever she thought he was exceeded the spoken language.

As her nervous rambling sank in, he braced his hands on the back of the sofa. "Six years is a long time to go without sex." As soon as the words were out of his mouth, he gave himself a hearty mental kick. *Way to go, man. Because if kissing scares you both witless, then the right thing to do is bring up sex.*

"Oh." She blinked at him, surprised. "That's not what I meant. I'm not abstinent, but there's a big difference between scratching an itch and starting something that matters."

*Something that matters.*

He stood in stunned silence. So she'd felt it, too. He'd been in such a haze of need that he hadn't put it all together, how she made him feel, what she made him want. What they'd done was more than physical, more than a kiss. It was a door opening.

And Levi had no intention of walking through it. It wouldn't be fair to Kate. Because the curse of being a Colton wasn't the only legacy Jethro had handed him, nor the most damaging. He'd learned the hard way from one failed relationship after another that, despite his best intentions, he was incapable of sustaining any kind of meaningful connection with others outside the realm of doctor/patient relationships. Kate talked about scars from the past, and that was his.

Only in doctoring had he found a way to connect to other people. It was more than a calling. It was his path to atonement. His lifeline to humanity. "I'm sorry." Not about kissing her, necessarily, but because he couldn't deliver on the promise of it.

"Not as sorry as I am. You have to understand, my heart doesn't beat like that anymore." She flitted toward the sitting area and grabbed the tray. "I have to go."

He supposed he should be grateful that she was leaving his room, grateful that she didn't want to start something with him that he'd screw up sooner or later. His heart didn't beat like that, either…never had. But, inconceivably, desperation welled up inside him to chase after her. He wanted more than anything to prove she was wrong, not about him, but about herself. He might never be able to love, but she had far too much life and brightness in her to believe herself as damaged as he was.

Somehow, he stopped himself from giving chase. He had to force himself to stay away from her. And by God, he had to stop feeling so much. He'd spent his life striving to stop caring about things out of his control. It was the reason he'd come to Dead River Ranch—to look his father in the eye and prove he was nothing like the man so he could put the ghosts of his past to rest for good. To stop feeling the pain and longing and grief so deeply and regain control.

But every waking hour since he'd arrived, all he'd

thought about was Kate. He couldn't get her out of his head or out of his heart. He couldn't stop wishing he could be the man she deserved. He couldn't stop wanting her. Beyond a kiss, beyond sex, beyond the scope of his stay at the ranch. Like it or not, Kate McCord had grabbed him by his spirit and she wasn't letting go.

The question was, what was he going to do about it?

# *Chapter 9*

Kate's small, windowless bedroom might as well have been a coffin for all the solace it provided. She'd done her best to shine up the space with dried wildflowers, pretty pictures from magazines and an elaborate crocheted table runner—handmade by Faye and given to her as a birthday gift—on her dresser. But tonight, the room was far too small to handle a mind overflowing with warring emotions.

It seemed incomprehensible that she could simultaneously feel both a renewed grief for all she'd lost right alongside blazing desire for Levi. Yet, here it was an hour since she'd fled Levi's room and she was still reeling, her heart torn asunder.

Levi's arrival at the ranch had been too much, too fast on the heels of Faye's passing. It had been a long time since anyone had asked her anything beyond the easy questions. Even longer since a man had looked at her as though he saw right into the core of her being, the intensity of his gaze pouring over her as sweet and heavy as melted chocolate.

She felt overwhelmed and off track. This wasn't a part of her plan.

Then again, it was ridiculous of her to believe for a second that she was in control of her destiny. She knew better than that. She'd naively thought she held the reins of her life until William's and Olive's deaths, when Mother Nature taught her what a dangerous illusion it was to feel in control.

She still needed a plan to get on her own two feet, because spending the rest of her life at the beck and call of a wealthy family and two tyrannical bosses sounded akin to the fourth level of hell, but she knew better than to become invested in her future with any emotion other than relentless determination.

She'd been doing great until Levi showed up with his haunting eyes, dry wit and body that begged to be worshipped. He'd fawned over her desserts, dredged up her past with probing questions and forced himself into her awareness, leaving her restless for more.

Then he'd kissed her as though his very existence hinged on the connection of their bodies.

She vaulted off her bed, cursing as lust with a chaser of fear rippled through her at the memory. That kiss had rocked her off her foundation in a serious way. It shouldn't have. She'd kissed other men since William, even some kisses of the toe-curling variety with men who were clearly experts in the skill.

But never had a kiss filled her with fantasies about shooting for the moon and grabbing hold of a new life, a new love, a fresh start. She'd barely recovered from her last shot at love and happiness—if she could call herself *recovered* yet.

She paced from one side of her double bed to the other, her body quivering with lust and stress, her mind whirring at a mile a minute, trying to make sense of it all. Before she realized it, she was standing in front of her wardrobe, reaching for the drawer that held her most prized possessions.

After a moment's hesitation, she pulled the drawer open. She'd stowed the photograph of Brittany and Cole here for safekeeping until she could return it to Mr. Colton's room. She moved it out of the way and touched her fingertips to the box below. Did she dare go there tonight, to the darkest place in her heart, but also the most familiar? Perhaps this was what she needed to erase the memory of Levi's kiss and reinvigorate her resolve to stick with her plan.

She withdrew the box and sat on the end of her bed. Tears crowded her eyes before she'd gotten the lid off, the box was so loaded with symbols of her pain. She swiped at the wetness at the corners of her eyes and gave herself over to the journey through her past.

By design, a photograph of William sat on top. When she dug into her memory box she liked to look at him first and remember how it had all started in her previous life. She'd had such a crush on him in high school. He took her out on their first date the day after she turned eighteen. She was tickled to be dating an older man, as if twenty-eight was so mature an age.

The picture was of him in a heavy jacket, pants and boots, sitting on the front porch steps of the modest house they bought while engaged. He'd been winded after shoveling snow, but his dark brown hair was slicked down and his handsome Irish face—blue eyes with thick, long lashes, pale skin and thin lips—glowed in exasperated amusement. She'd chuckled and taken a picture as evidence, or so she told him. He hadn't been keen on manual labor so snow-shoveling duties usually went to Kate. But she was pregnant and had plied him with the promise of his favorite cake: pineapple angel food with a coconut glaze.

Their relationship was far from perfect but she'd loved him with all her heart. So much so that she didn't understand how she could also love a baby with all her heart. The math didn't add up.

She picked up a photograph of her and William taken during her pregnancy. At the time, it'd seemed so funny that she'd been worried about having enough love to share, because before her belly had rounded or she'd felt the first flutter of movement, she'd fallen head over heels in love with her baby. Each unique love made its own space in a person's heart, she'd discovered.

It was only a few months later that she learned the cruelest lesson of all. The spaces in a heart created by the people you love don't disappear with their deaths. They remain there, achingly hollow and ever aware of the loss.

She'd never gotten to hold Olive, who'd been eight weeks from her due date when she died right there inside Kate on the side of the road in the dark of night during one of the worst rainstorms in Wyoming history. The storm had worsened unexpectedly, and when they were too far into the open country to turn back. The falling tree, the rain-slick road. Behind the wheel, there had been nothing she could've done to avoid the oncoming car.

Setting the stack of photographs in the box aside, she pulled out the baby blanket that had been part of the care basket she'd received at the hospital from the Angel Support Network, the volunteers who gave grieving mothers of unborn babies something tangible to hold on to.

She held the fuzzy pink blanket to her face. It hurt like no other pain in the world, thinking about the baby she lost, the precious life she never got to know. But the hurt wasn't as raw as it once was. It didn't suck her into despair anymore. Not like those first few months. In a way, she'd come to accept the grief as permanent and didn't fight it anymore. It was as much a part of her as her talent for baking.

She purposely hadn't told Levi about losing Olive. She'd sensed he needed to know she understood what it meant to grieve, which was why she told him about William, but bringing attention to her loss as a mother would've been too much, shifting the focus to her, snatching away from him the moment he needed.

She could tell he was going through something profound, looking at the same motel she'd glanced at every time she'd gone to the supermarket in the years since she made Dead her home. Nothing but an eyesore, she'd thought. Some roach-infested hole of a place that ought to be demolished.

Levi had called it home. And she could tell by the look on his face, the tears threatening in his eyes, that there was more to the story than that.

She draped the blanket around her neck and hugged her knees close as the first tears dropped from her eyes.

She'd thought her life was going in one direction, merrily and without incident. At twenty, she'd thought she had the world by the reins.

She and William had cashed in everything so she could go after her dream of owning a bakery. The little shop struggled, but then, what new business didn't? But the lack of income stressed William out more than he'd expected. It stressed her out, too. They hadn't had a perfect marriage to begin with, and her struggling business only magnified the weak points in their relationship. Still, they were doing their best and neither was anywhere near ready to give up.

The weekend he died, William had decided to join her in Dead at the last minute. She was slated to promote the bakery at a local church fair and was delighted that he'd opted to come. *Maybe this is the upturn,* she'd thought. *If we both keep trying for baby Olive's sake, we'll be fine. Happy, even.*

She covered her hair with the baby blanket and rubbed her tears on it.

Her parents adored William as though he was their own. Once, on a night he'd had too much to drink, her father had joked that if she and William ever got a divorce, they'd have a tough time picking sides. Their grief over losing him and their only grandchild hadn't left any room for them to support her.

There had been no justice for William's and Olive's deaths. Mother Nature was above the law. But Faye's death could be avenged. It wasn't too late. Jenny may have stolen a copy of the kidnapping-for-hire letter, but Kate wasn't ready to quit. Burying her nose in the blanket, she let the ghosts of the people she'd loved crowd around her, settling her not so much into a state of peace, but one of determination to make things right. Maybe then she wouldn't feel so haunted.

She stood, wrapping the blanket around her shoulders like a shawl.

The ranch hand who'd carelessly taken Faye's life during baby Avery's kidnapping wasn't working alone. Someone had hired him to commit the crime, someone who knew the Coltons well enough to realize that the kidnapped baby wasn't Amanda's daughter, Cheyenne. Kate had overheard Mathilda talking with the sisters and knew the head housekeeper had been asked to present a list of ranch employees and their alibis to the police.

And Kate knew where to find a copy. It was time to whittle down her list of suspects.

From her nightstand, she grabbed a flashlight, then slipped silently into the hall. The hour was late enough that the staff had retired to their rooms. Though she heard the muffled sounds of televisions behind closed doors, she didn't run into anyone as she stole down the stairs to Mathilda's desk off the employee dining room.

The dining room was dark and empty, as was the kitchen. She tightened the blanket around her and traded the light of the flashlight for that of the delicate green glass desk lamp gracing Mathilda's desk.

The top of the desk was clear. Biting her lips in concentration, she eased the top left drawer open ever so carefully and leafed through the files. Nothing but employee evaluations and personnel files.

She repeated the torturously slow pull of the middle drawer. Below a spiral-bound address book, she hit pay dirt. A typed spreadsheet of ranch employees, organized by years of service and detailing where each was on the day of the kidnapping. "Bingo," she whispered, flipping through the pages and skimming the names.

After she made her own copy, she'd add a few names to the list—Darla, Trip and Tawny, and people in town who were vocal in their dislike of Mr. Colton. After all, it wasn't only servants and ranch hands who were capable of committing murder.

She soft-stepped to the printer and turned it on.

The overhead light burst to life. Kate whirled to face the door and looked into the eyes of the last person she would've wanted to catch her snooping. "Mathilda, I was—"

"Rifling through my papers? I'd say I hoped you had a good reason for this, but I can't imagine there is one." She picked up Kate's flashlight and rapped it against the palm of her other hand.

Kate's mouth hung open, her mind coming up blank on viable explanations as Mathilda plucked the list from her hands. "First the letter and now this? Do you really think you're qualified to be digging into a kidnapping and murder investigation? It seems to me you're in way over your head. I know you miss Faye, but this—" she swept the hand with the flashlight toward her desk "—this is unconscionable."

Kate cleared her throat, finding her voice. "I'm sorry. It's just that I have to try to help. What if one of us is next? What if the person attempts the kidnapping again?"

"Of course you're worried, dear. We all are. You need to trust that the Coltons and I are working with the police to catch the person responsible." She tucked the flashlight under her arm and reached toward Olive's blanket. Kate scooted out of reach. The blanket was too sacred for anyone else to handle.

Mathilda's lips flattened into a straight line. "Tell me, did you dispose of the letter, as I recommended for your safety?"

Blame it on karma or her country upbringing because she couldn't throw Jenny to the wolves. "I lost it."

Mathilda folded her arms across her chest. "Why don't I believe you?"

Kate tried to make her face look sincere, trustworthy. "It's the truth."

"Hmm, I see. Off you go to bed, then." She returned the flashlight to Kate. "My advice to you—stay away from business that makes you look bad, as this does. It's beneath the dignity of the Colton name to have their staff performing vigilante justice on their behalf. Theirs is not a household built on sins and secrets."

"Yes, ma'am." Kate performed a slight bow and turned for the stairs, thoroughly defeated. Mathilda and her old-school sensibilities thought it sacrilegious to believe an estate as wealthy and prosperous as the Coltons' could be anything except stalwart, but with last month's kidnapping and murder, a house of sins and secrets was exactly what it had become.

Three days after kissing Kate, the alarm on Levi's watch beeped him awake at the same ungodly hour—four-fifty-five in the morning. He rolled to his back and stretched his feet over the arm of the sofa as he struggled to convince his body to work. It boggled the mind how Kate managed her long workdays week after week, month after month.

The night they kissed, he'd endured hours of restlessness in the loathsome guest suite, talking himself down from the panic swirling around the implacable needs she'd evoked. At a loss for how to cope, he'd sifted through the box from Luella again. All that had done, though, was pile on a fresh flood of grief and frustration to his already-haywire emotional state.

He hadn't felt that out of control in a lot of years and it pissed him off something fierce. All that unnecessary emotion was weakness. And the only thing that weakness brought with it was pain. Vulnerability and pain and lapses in judgment—three things that nearly got him killed after his mom's funeral.

Time to rein it in and regain control. He didn't have to feel anything for Kate that he didn't want to. Enjoying a beautiful, vivacious woman's company did not bind him to her for life. She didn't want to do any more than scratch an itch and, while he wouldn't have phrased it so crassly, neither did he. So why shouldn't they give in to what they wanted and forget the rest?

It was while stewing on that epiphany that a plan had taken root in his mind—one that involved seducing Kate on terms they could both live with. That night, he'd abandoned the guest suite and trekked through the dark house to the sofa in the employee dining hall. The sofa was comfortable and the smell and feel of the room soothing. Most importantly, sleeping there gave him a solid half hour alone with Kate each morning before the household woke.

It centered him to feel in control again. With his mind fixed on Kate, he barely afforded any thoughts to his mom, Jethro or the Desiree Beal mystery.

The first two mornings Kate had tromped down the stairs to find Levi waiting for her in the kitchen, she was skittish, as he'd expected. He kept their conversations light while sipping coffee and watching her bake. For two days, it had been enough to be with her, chatting.

Today, though, it was time for the next step in his plan. He rose from the sofa, stretched and rolled his shoulders, then snagged his toothbrush and toothpaste from the table and plodded to the restroom.

He was back in the employee dining room, sitting at the table, in time to hear the heavy footfalls and cranky muttering that preceded Kate's appearance at the bottom of the stairwell. He couldn't help but smile, listening to her grumble. Her pre-coffee grumpiness was adorable.

Her gaze went right to him and she straightened. "You're back."

Her cheeks were a freshly scrubbed shade of pink, and her hair had been pulled into a messy ponytail that reminded him he'd never seen her with her hair down. He'd be changing that soon, if he got his way.

He stood. "You knew I would be. I love watching you bake bread."

Her scowl eased a smidgen. "Then I hope it's not too big of a disappointment that I'm making cinnamon rolls today."

Dang, did that ever sound good. He'd have to add an extra hour of cardio to his workout to counterbalance cinnamon rolls for breakfast. "With icing?"

He didn't actually care about icing, but knowing about Kate's preoccupation with dessert perfection, he had to ask, if only to enjoy her reaction.

Sure enough, she scoffed and stomped toward the kitchen. "You can't even call them cinnamon rolls if they don't come with icing."

He hung back from following her until he'd tamped down the urge to pull her into his arms and kiss away her grumpies. The plan was to touch her this morning in small doses, not abandon his strategy to reckless desires. Once he'd regained control, he took his usual seat on a stool near the center work island and watched her fix coffee.

"You slept here again last night, didn't you?" she asked.

"I don't find the guest suite very hospitable."

"I'm sure you're the Coltons' first guest to feel that way, but I agree with you. Those pieces of antique furniture with skinny legs don't seem all that trustworthy."

"Right? That's exactly what I was thinking. And all that embroidered silk looks rather disreputable."

She poured his coffee. "I'd go so far as to say it's ignominious."

He gripped both hands around the mug to stop from reaching out and pulling her up against him. "There's a word you don't hear every day."

"It was an answer on a crossword puzzle."

"Like *quibbles.*"

They shared a smile loaded with awareness, not only of their physical chemistry, but of how much they enjoyed each other's company.

The image emerged in his mind of the two of them in pajamas on a Sunday morning, drinking coffee and solving a crossword together. Traitorous imagination. That wasn't what he wanted from her, and it certainly wasn't what she wanted from him. He shook the fantasy away.

Stick to the plan.

"Would you like to hear a secret about that guest suite?" she asked.

"I'm all ears."

"When there aren't any guests visiting, Jenny—one of the maids—sneaks in and sleeps in the bed."

He chuckled. That juicy bit of gossip perfectly matched the impression he'd gotten of Jenny. Boy, would she be in for a rude awakening if she ever got the chance to discover that money did not actually bring about eternal happiness. "I met her outside Jethro's room, remember? She was quite…friendly."

Kate's spine stiffened. "Be careful around her. She's a user. Looking for an elevator daddy to raise her station in life."

"You mean a sugar daddy?"

She wagged the coffee scoop at him. "Don't go disrespecting my favorite ingredient like that. I've staked my livelihood on the many glories of sugar."

"And I am ever so grateful for your talent with it."

She set a mug in front of him. "I'd forgotten how inspiring it was to bake for people who truly appreciate it. Thank you for reminding me."

It was a crime that she'd been allowed to forget how wondrous she was, in or out of the kitchen. Shame on this ranch for not exalting her as they should have.

Time for his first move. Before she could dart off, he reached out and fingered the sleeve of her chef jacket at the cuff. She allowed it to happen, swaying closer to his body, so close that her legs came within a hairbreadth of touching his knees.

"We need to talk," he said.

"We are talking. So far we've covered cinnamon rolls, villainous furniture, crossword puzzles and sugar."

He brushed the back of his hand against the back of hers and shook his head. "We need to talk about you and me and what we both want."

She responded with a ragged inhalation, turned on her heel and headed for the refrigerator.

He pushed off the stool and stood. "Hear me out. We haven't talked about the other night and you know we need to."

She removed a covered bowl, then stood facing the closed refrigerator door. At least she was listening without cutting him off at the pass.

"So you're scared. I am, too," he continued. "I don't know what the right move is or what the future holds. But I do know that you being here at Dead River Ranch is the only thing making this place bearable to me." In his voice, he recognized the beginnings of the same damn fear and yearning he'd felt the other night. He stopped and breathed, calming down, getting a handle on himself. "We can control this. We want each other and, Kate, I can't think of one good reason why we shouldn't—"

"Scratch each other's itches?"

He braced his hands on the refrigerator door, caging her between his arms. "We can agree to keep it under control."

"That never works, and you know why? Because control is an illusion." She ducked under his arm and brushed past him. "We're all at the mercy of nature and the heavens and bad people."

It was a crime of the highest order that the world's cruelties had been allowed to turn her so cynical. Then again, who was he kidding? He was the most cynical person he knew. Still, he hated to think of her losing hope. “What if I prove you wrong?”

She slammed the bowl on the counter. “What if I prove *you* wrong?”

“Not going to happen.”

“You know the only thing I can control? My cooking. And that’s what I need to get busy doing right now.” She made a beeline to the pantry.

But she underestimated his resolve. Hell-bent on proving he was right and satisfying both their needs, he prowled after her.

## *Chapter 10*

Levi stood at the pantry's threshold until Kate acknowledged him with a glance. Then she stilled, a hand on the flour bin. He pressed close, splaying a hand over her lower back and dipping his mouth to her ear. "You still owe me a croissant-making lesson."

She turned, the bin out in front of her like a shield. "That's not a good idea anymore."

"A promise is a promise. Name the time."

"There's no good time. The kitchen's always crowded with people."

"Nice try. I've been in here at midnight and it's empty. And it's empty now." He brushed her lower lip with his thumb. Change of plans. Forget waiting until the croissant lesson—he was going to kiss her right here.

He took the flour from her and set it on a shelf. Despite her obvious nerves and the hesitancy she'd voiced, she didn't tell him to stop. She didn't duck away. Emboldened, he cupped her cheeks with his hands, looked into her anxious eyes, then captured her lips with his.

She went stiff until he stroked her lip with his tongue. Then she melted into him, surrendering her body to his will. She made a whimpering sound into his mouth that vibrated against his tongue, but it was the feel of her hands lifting his shirt to feel his stomach that fueled his driving need to claim her body. To never let her go and the world be damned.

He pressed her against the pantry shelves, pinning her with his hips, taking more. As much as she would give him for as long as she would give it. Forever.

He wrenched his mouth away, his final thought echoing ominously in his head. *Forever?* He didn't know that word was in his relationship vocabulary. He fought to hide the panic from his expression but feared he failed miserably.

He tried to back away, but she took his head in her hands and locked him to her. "Look at me," she said, her voice low and thick.

He pulled his gaze from the doorway he'd been staring blankly through to look her full in the face, at her dilated eyes and mouth that was moist and slightly swollen. The most erotic vision he'd ever seen.

"Did that feel like control to you?" she asked.

Hell, no. One minute he was going along with the plan he'd laid out and the next he'd lost complete command of his senses. How had he allowed that to happen again? He touched his lower lip with his tongue, absentmindedly wondering if his lips were as marked with passion as hers were.

She pushed him away and grabbed the bin of flour again. "No more kissing. Neither one of us could handle what came next. You know I'm right."

She made to slink around him and leave the pantry, but he lassoed her waist with his hand and backed her up against him, breathing into the hair at her temple. He needed to counter her argument with logic about control and plans and scratching itches.

Too bad his blood was flooded with hot, thick testosterone and all he could think was *more*. "I still want you."

She pressed her back and butt into him, and when she twisted her neck to look him in the eye, her expression glinted with challenge. "Fine. Tonight, after everyone's asleep, I'll teach you how to make croissants."

Not what he was expecting, but he'd take it. He nipped at her ear. "Also happening tonight—I'm going to kiss you again." His hands roved over her stomach, and it was only the idea that he needed to remain under strict self-control that kept him from moving them up or down. "I'm not going to let a little fear stop me from getting what I want."

She peeled his hands from her body and stepped into the kitchen, drilling him with a hard look from over her shoulder. "All I can tell you is to be careful what you wish for."

Kate had really gone and done it this time. She'd let her stubbornness paint her right into a corner. No doubt she was going to prove Levi wrong about control, but at what price to herself?

Levi had left the kitchen immediately, probably knowing better than to push his luck. Kate paced around the center island, getting a grip on her irritation before Agnes and the other waitstaff appeared.

The crux of her problem was that she liked everything about Levi. That kiss in the pantry had lit her body up like the wildfire currently ravaging the Wyoming countryside, and had the potential to be as catastrophic. The plan she had for her life didn't involve getting tangled in a relationship. And it certainly didn't involve getting fired for sleeping with a member of the family she worked for.

She knew full well that she was going to sleep with Levi tonight. She was too far gone in lust to pretend she had the willpower to stop it from happening. Why couldn't he have been some guy she'd met in a bar—the relationship equivalent of dessert? That would've solved all her problems. Because then she would've never discovered how cute he looked first thing in the morning when he woke up or how much his praise of her desserts affected her. She wouldn't have learned about his relationship with his mom or his past or how handsome he was with a stethoscope slung around his neck.

If they'd met in a bar, the physical attraction would've still been there, as would their joking chitchat that she enjoyed so much, but chances were, they wouldn't have exchanged last names. They would've been able to keep it simple and physical. Temporary.

Why did he have to be a Colton? And why did she have to care about him so darn much?

A metallic, rumbling sound caught her attention. The water in the kettle boiling. She'd forgotten to make the coffee. Huffing, and grouchier than ever, she unplugged the kettle and poured water into the French press. Maybe she'd have a better idea of what to do once the coffee hit her brain.

A strange smell wafted from the steam. Gross. Fishy.

She opened the kettle lid. Inside sat a shrimp shell.

Gasping, she slammed the kettle on the counter and scurried away. Nothing Mother Nature could throw at her would kill her quite as fast as shellfish. Stunned at the bizarre turn of events, she stumbled to her pastry-utensil drawer, where she kept an EpiPen.

It wasn't there.

With a curse, she broke out in a flat run to the stairs, not letting up until she reached her bedroom. She didn't feel any symptoms of anaphylactic shock coming on, but she'd breathed in steam from the kettle water and knew better than to take a chance. She dived for the drawer in her nightstand and had the EpiPen jammed in her thigh before she had time to fret over the pinch of the needle.

Panting, she pulled the EpiPen out and sat on the edge of her bed. She wasn't sure how much time had passed before her mind stopping whirring and she could form coherent thoughts again, but when the haze of shock and fear had subsided, all she could think was *who?*

Not that many people knew of her allergy. Shrimp, crab and lobster weren't exactly staples on the staff's menu. Besides Agnes and Mathilda, whom she'd told as a precaution, no one else needed to know. Then again, Agnes was a terrible gossip, so anyone in the house would be privy to the information the Dragon Lady spewed during her rambling kitchen monologues.

A better question would be *why?*

Kate had only one suspect in mind. Jenny. And if

she was the culprit, then the why was obvious. Petty revenge on Kate for taking the photograph from Mr. Colton's room before Jenny had a chance to. That girl was turning into a big thorn in Kate's side. Dingbat that she was, she was probably clueless as to how dangerous a single shrimp shell could be to someone with a severe allergy.

Kate stood. Enough was enough. It was time for Jenny to get an education.

She stomped through the hall to Jenny's room and banged on the door. No one answered.

"Something I can help you with, dear?" Mathilda smiled at her from the stairwell landing.

"Have you seen Jenny today?"

"Yes. Miss Gabby was up and out of the house early, so I sent Jenny to clean her suite. Is everything all right?"

"Yes, ma'am. Thank you."

Kate stormed through the house. The door to Miss Gabby's suite was open. Jenny was near the window, pretending to dust while she rifled through a stack of papers on the desk.

Kate stepped in and closed the door. "That was a dirty trick."

Yelping, Jenny whirled to face her. "You scared me."

Kate folded her arms across her chest. "Not as badly as you scared me with that shrimp."

"Shrimp?" Jenny had the gall to look genuinely baffled.

"I found a shrimp shell in the water kettle this morning. You're the only person I can think of who would have it out for me. But it didn't work. You didn't take the fishy smell into account."

"I have no idea what you're talking about." She punctuated her words by waving the feather duster.

"My shellfish allergy isn't something to mess around with. It could kill me, Jenny. Would you really want that on your hands?"

"I'd never do something like that. I didn't know you were allergic to shellfish. Where would I get a shrimp shell?"

"Agnes served shrimp again last night to the family for dinner. Anyone could've gotten a shell from the trash."

Jenny rolled her eyes and wiggled the fingers of her left hand. The diamond ring sparkled in the light of the rising sun. "Do these look like hands that dig in the trash?"

She had a point. Kate felt her anger draining. Maybe it had been an accident, like someone had washed the kettle and a shell got mixed up with the rinse water. It was an icky idea and scary because of the ramifications to her immune system, but still possible.

Jenny grabbed the stack of papers from behind her. "If it was me who'd done that, would I share this with you?"

"What is it?"

"A file on the Cole Colton kidnapping. It looks like the sisters hired a private investigator."

Kate's curiosity got the better of her. She walked to the desk and watched Jenny flip through pages of old photographs and police reports, her heart growing heavy with renewed sadness over what had happened to such a beautiful, innocent baby. If the sisters were indeed hiring an investigator to look into Cole's case, then good on them. Maybe Mr. Colton could die in peace, finally knowing the truth.

"I didn't know Agnes had worked here at the time of the kidnapping," Jenny said, pointing to a line on a police report of witnesses who had been interviewed.

Kate skimmed the list and saw another name she recognized besides Agnes and Mathilda. Her mouth went dry.

Desiree Beal, listed as the sister of Brittany Beal Colton—Mr. Colton's first wife and Cole's mother. She stifled a gasp. Why had Levi's mom hated Mr. Colton's sister-in-law? It didn't make sense. She had to tell him immediately.

"I don't get it," Jenny said.

"What?"

"If the sisters find Cole, they'll have to share their inheritance when Mr. Colton dies. Why would they want to do that?"

Kate stared, dumbfounded. "All you care about is money."

"There's nothing wrong with that, so don't you go judging me. Money makes the world go round."

Of course Jenny hadn't tried to poison Kate. There wouldn't have been any monetary gain, and Jenny was nothing if not single-minded.

In the name of all things holy. What if Jenny had been the mastermind behind Faye's death? Nobody loved money as much as Jenny. What if she was the one who'd planned to demand a ransom from Mr. Colton? Kate took a step back, eyeing Jenny.

Was Jenny diabolical enough to try something like that? She was certainly greedy enough. What if she stole that kidnapping-for-hire note to get rid of the evidence? *Faye,* she silently prayed. *Give me a sign. Is this the person responsible for your death?*

Holding her breath, she took another step toward the door.

Jenny looked up from the papers and furrowed her brow at Kate. "What's wrong? You look like you've seen a ghost."

A cold chill crawled up Kate's neck.

# *Chapter 11*

Levi smelled the baked sugar-and-spice scent of cinnamon rolls coming down the hall. He straightened and ran a hand over his hair in anticipation of Kate's arrival.

Jethro must've smelled them, too, because he clapped his hands with eagerness and bounded off the bed. "It's about time the pastry girl showed up."

"Her name is Kate."

Jethro cleared a magazine off the bedside table to make room for the tray. "I don't care what her name is. She's late."

The cinnamon rolls appeared on a tray carried by a nubile young maid. Not Kate. What a letdown. The breakfast pastries looked good, but without Kate there for him to lavish praise on and to watch her eyes glow with pride while he and Jethro gobbled up the sweets, he almost didn't want to eat them. Almost.

Jethro slumped against the side of the bed. "Where's the pastry girl?" he asked the maid.

"She's busy in the kitchen, sir. She asked me to bring the tray up. If you'll sit back on the bed, I'll serve you."

"I'm not a damn invalid. I'll serve myself when I'm ready."

The maid was savvy enough to know when it was time to leave. Once she'd fast-walked from the room, Levi grabbed a fork and slid gooey, icing-topped rolls onto two plates.

The chime from the intercom sounded. Jethro licked icing from his finger, then punched the button. "Jethro, here."

"Sir, did the cinnamon rolls make it to you okay?" The sound of Kate's voice, coupled with her latest dessert creation, put a smile on his face right quick.

"They made it and they smell phenomenal," Levi said. "We were about to dig in."

"Where are you? Why aren't you here?" Jethro barked.

"I got busy prepping tonight's dessert. It's a special surprise."

"Everything you've made has been special," Levi said. "I've been waiting for this exact moment since you told me you were making these this morning."

Jethro cast him a long, inquisitive look. So Levi liked her and it was obvious, so what? Kate was really darn likable. Rather than challenge Jethro's stare, Levi shoveled a forkful of pastry into his mouth and groaned at the blissful sugar rush.

"Don't forget about lunch dessert, too," Jethro said. "And don't tell me you're going to be off running errands again. Last time you went to town, the cookies ran out and Agnes served me store-bought ice cream. Plain vanilla. It was horrible."

"You're right. That does sound horrible. Don't worry. I have no plans to leave the ranch anytime soon."

"Good." Jethro clicked off the intercom and narrowed his eyes at Levi, though Levi had no earthly idea why.

The two men settled into silence as they ate. Not for the first time, Levi marveled at how their mutual love of Kate's desserts had given them a common ground on which to meet. Levi had come to the ranch to prove himself Jethro's opposite, but all he'd managed to discover were the many ways in which they were the same. They looked alike, sounded alike and both had a sweet tooth. Like Jethro, Levi couldn't love, he had a temper and his stubbornness was both his gift and his greatest flaw.

The similarities were uncanny.

A knock sounded on the open door. "Sir?" Gray, the ranch foreman, stood in the threshold. "We've gotten word that the fire's turned. It's headed in our direction and could reach the ranch in three or four days. It's time to start evacuating the animals."

Jethro got up, jerked off the oxygen tube from his nose and shrugged into a flannel shirt.

"Where do you think you're going?" Levi asked.

"This is my ranch and I won't lounge in bed while the fire comes right up on it and destroys my life's work. I'm feeling well enough to oversee evacuations." With that, Jethro strode from the room.

Levi followed him into the elevator he'd seen the Coltons use, but had never deigned to step foot in. "You're not strong enough for this, and being around the animals' germs might give you an infection. With your compromised immune system, that's too risky."

"Go ahead and leave if you can't handle the risk. In fact, it's high time you got the hint that I don't need you. I never did and I never will." The elevator opened onto the ground level. Jethro shouldered past him. "Get the hell out of my way. I've got a ranch full of livestock and people to save."

He strode with long steps toward the front door, calling orders to the men and women scrambling around.

Levi watched him go, hating the power of Jethro's words to wound him. But through his hurt, he recognized the tough spot Jethro was in. Jethro was a surly, unlovable jackass, but he was also human, and his home was being threatened. If Levi were in his position, he'd put his health on the back burner, too.

Tamping down the urge to argue with Jethro for the sake of getting his way, Levi charged after him. "Two hours, tops, then you're going to take a break or I'm going to make you."

Jethro opened the front door and stepped outside. "I'd like to see you try." With that, he slammed the door behind him.

Levi threw the door back open. "Challenge accepted, old man. You've got two hours."

With the fire approaching, if Levi was going to go see Luella, it would have to be right now. It seemed like such a selfish thing to do while the ranch workers rushed to get the animals to safety, but he had to know the truth about his mom and Desiree Beal. And it was a good opportunity to make sure Luella knew how dire the fire danger was. Maybe she'd let him buy her a bus ticket out of town until the danger had passed.

He snagged Dylan by the arm. "Jethro's hell-bent on helping with the evacuations, but I've given him a two-hour limit."

Dylan poked the brim of his hat up. "Good luck with that."

"I've got a friend in town I need to check on, but I'll be back by then."

"Do what you gotta do. That's our new motto around here until the fire danger passes."

A chirp of smoke detectors and the flicker of the nearest lamp warned them that the power had cut out. "Pick up some batteries in town while you're there, would you? And all the water you can carry."

"Will do." Levi jogged up to the guest suite and grabbed the box Luella had given him, thinking that seeing the photograph might give her memory a nudge.

Back on the ground floor, he indulged in a brief mental debate before pushing through the swinging doors into the kitchen. Several kitchen workers hurried around, not paying him any mind. He walked to the center island, where Kate was laying sandwich meat onto slices of bread, assembly-line style. She glanced up at him. "Hi."

"Hi, yourself. I bet you've already heard that the wind changed direction and the fire's expected to head this way."

Her face blanched of color. "I did hear, yes."

"I'm going to run to town to check on Luella, ask her about the newspaper clipping and make sure she has a way to evacuate. Do you need anything from the store?"

"I'm set." She glanced around as though to make sure Agnes wasn't paying attention, then she gestured for Levi to follow her into the hall.

She crowded close enough that Levi could see a dusting of flour on her cheek. "I found out a couple things this morning you need to know. I stumbled across a folder of information on Cole's kidnapping. It looks like Mr. Colton's daughters have hired a private investigator to find him. I thought that might bring up some stuff for you, so I wanted you to be able to brace for it if they find him."

He managed a nod of thanks, swallowing back his irritation. Not about her revelation. Gabriella had told him about the private investigator when she'd come to the hospital to solicit his help, and then Catherine had mentioned it again the first day he arrived. What got his hackles up was Kate's concern, which meant he'd done a terrible job of keeping his emotions under wraps. Around her, he felt as transparent as glass, and it ticked him off in a royal way.

"I learned something else from the P.I. file." She rocked to her tiptoes, a hand on his shoulder, to get closer to his ear, and whispered, "Desiree Beal was the sister of Mr. Colton's first wife. She was Cole's aunt."

Levi let the news sink in. "So Brittany Colton's sister was at her funeral. That makes sense, but why would my mom call her a name?"

"I don't know. With any luck, Luella can give you some insight."

"I'm not pinning my hope to it, with as fried a brain as Luella seems to have, but it's worth a shot. I'd better get moving. Jethro's insisting on working, so I gave him a two-hour ultimatum. I need to get back by then to hold him to it."

"Good luck."

He wanted to kiss her goodbye, but he settled for

sliding his fingers over her hand. "We're still on for tonight?"

"Unless the fire threat gets worse or you chicken out."

The teasing nature of her words brought a smile to his lips. "Getting sassy, McCord? You should know that once I'm determined, there's no changing my mind."

"I'm counting on it."

In town, Levi parked in the supermarket lot, his heart slamming against his ribs at the realization that he'd have to walk through the parking lot of the motel, then up the stairs. He'd have to smell it, feel it around him, the heat of August coming off the peeling paint of the walls, the grit beneath his shoes, the sound of televisions playing behind closed doors. He'd have to get close enough for it to surround him, a thought that sent him straight into the supermarket to pick up water and batteries first, along with a bag of food for Luella.

After that, there was nothing to do but retrieve the box of his mother's possessions and walk across the street.

Luella was sitting on the second-floor walkway in a metal-and-plastic folding chair, smoking. She didn't seem to notice Levi. She watched the traffic in the supermarket parking lot as though she was watching the clouds.

The wildfires gave Levi a much-needed buffer against his memories. He mounted the concrete stairs, and rather than grit beneath his feet, all he stepped on was ash blown in from the winds. Rather than the smell of cigarettes and the grime of poverty, the acrid odor of the fires permeated every inch of air.

When he crested the stairs, Luella turned her blank stare on him.

"Hello again, Luella. I brought you some food." He set the bag on the ground near her chair.

She opened her mouth to talk and, after a few rattling coughs, said, "That was right nice of you. You on your way out of town like everybody else?"

"No. Not yet. Do you have plans to leave?"

She took a slow drag on her cigarette. "No plans."

Levi walked a few doors down and snagged a white plastic chair, shaking ash from it. He set it next to Luella and took a seat. "I could help you arrange for a bus ticket or something, if you wanted."

"These old bones are fine right here. There ain't nothing for me in the rest of the world no more."

He nodded. That was probably true. "I looked through the box you gave me and I have some questions."

"You always were a nosy kid."

He'd never heard that assessment of himself before. He'd done his best to stay out of his mom and Luella's way. Guess she felt differently. He lifted the box's lid and withdrew the newspaper clipping. "I found this and I'm curious about why my mom wrote this about Desiree Beal."

She looked for a long time, dragging on her cigarette. "That was before you were born."

Into the silence, Levi added, "I always thought she and Jethro had a brief affair, a few months at most, that resulted in her being pregnant with me, but this photograph was taken two years before I was born."

"That's not true."

His heart sank. What if Jethro wasn't his father? Worse, what if Kate was right and he really was Cole

Colton? His whole life would have been a lie. "What part am I wrong about?"

"Eileen was in love with Jethro Colton from the minute she laid eyes on him one day when she spotted him at the diner. And he was taken with her, too. Any chance he got, he came to town to pay her a visit."

"How did she take it when he married Brittany Beal?"

The question earned him a wheezy laugh. "Like you'd expect. We boozed our way through his wedding day, watching the church from across the street, and we kept on boozing it up until that Brittany girl died."

"Their affair stopped when he got married?"

"Sure did."

"She got pregnant with me, though, right? So they had to have gotten back together eventually."

"On again, off again. They never could decide whether to keep scratching each other's itches or leave the other alone."

Her wording stopped Levi short. His gut twisted. Scratching an itch with Kate suddenly felt wrong, cheap. Ugly. Something Jethro did with his girls on the side. Kate was worth so much more than that. He shook himself to the present. "I still don't understand what my mom's beef was with Jethro's sister-in-law."

Luella dropped the butt of her cigarette on the ground and stubbed it out with her shoe. "What happened was that we didn't know that woman was his sister-in-law until it was a lot later. After Brittany's funeral, Eileen insisted on going to the ranch to give Jethro our condolences. I was the one with the car, so I drove. Of course, she was hoping maybe he'd invite her in and she could console him privately, if you catch my drift."

She waited for Levi to nod before continuing.

"Except there was this other woman there." She tapped the newspaper photograph. "And every time we went back, there she was. Your mom was getting madder and madder about it. Like a dog with a splinter, she wouldn't let it go. One night, she decided to confront Jethro about this new piece of tail he was sleeping with when we see that woman in her car out in front of the ranch, nobody else around. It was after dark and we'd never seen her leave before so we followed, all the way to a diner in Jackson."

Levi rubbed his chin, picturing it. "That seems pretty extreme, even for my mom."

Luella sniffed. "Well, you asked."

"I'm sorry. Go on."

"Eileen got cold feet about saying something nasty to the woman, but we stayed in Jackson for a while because my car broke and your mom was so upset that Jethro had chosen somebody else over her that she had a few bad weeks, if you know what I mean."

She waited for him to nod again. "What happened next is a little fuzzy. All I remember was your mom got out that newspaper—she'd saved it for the picture of Jethro—and recognized the woman. We was both sickened to learn it was Jethro's wife's sister, so we drove to the diner we'd last seen her in to give her a piece of our mind."

"Was she still there?"

"Yeah, she was there. And she had a baby with her and a wedding band on. Both Eileen and me figured Jethro had knocked her up and married her."

"If he'd married her, then would she be living in Jackson?"

She leaned forward and hung her hands between her legs. "How should I know? All that matters is that Eileen was spitting mad. We drove home to Dead and went on a bender for the ages. You see, your momma wanted to be the one Jethro married and gave his baby to, and I guess it half worked out because only a little while later she had you. You never did get her in tight with Jethro like she wanted. But you were handy enough to have around."

*How sweet.* It was time to get to the answers he was truly dreading. "Do you remember my mom being pregnant with me? Did you ever feel me kick or anything?"

If his age had been faked, if he was Cole Colton, then she would've had to fake the pregnancy, too.

"You're asking a lot of things I don't know."

Luella stood and lit another cigarette, clearly agitated, but Levi needed answers. "Do you remember her going into labor?"

"Wasn't like we was joined at the hip or something. I remember driving her to the hospital."

"Were you in the room when she delivered me?"

"Hell, no. You crazy?"

He bit the inside of his cheek. "Do you remember me coming home from the hospital?"

"No. I had a boyfriend at the time and was living with him. I suppose I came and visited. I remember bringing a set of baby clothes I bought."

"Did I look like a newborn to you?"

"Why are you asking all these questions?"

He stood and his head started to spin. Why couldn't she give him one little nugget of proof that he was who he grew up thinking he was? First the mystery of the car accident, then this. It felt as if nothing in his past was real, just illusions and nightmares. "I'm trying to get it all straight in my mind."

"Listen, I need some money for food. I know you already brought me some but life's expensive. Barely got enough for smokes these days."

Mechanically, he reached for his wallet and handed her two twenties. "Thank you for talking to me today."

She stuffed the money in a pocket and shuffled to the nearest closed motel-room door. "Like I said, you always were a nosy kid."

He was halfway across the parking lot when Luella called his name. He turned.

"I thought of something," she said. "About your mom before you was born. She had diabetes when she was pregnant with you. Had to test her blood sugar all the time. I remember how she wasn't afraid of the needle and I was. She used to laugh and try to get me to look. I remember that."

"She had gestational diabetes?"

"Whatever you call it, it made her sicker than sick, but I still wouldn't help her with that needle."

Relief. He wasn't Cole Colton. He was still Jethro's bastard son, but not this savior or missing treasure of a person the sisters thought they'd have once they found the prodigal son. If Cole Colton was alive and well, Levi wondered if he wouldn't be better off staying lost and happy, without knowing the truth about who he was or what had happened to him. So many times, Levi wished he didn't know.

"Thank you, Luella. Stay safe with this fire coming."

She shuffled to her room, hands in her pockets, probably fingering the money Levi had given her.

Levi's spirit felt lighter as he got into his car, as

though he'd taken a critical step toward healing. The same way his kiss with Kate had shaken his spirit awake, the talk with Luella had dragged him into the light. He didn't want to scratch any itches with Kate. He wanted her, period. All of her, unconditionally.

For the first time in his life, he had a shot at a functional relationship. He had a shot at love. Kate made it feel possible. His mother was the only person he'd loved, and that love had been so knotted up with hurt and sadness he couldn't claim to have any real knowledge of what the emotion felt like. Not really.

He saw love at his job all the time. Between his patients and their spouses and families. Husbands who spent nights in uncomfortable chairs to be near their wives; parents who fought for better treatments for their children; people who put their lives on hold to become caretakers. Like Levi and his mom's love, that love was steeped in pain and sorrow.

When you loved someone, they didn't have to love you back. There was no guarantee your sick family member would live or even fight to live. Love, at least every experience he'd had with it, was hard and riddled with unpleasantness.

What he felt for Kate was nothing like that. She was sheltering and life-affirming. When he was with her, he was the happiest he'd ever been. He had to fight for the chance to be with her, even though the likelihood that he might come up short terrified him. After all, a huge part of him was broken, and he wasn't sure it could be fixed.

Worse still, what if he broke her, too?

But what if he didn't?

He took another long look at the Roundup Motel. His

mother had had a heart full of love and demons at the same time. He wasn't so different from her. Neither was Jethro. And neither was Kate.

Haunted by the past, by people they'd loved and couldn't have, and regrets. Cruel fate thrust itself on them all. It was too late for his mom and Jethro to change. But Levi had time and a will as stubborn as forged iron. He'd told Kate that morning, and he believed it to the depths of his soul, that when he was determined, nothing could stop him.

So if he decided it was time to heal and find a way to learn how to love, then by God, there wasn't a force on the planet that could derail him.

## *Chapter 12*

Levi returned from town to find the ranch in chaos, with people hustling in every direction on foot, horseback or in vehicles of every shape and size, hauling feed or water to corrals, running this way and that with buckets or ropes.

Those he could snag to ask about Jethro hadn't seen him recently, which Levi took as a good sign. Perhaps the old man finally gained some common sense and was resting.

Dylan, Amanda and one of the other ranch hands were already gone with trailers of livestock. As soon as Levi checked on Jethro, he'd get outside to help in any way he could. It would be good to get his hands dirty while he considered all he'd discovered that day about his mother and about himself.

He strode through the front door, already scanning for a glimpse of Kate.

The usually busy mansion was silent save for a television blaring from the great room on the second level. He almost turned in the direction of the kitchen but regained his senses before he'd taken two steps. Business before pleasure, he reminded himself.

Jethro's ex-wife Darla and her two kids lounged on sofas in the great room watching television. Apparently the wildfire didn't weigh as heavily on their minds as catching up with their daytime talk shows. The boy, Trip, turn lazy eyes in Levi's direction.

Levi couldn't think of a single thing to say to them, so kept moving to the third level. Jethro wasn't in his room. Looking at the perfectly made bed, irritation flared within him. Jethro, it seemed, had ignored Levi's orders and was probably out on the range helping with the livestock evacuation.

With a curse, he turned on his heel and took the stairs two at a time. He stopped at the great room. "Have any of you seen Jethro today?"

This time, all three TV watchers looked his way. Darla blinked, a stupid expression on her face, as if she couldn't quite believe someone was speaking to her. The daughter, whose name Levi couldn't remember, shrugged her shoulders.

"Haven't seen him today," Trip said in a nasally drawl. He waved his hand toward the window. "He's probably working, as usual."

Biting back an insult about his surprise that Trip had the word *work* in his vocabulary, Levi pinched the bridge of his nose and kept moving. If Jethro had gone off by himself and collapsed, nobody would be the wiser. Praying that Jethro was in the stable and not out on the range, Levi booked it the rest of the way down the stairs and outside.

He stopped the first man he came across, a ranch hand he didn't recognize. "Where's Jethro?"

"We couldn't stop him. He's been out all morning, bringing in the herd."

"And you couldn't assign someone to accompany him?"

The man looked sheepish. "He told us if anyone tried to follow him, they'd be fired."

Levi shook his head. What a tyrant. "May I borrow your radio?" The worker handed it over. "Jethro, this is your doctor speaking. Do you copy?"

He held the radio close to his ear, and after a moment, Jethro answered, "Copy, but I'm busy. What do you want?"

"What do I want?" Unbelievable. "You're supposed to be resting."

"You better watch your tone, boy. You're on my property, talking into my radio. I make the rules around here."

The ranch hand nudged Levi's arm and gestured west. Sure enough, there was Jethro, riding in on a large, black stallion with a lightning bolt of white on its chest behind a mass of trotting cattle, driving them into a pen.

"You've got to be kidding me," Levi muttered. Into the radio he added, "I see you on that horse. What are you thinking, jeopardizing your health like that?"

Jethro snickered. "My health? I don't have any health left to worry about. I've got more than half my herd on the range, and they need bringing in before it's too late."

Levi's eyes narrowed. Rather than anger, his system pulsed with icy resolve. "When you're done there, you ride in. Time for a break."

"Like hell it is." Jethro afforded Levi a glare from across the grounds as he leaned from his horse and shut the gate of the pen. "I feel fine."

Levi stomped toward him, radio to his lips. "Jethro, I'm warning you." Despite the distance between them, he could make out Jethro's middle finger standing proud as he turned his horse around and beat it across the plains as if the wildfire was nipping at his heels.

Cursing, Levi jogged to the ranch hand and handed off the radio. "Got any saddled horses around?"

The man poked the brim of his cowboy hat higher on his brow. "We could muster one up. You going after him?"

"Hell, yeah, I'm going after him." It'd been years since he'd last been on a horse but a skill like that never left a man once it had burned its brand on his soul.

The two men started for the stable. "Bet he'll love that."

Levi huffed. "Either way, I don't care. I learned a long time ago not to give a whit about what Jethro Colton thought of me."

The worker slapped Levi on the back. "And I reckon that's why you're the first and only person who's ever gotten him to do a single thing he hasn't wanted to."

It was a dubious distinction, and Levi didn't bother to mention that he'd failed miserably in convincing Jethro to follow his orders a few moments ago.

Not five minutes later, Levi was handed the lead rope for a glossy-maned brown-and-white American Paint named Moonshine. He wore sneakers instead of boots, but the second he hoisted into the saddle, he was right back to being the Wyoming country boy he'd been raised as.

Walking through the yard, Catherine stepped in their path. Her eyes were puffy, as though she'd been crying. "You're going to get him?"

"Yes, ma'am." Oh, yeah, his roots were coming back to him real good now.

"I tried. He won't listen to me."

Levi filled his expression with the same stubborn resolve coursing through his veins. "He'll listen to me. I'll bring your dad back to you before he runs himself into the ground."

Nodding, she stepped out of Moonshine's way.

Levi walked the horse to the trailhead Jethro had taken, warming the animal up. "All right, Moonshine. We've got a patient to catch. You ready?"

Moonshine tossed his head, which Levi took as a yes. He nudged the gelding's flanks and they were off, churning up the countryside straight into the afternoon sun.

One thing became crystal clear only minutes into the ride—it'd been far too long since Levi had done anything near as fun as riding horseback. He'd forgotten how jubilant it felt to fly over the rich Wyoming soil. Riding had been one of the few aspects of his childhood that had been easy. It'd been the only time he felt carefree.

His mom had insisted he learn to rope and ride and work a tractor when he was in grade school, so certain was she that any day Jethro might realize he was in love with Levi's mom and invite the two of them to live on his ranch.

She'd hired Levi out to any farmer or rancher in Dead as a stable boy, farm hand, whipping boy—whatever he was told. Sometimes he got paid with cash, other times a hot meal. Anytime he had the chance, he volunteered to work with the horses. Often, that meant mucking stables, but every now and then he got to ride. He lived for those hours of freedom in the saddle.

By high school, the hard work had conditioned his body and mind to handle anything life could throw at him. Taught him he was tougher than most. He liked to think it'd given him an edge during college and med school over the rich kids, who whined about long hours and little sleep.

Today, it didn't take his body long to remember the loose-hip rhythm of the ride. With the wind in his hair, the world came alive all around him. This was the good stuff, and there was no place to find it except in the wide-open stretches of Nowhere, U.S.A.

Kate would love this. The speed would suit her.

It struck him that he didn't know if she'd learned to ride. Other than the loss of her husband and bakery, she hadn't volunteered many details about her history, and she'd evaded his every question. Was *McCord* her married name or maiden name, and how long ago had her husband died? That he knew so little about her was suddenly, overwhelmingly, unacceptable.

Good thing he had their cooking class on croissants to look forward to. Maybe he could coax her to open to him while they baked her favorite pastry. He had to try. And if baking didn't do the trick, then perhaps kissing her again would.

He steered the horse around a copse of trees and spotted Jethro on his black stallion, persuading an older calf away from the boulder it was cowering near. Levi urged the horse forward.

Jethro heard him coming and scowled over his shoulder before shaking his head and taking off. "Get the hell away from me. You're as bad as the rest of them."

Levi urged his horse faster. "Worse, I'd say, because I'm not afraid of you."

"You should be." With that, Jethro darted along the lip of a dry riverbed, then turned his horse on a dime and headed in the opposite direction.

Levi did his best to keep up even though Jethro's many years as a rancher had made him the superior horseman. The chase rapidly spiraled into a test of horse handling as Jethro navigated between narrow boulders and around dense clusters of trees. Teeth gritted and too full of pride to give up, Levi kept him in his sights until he rounded a felled tree trunk that Jethro's horse had jumped. Finally, Jethro had managed to slip out of view.

With a curse, Levi pressed on. The ground yielded the occasional horse track and, though he had to slow Moonshine to see the markings, he'd soon spotted Jethro again. A wave of relief rolled through him.

Jethro's horse was standing on the edge of a drop-off. Levi picked up the pace again, expecting Jethro to bolt, but he remained where he was. When Levi trotted his horse alongside him, Jethro afforded him only the slightest flinch of his head. The drop-off looked across a valley thick with patches of trees, yellowing grass and weathered boulders. Beyond the valley, the forest fire raged on, smudging the horizon black.

Levi puffed his cheeks and took the time to let his irritation simmer down. "You shouldn't be out here. I know you feel better, but this is too much. You need to rest."

Jethro's focus remained fixed on the northwest horizon. "The fire's going to be here in a day or two." His voice was pensive but strong. If being in the saddle tired him, then he did an ace job hiding it.

"That's not what the news is saying. They're saying four or five days, if at all."

Jethro let out a derisive huff. "A bunch of sissies in suits could never know this land like I do. The wind's going to get stronger before it dies down, and the fire's going to come straight at us like a missile. We should've starting evacuating the animals a week ago. Damn cancer has me off my game."

"It wouldn't if you got the help you need. A marrow donor and regular blood transf—"

"It's too late for that."

Jethro was right about it being too late to beat the cancer. It was only a matter of time before leukemia won out. But Jethro had to see how even the small measures Levi had taken had already improved his energy and managed his pain. "I know it can feel that way at times, but I'm not talking about curing you. I'm talking about your quality of life."

"I've had plenty of quality to my life. I want to die on my land, not in a hospital. All I'm worried about now is the legacy I leave. This ranch burns to the ground, the legacy I wanted to leave my daughters goes with it."

It shouldn't have felt like a tourniquet squeezing his chest to hear that. It should've bent around him like water around a rock. His armor should've been stronger than to let a mild, backhanded insult get to him.

After the life Levi had led, his armor should've been near impenetrable.

He tugged the reins, turning his horse sideways. Turning his face away from Jethro's line of sight before he caught a glimpse of Levi's pain and saw a weakness he could exploit.

Levi ran his tongue along his teeth and watched black tendrils of smoke lick the edge of gray-blue sky. "Amanda, Catherine and Gabriella secretly hired a private investigator. They don't want you to know that they're searching for your son, Cole, because they want to surprise you before you die. That's got to make you happy, right? To have your chosen son back, the one you wanted. The missing piece of your legacy restored." Fury tightened his throat, suffocating him.

Feeling as black as the smoke in the distance, he turned to pin Jethro with a glare of judgment. But what he saw stopped him cold.

Jethro had slumped forward over the saddle, listing precariously, his face pressed into the side of his horse's mane. The horse was spooked by the sudden change in its rider. Its hooves pawed at the edge of the cliff, fighting for purchase. Rocks and earth crumbled away from the ledge.

Levi urged his horse forward and lunged, his arm reaching for the dangling reins of Jethro's horse as he attempted to use the nose of his own steed to herd the spooked horse back from the ledge. It didn't work.

The horse's front two legs slipped over the edge. It squealed, clearly terrified.

Levi didn't hesitate. He vaulted from his saddle, but the sudden movement proved too much for the already-hysterical horse. It reared up on its hind legs as Levi wrapped his arm around Jethro's waist and pulled.

Levi slammed into the ground on his side, with Jethro's slumping weight crashing on top of him. He dug his heels into the ground and rolled, taking Jethro with him, hopefully out of range of the horse's hooves, but with Levi on top as a shield, just in case. The horse crashed down next to them, inches from Levi's arm.

He squeezed in tighter, creating a force field around his unconscious patient.

The sound of hooves thundering away had him raising his head to see the rear flanks of Jethro's horse disappearing across the land in the direction of the ranch. Thank goodness Levi's own mount remained.

Levi pushed up on his hands, breathing hard. He jammed two fingers onto Jethro's throat, feeling for a pulse. When he found it, relief jolted through him, shockingly profound. He turned his face up to the sun and closed his eyes as a hard, wheezy laugh burst out of him.

What the hell had gotten into him?

He'd been desperate to protect Jethro Colton. *Desperate.* He'd literally thrown himself over the old man to safeguard him with his own life. A man who refused to acknowledge they were related. He'd used his back as a shield against the horse's panicked hooves so Jethro would be safe. Why?

Come to think of it, *why* wasn't really the question. That answer was the same as it was for the question of why he'd become a doctor. Because he was in the business of saving lives.

What had him floored was the raw quality of his fear and desperation and then, after the danger had passed, his relief. It was those feelings that had transformed an act of altruism into something personal.

He folded over his unconscious father, hands bracing against the ground on either side of his head. "You heartless bastard. You're making me care about you. But I don't want to. Can't you see that, damn it? Can't you—"

Emotion cut his words short.

Jethro moaned and his eyes fluttered open.

"Jethro, can you hear me?"

He muttered something unintelligible, his eyes staring blankly at the sky. Levi jogged to his horse and rummaged through the saddlebag for a bottle of water, then dribbled a few drops into Jethro's mouth.

"Jethro, are you in there?"

Jethro grunted.

"You blacked out and your horse spooked. If you can understand what I'm saying, then say something. Right now."

That roused him. He licked his lips several times, blinking, then turned his head. His gaze swung to meet Levi's. His cheeks and lips twitched as though he was working up to saying something. Levi leaned closer.

"Levi Vessey, you're an idiot."

Levi's heart took a dive. What did he expect—Jethro's gratitude? An admission that Levi was his son? Shaking off the hurt, he swiped the radio from Jethro's belt and stood. Gray answered his radio call.

"Yes, I've got Jethro here. He collapsed on the eastern rim of the property. I'll send you our GPS coordinates from my cell phone. Bring the truck."

After answering a few of the foreman's questions, he ended the call and punched buttons until he'd sent the coördinates to the foreman's phone. Then he dialed a second number. "Mia, it's Levi. Jethro collapsed on the range and I'm having a truck bring him home. Do you have time to meet that truck at the house?"

"Of course," Mia answered. "Won't you be with him?"

"No. I've got to bring in my horse. I'll meet you in his suite as soon as I can." Thank goodness for the horse because what he needed was time to clear his head on a long, solitary ride. Time away from Jethro's vitriol. Away from the sisters' pleading eyes and the staff's big ears.

Jethro levered onto his elbows to stare across the ravine. Levi kicked the bottom of his boot to make sure he was listening to this next part he told to Mia over the phone. "And, Mia? Jethro's not going to give you any trouble. He's going to let you settle him in bed, take his vitals and get him on oxygen and a painkiller. We need to get some fluids in him, too, so start an IV drip, please."

"Certainly."

"If he throws a tantrum, call me."

Jethro rolled his eyes at that. Ornery SOB.

After the call ended, he set the phone on Jethro's stomach. "Stay put. Don't try to sit. You'll be lucky if you don't contract pneumonia or some other infection from this little field trip."

"You should've let me die." His voice was weak and raspy, defeated. "Off that cliff would've been a better way to go than this. I hate this." Levi bet he did. Nobody liked to be weak and need help, least of all a man as independent as Jethro.

"What are you doing out here, anyway?" Jethro

asked. "Why waste your energy coming after me? Doesn't make any sense."

"I rode out because..." He didn't want to say it. He owed this man nothing. Especially not the courtesy of the truth that he'd been worried, and rightfully so, it turned out. And that he hadn't let him fall off that cliff because he cared despite all the reasons he shouldn't.

At a loss of how to explain, Levi stalked to his horse. It was munching on grass near the edge of the clearing. He didn't expect the animal to bolt at this point, but he tied a lead rope to a tree branch anyway.

"I didn't know you could ride a horse," Jethro called before pausing to catch his breath. "You keep surprising me."

It was an unexpected thing to say. Levi looked his way. Jethro's eyes were fluttering closed again. His arms were limp at his sides. Levi dug a thick blanket out of the saddlebag and covered him up.

Jethro sighed. "I don't know what to do with you," he rasped.

Levi stood, shifting until his body blocked the sun from Jethro's face. A face so much like his own that every time he looked at him, the similarity eradicated any lingering doubt of Jethro's paternity and gripped Levi with a choke hold of frustrated longing. "I don't know what to do with you, either."

Jethro grunted softly. "I guess we're even."

"I suppose we are."

"You're falling in love with the pastry girl."

Yes, he was. "You have to stop calling her that. Her name is Kate. And the way I feel about her is none of your business."

"She's my employee, so it is my business. If you two

run off together, I'm going to have to find someone to fill her spot, and it's not as easy as you might think."

"If you don't let me take you to the hospital for blood transfusions and a marrow transplant, you'll be dead soon anyway, so what do you care?"

"You're not going to let up about that, are you?"

"Not when I know I'm right."

Jethro let out a wheezy snort accompanied by a weak smile that faded fast given his fatigue. "Stubborn as a mule, aren't you?" He closed his eyes again, sighing deeply. "You get that from me."

Levi swayed, as if being mentally knocked off balance came with a physical manifestation.

He fisted his hands and traced the horizon with his stare, squinting into the ash-orange brightness, until he knew he could speak with a level tone. Then he looked down into the face that had haunted the periphery of his life since his birth. "Yes." He swallowed hard. "I know."

Kate didn't bother to knock when she reached Mr. Colton's suite. The rattle of dishes on the tray she carried was enough of an announcement of her presence. Levi smiled at her from a bedside chair next to Mr. Colton's bed. Mr. Colton was lying on his back, eyes closed, an oxygen tube resting below his nose.

"Hi. I've been thinking about you," Levi said.

She'd been thinking about him, too. In fact, the more she thought about him the harder a sell it became, reminding herself why she shouldn't give herself over to him, body and soul.

The electricity was on the fritz, so the curtains had been opened wide, lending a muted gray-orange light to the suite. She arranged the tray on the breakfast table that was still set up in the sitting room, then looked up to see Levi standing in the doorway between the sitting room and the bedroom, watching her.

She pushed a strand of hair behind her ear, nervous at his scrutiny. "How's Mr. Colton?"

"Sleeping and fighting a fever. Breathing that polluted air didn't do his body any favors. He'll be lucky if he doesn't come down with a lung infection given his weakened immune system."

"I heard what happened."

He shook his head and sat on the sofa. "It was a good thing I wasn't five minutes later because he blacked out and fell off his horse."

She sank next to him. "My God."

"Yeah. Tell me about it. You know what I did? His horse was bucking and I jumped on him. Didn't think twice before I risked my spine to shield him. I still can't believe I did that. I'm trying so hard not to care about him and it's like I can't help it."

Solemn astonishment lightened his eyes. Acting on impulse, she twined their fingers. He smiled and held tight to her hand. It felt so good to connect with him that it bordered on relief. She'd been alone for so long that she'd forgotten the power and pleasure of holding hands.

"You're a doctor. Caring about people is in your nature."

"At this rate, I'm more of a hospice nurse. Keeping Jethro comfortable, watching him die. It goes against every doctoring instinct I have. With him like this, especially, it's so tempting to call Life Flight and get him to the hospital for the care he needs."

She added her second hand around his. "You're doing the right thing, honoring his wishes."

Levi chuffed. "His wish is to die in his house instead of a hospital, but I've looked across the valley and I've seen the signs in town—the fire's coming. Or at the very least, mandatory evacuations. I can't leave him here alone, and I know Gabriella, Amanda and Catherine won't, either. When Jethro wakes, the two of us are going to battle it out about an evacuation plan. The old man might be cruel, but he loves the daughters dearest. He'll agree to leave the ranch if it means keeping them safe."

"The daughters dearest?"

"Growing up, that's what I called them. They'd roll into town in their tricked-out luxury car and every head would turn like they were the royal family. One summer, I was working at an orchard and I had to wait on them a few times…Jethro, too. He'd bring his daughters for cider and hayrides and, I guess, to feel like they were common farm girls for the day or whatever delusion they fancied.

"The other guys who worked there and I had to scramble around to make sure they were comfortable and happy, busting our tails for the princesses and their daddy. One day while we were picking apples for them to take home, my buddy Frank called them *the daughters dearest* and the name stuck."

"That must've been so weird and awful for you, like they were rubbing it in your face that you weren't welcome in their family."

He shrugged and one corner of his lips pulled up in a resigned, lopsided smile. "It wasn't fun, that was for sure. But I'm glad I came back to Dead. I'm not sure I would have said that the first few days. It's hard being here, watching Jethro die, getting to know my half sisters. Hard and strange and confusing. But this was right for me to do, making my peace." His eyes, wide and intense as ever, held her gaze. "Meeting you."

A thrill rippled through her body. The same scary, wonderful feeling she experienced every time he looked at her as though he could see into her soul. As though he saw straight to the essence of who she was and loved her anyway. *Whoa, girl.*

She cleared her throat. "How did it go today with Luella? Was she helpful?"

He sat back, absentmindedly rubbing her hand with his thumb. "She was. According to Luella, my mom's obsession with Jethro started before his marriage. She saw Desiree Beal at the ranch after Brittany Colton's funeral and thought she was his new mistress. That's why she hated her."

"Wow. That explains the writing on the photograph from the newspaper."

"Exactly. She and Luella followed Desiree to a diner in Jackson and kept tabs on her for a while. Later that year, they went back to Jackson and saw Desiree wearing a wedding ring. She had a baby with her, like maybe Jethro got her knocked up or something. Who knows what really happened, though, because my mom and Luella were so wasted all the time, even back then."

Kate was blown away. It took her a minute or so of processing to formulate one of the many questions bouncing around her head. "So you, Gabby, Cath and Amanda might have another half sibling floating around somewhere?"

"Trust me, I never made the mistake of thinking I was the only bastard he fathered."

"Don't call yourself that."

"It's the truth, for better or worse. If there's one thing I've learned in life, there's no getting around who you truly are. Blood ties never break."

A knock sounded on the open suite door. Mia poked her head in. Kate slipped her hands away from Levi's and leaned away from him.

"How's the patient?" Mia asked.

"He's been in and out of lucidity. Catherine's staying with him tonight. Come on in. Sit down."

Mia settled in the chair across from the sofa. "Catherine and Mr. Colton are close. She puts up with his grouchiness better than anybody." She wrung her hands as though debating whether to say something more.

Levi must've noticed, too, because he asked, "What's on your mind?"

"I'm sorry to bother you with this right now, but I kept waiting for the right opportunity today to tell you something, and I couldn't seem to find it. And now I'm out of time."

"Now's good, actually," Levi said. "What are you out of time for? Are you going to evacuate?"

That had been Kate's guess, too, but Mia shook her head. "Not exactly. Before I came to the ranch, I worked with firefighters, fire jumpers in particular. I was called yesterday by a nursing friend of mine who's working on the front line of this current fire and she needs help. They're short of nursing staff, and with the blaze spreading faster than they can contain it, firefighters are sustaining a lot of injuries. With you here at the ranch, I'm hoping it won't be too detrimental for me to go where I'm needed most."

"Of course you have to go," Levi said. "Don't worry about Jethro or your work at the ranch. I've got a handle on things here, and I'm not planning to leave anytime soon unless I can convince Jethro to go to a hospital or evacuate, if it comes to it."

"Thank you," Mia said. "Mr. Colton might not act like he appreciates you, but I know he does and I know his daughters do."

"It means a lot to me for you to say that." He stood and shook her hand. "Stay safe and good luck."

"To you both, too."

In silence, they watched Mia walk from the room.

He dropped onto the sofa and took up Kate's hand again. "Mia's good people," he said.

"She is. And braver than me. I'd never voluntarily run toward a raging forest fire." Merely thinking about it sent a shiver down her back.

"Do you have an evacuation plan in place?"

She wished. Running from Mother Nature's wrath sounded like the best idea ever, but the hand she'd been dealt in life didn't include the ability to pick up and leave at a moment's notice. "I don't have anywhere to go or a car to get there."

"Your family?"

"They're in Cheyenne, but we're not close."

He leaned near and turned his nose into her hair. "I know all about family like that. Would you consider evacuating to my apartment in Salt Lake City? You could take my car and blast out of here tomorrow."

The offer left her breathless. Accepting a man's help, driving his car and moving into his home—even temporarily—was the exact opposite of her plan to rise like a phoenix from the ashes of her past and blaze a new life path on her own.

She wasn't in a position to help him with rent and

wasn't sure she even had enough money to pay for gas and food for the road trip, much less the duration of her stay. It had the potential to drain her of all her savings. "Thank you, but I could never accept such a generous offer."

"You could and you should, especially if the fire picks up speed or evacuation become mandatory."

The expression on his face was so sincere, she kissed his cheek. How such a kind, decent man had emerged from the childhood he'd endured was a mystery. She wondered if he had any idea how incredible a person he was. Somehow, she doubted it.

"For the record, my offer isn't all that generous. Selfish is more like it, because then I won't be worried about you getting caught in the fire and yet I'd know exactly where to reach you." He released her hand, slid fingers over her thigh and dipped his head near her ear. "And imagining you sleeping in my bed—" he let out a huff of air that billowed on her neck, sending goose bumps over her skin "—that would be repayment enough."

She could easily imagine sleeping in his bed, too. The pillow would smell like him, as would the sheets. As her erotic imagination bloomed, her inhibitions disappeared, and along with them, her doubts about what she wanted from Levi that night.

They locked eyes and the smoldering desire she saw in him filled her with a new kind of dizziness that had nothing to do with tender affection for the good, smart, funny man Levi was. She stroked a hand along his jaw, enjoying the grate of stubble, imagining it abrading her thighs.

Oh, yeah. She wanted him bad. Breathless bad. Good-sense-out-the-window bad.

That was a tricky problem because, already, she was barely hanging on to the rational thought that it wasn't prudent to straddle Levi and lay a wet kiss on him right there in the sitting room of her boss's private suite. Already she was forgetting what they were doing had to be temporary and superficial. It didn't feel superficial at all. Not even remotely.

He kissed a trail up her neck as his hands roved over her arms and middle. "You have too many clothes on. Don't you ever take off this damn chef jacket?"

Despite how vehemently he'd sworn that morning that he had complete control over every situation he was in, the breathless urgency in his voice told her he was as far gone in irrational desire as she.

She pushed against his chest, coming up for air. Now wasn't the time and this definitely wasn't the place. "I have to get to the kitchen. Agnes is expecting me."

He brushed his thumb over her lips, studying her. "Okay, but for the record, I don't care who sees us anymore."

If only she had the luxury not to care. "I brought you lunch...and dessert."

He looked over the top of her head at the tray. She grinned at the brief flare of surprise in his expression when he saw her bold choice for dessert.

"This might be one of those days I eat dessert before the meal." His voice had turned husky with awareness.

"You do that at every meal."

She walked to the tray, then dropped a whole, ripe peach in his hand and bent close to his ear. "Tonight, I'm going to teach you a lesson about croissants and control. Consider it an audition for those skilled hands you were bragging about."

# *Chapter 13*

Levi couldn't believe how daring and carefree it felt to be sneaking through the darkness knowing a beautiful woman was waiting for him downstairs. The thrill felt akin to ditching class, which he'd been known to do a time or two.

He walked through the formal dining room without glancing at the portrait of Jethro and his daughters and pushed open the swinging door to the kitchen. Kate stood at the counter, her cursed chef jacket on and her hair back. The only indication of her awareness that this was anything other than an ordinary cooking lesson was the plate of sliced peaches she was nibbling from.

She smiled at him. "You're right on time."

Only the under-the-cabinet lights were on, and the dim light cast her face in the most alluring pattern of shadows. Her deep, dark eyes held a thousand secrets and a thousand truths, all waiting for him to explore.

"If I was trying to be suave, I'd tell you that was unplanned. But the truth is, I've been pacing in my room, watching the clock. Waiting for this. For you."

She popped a peach slice into her mouth. "Wash your hands so we can get started. We have a lot to do before the night's over."

Did they ever. While he was at the sink, she removed a plastic-wrap-covered bowl from the refrigerator. "The pastry base has to rest, so I made it earlier."

"So much for my lesson."

"Mixing the dough isn't the part that requires perfect control or skilled hands. All it takes is the patience to let it rest long enough, and I can tell you would've been terrible at that part."

He picked up a rolling pin and swung it like a baseball bat. "Touché. So what do we do first?"

She overturned the bowl on the counter. "First we roll."

The dough was thick and sticky. She sprinkled flour everywhere, then took the rolling pin from his hands and demonstrated. Before long, Levi was engaged in the arms-and-chest workout of his life, pressing and rolling, over and over, until Kate was satisfied with his technique. If he'd had any doubts about her mastery of baking before, he sure didn't now. She was brilliant and confident and a patient teacher.

Just as he thought they were done with the rolling part, she added a thin sheet of frozen butter the length of Levi's forearm to the dough, then directed him on how to work it into the dough base with more rolling and folding. Then rolling again.

She set a hand between his shoulder blades. "You've got to put your back into it. Make the pressure of your strokes more even."

Her nearness combined with all that talk about stroking had stirred his body to life. Though he relished this opportunity to work in her world and witness the passion and pride she put in her craft, he couldn't wait to peel her clothes off and feel her skin against his tongue. Her room, his room, it didn't matter. All he wanted was her, naked, in a room with a lock.

He moved the rolling pin under his hands, trying to remember all the pointers she'd given him, until the pin reached the end of the dough.

"That's good enough," she said.

"Good enough? I think it looks perfect. A masterpiece."

She pulled a face of affectionate exasperation. "Time for the tricky part. Your skilled-hands audition."

With a small knife, she cut the dough into triangles, then demonstrated the technique to roll them up carpet style, then bend into the classic crescent shape. "You're going to roll with your fingers and open palms, gently. Like a caress."

Levi's body must've misunderstood what was getting stroked and caressed because all of a sudden he didn't give a hoot if they never finished baking a single croissant.

He clumsily gave it a whirl with a second triangle of dough, not caring if she wrote off his hands as unskilled. He'd prove otherwise to her when they were done in the kitchen.

She frowned at his limp, wormlike creation. "This

is harder than it looks, so let me show you again," she said. "Put your hands over mine. Feel what I'm doing."

The command took him to the limits of his restraint. He moved behind her, gritting his teeth at the friction of his arousal brushing across her backside. If she felt it, she gave no indication. She was all business as he stacked his arms over hers, hands covering hands. He closed his eyes, drinking in her scent and body heat.

"Okay, ready." His voice was husky.

She drew a ragged breath and he took comfort that she wasn't as unaffected as she'd let on. "Here we go," she said. "Like a flick. You barely touch the dough."

She was right. It was the barest of movement and faster than he'd gone. Like a butterfly lighting over flowers. They rolled another triangle, faster and more efficiently than the first.

After that, he was on his own and back to being an utter failure at croissant rolling. By his third disastrous attempt, the profile of her face claimed his attention. He was mesmerized by the way she worked with such intensity, such cool control over her domain. The irony hit him that they were doing this little baking exercise because he'd postured about having control and she'd sworn it was an illusion. But here, in the kitchen, she was the commanding force and he was completely at her mercy.

As she rolled, she stretched her chin out, bringing to Levi's attention the delicate angle of her jaw where it met her neck. On the next two rolls of dough, he couldn't take his eyes off the juncture. When it was time to explore her body with his lips, that was where he was going to start.

As if feeling his gaze on her and not their baking, she

cast him a sidelong look with those dark chocolate eyes through thick lashes. The turn of her head had positioned her mouth close to his shoulder. She lowered and brushed her closed lips over the sleeve of his T-shirt.

He crushed the dough beneath his fingers.

She flicked a glance at his mangled creation. "You see now? Croissants are way more complicated than you thought. French doughnuts, indeed."

He forced his gaze up to meet hers. Oh, he saw, all right. He saw plain and clear the way her eyes had dilated and her cheeks flushed, the shallow rise and fall of her chest and how her parted lips trembled as though ready and waiting for him to sample them. She looked like he felt, strung out with heady desire.

He curled his fingers around the lip of the counter, holding himself in check. "*Complicated* doesn't begin to describe it."

Biting her lower lip, she set to work transferring their completed crescents to a baking sheet. Levi gawked openly at her as she moved, mapping the course of his journey over her body. Neck first, then between her shoulder blades and down her spine. Then he was going to pleasure her like no man had ever done before. He was going to use his body and every skill he had to leave his mark on her memory.

She set the baking sheet on the rack in the oven and set the temperature to warm, then turned and pinned him with a long, loaded look. "I guarantee you've never tasted anything its equal."

The invitation was clear.

Releasing the dough, he turned to face her, his fists clenched at his sides, his breathing so labored he probably looked as if he'd jogged ten flights of stairs. He loved edging it out like this, making himself wait. Controlling the blissful agony of anticipation and wallowing in the knowledge that the second he reached out, he'd have her in his arms, kissing her.

Kate knew what was coming. She held his gaze, her pink, full lips parted, her whole being vibrating with arousal. But she must've relished the way it felt to let it build between them as much as he did because she didn't move, save for the exaggerated ebb and flow of her breathing and the locks of her hair that trembled with each exhalation.

Everything around them fell away, time and space suspended, until all that remained was the two of them and what they wanted from each other.

"I am going to ravish you." He barely recognized himself in the low growl of words.

She released a strained exhalation. "So do it already."

Levi swallowed as Kate's words sank in. With a jerky movement that showed the rush of adrenaline and testosterone pumping hard through his veins, he reached with both hands and clutched the curves of her hips. She swayed, then splayed her hands over his chest muscles as though she liked what she felt. Everything about her was sensuous, including her awareness of his body.

He stepped into her, tugged her tight against him and slid his hands to cup her backside. He wanted to rip open her chef jacket and get his hands on her bare flesh where they belonged. Forget a room with a lock, he wanted her in the kitchen, on the counter, naked and whimpering with pleasure. Right now.

He lowered his lips to hers, kissing her with a barely restrained hunger. She moaned at the contact and opened to him, kissing him back. She tasted faintly of the peach she'd eaten. Peaches and wicked loveliness.

He bent her over the counter, delving deeper into her mouth, devouring her. Nothing in his adult life had ever felt this good. Nothing.

He tore from her lips and fumbled with the buttons on her jacket. "I hate your chef jackets. I have to touch you." He yanked, popping the last of the buttons off with a brutish disregard. He flung the jacket open.

A T-shirt. Damn it.

She grabbed his wrist and threaded his hand under her shirt. He felt his palms up her stomach to the underside of her breasts, then nosed her hair out of the way to get his lips on her neck.

The scent of her skin was intoxicating—sugar-cookie sweet. He opened his mouth wider and bit the pressure point where her neck met her shoulder. The shiver that seemed to radiate through her body made him greedy for more. She might've been in control when it came to baking, but this was his domain. Levi knew his way around women's bodies. Every pressure point and muscle, every movement that would elicit a spark of pleasure.

She arched until his palms felt the bumps of her ribs beneath her skin. He wanted to feel the shape of each and every bone. Measure them with his mouth, rename them just for her. How many bones had he felt as a doctor? Hundreds, thousands? But with Kate, his awareness of them had never been so vivid, so steeped in desire.

His body pulsed, hard and demanding. He couldn't get enough of her. Not only her body—he couldn't spend enough time with her or talk to her enough. There weren't enough hours in the day, enough days in the year for him to be satisfied. Nothing, he was sure, would ever be enough when it came to her.

With Kate, there was no saturation point. Only need.

The kissing alone trumped every sexual encounter Kate had experienced. Heck, prepping croissants with him had trumped every encounter. Bent over the center island, she reached between them. He'd wanted access to her skin and it was her turn to access his.

His abs and chest were impressive, but she hadn't touched a man where it counted in more than a year and she was greedy to explore. A flick of her fingers and the button of his jeans gaped open. She pressed the zipper open with her thumb and rubbed him over his blue cotton boxers.

Sweet surrender, he was built for a woman's pleasure. Mouths locked together in a kiss, they groaned in unison when she wiggled behind the elastic band of the underwear and wrapped her hand around his hard, hot length. Damn, she'd missed that.

She pulled up and, like a marionette, his whole body rose, cresting upward. Drunk on the power she held over him, she worked him with her hand while he panted, leaning against her, taking it.

She angled her mouth to his lips and suckled his lower lip until he roused and kissed her ravenously. Then his hand clamped around her wrist until she released him. He yanked her leggings down, then lifted her to the counter and shucked her clogs and leggings to the floor. "Lie back."

She did as she was told, shivering at the feel of the cold granite through her undershirt. His hands went to her knees, spreading her wide. She squirmed, not sure she'd ever felt so empty and desperate before.

He indulged her with a few swirls of his tongue before drawing back. He reached next to her, to the plate of peach slices. Her body tensed in delicious anticipation. Food play was something she'd never done before and she'd always been curious.

He circled her belly button with a slice and then she felt the drip of liquid into it. He lowered his mouth to her belly and lapped it up. "Look who's dessert now."

The peach slice traveled lower until she felt it against the very epicenter of her arousal. It was cold against her flesh and the perfect hardness. He moved it over her again and again, pleasuring her until she arched with a whimper. She propped her feet on his shoulders, giving herself over to him and his naughty, wonderful game.

She thought she'd reached maximum euphoria until he added his tongue to the mix. She brought her hand to her mouth, biting the side of her finger to keep from moaning too loudly. Her legs turned to jelly and her feet slid off his shoulders as he got down to business. The peach disappeared. He scooted his upturned hands under her backside and brought her up to meet him, working her flesh with his mouth until he'd brought her right to the edge.

He straightened, releasing her backside.

"No, come back. I'm so close." When he didn't comply, she levered up on her elbows.

He was staring down at her as he rolled a condom on. Below his dark, lusting eyes, his mouth hung open to accommodate his hard breathing. Sweat beaded on his forehead and her moisture glistened on his chin. He licked at it, looking beastly and male and absolutely gorgeous. "Do you feel ravaged yet?"

She hooked her foot around his lower back and pulled him between her legs. "Nearly. There's just one more thing I need."

He grinned at that. Holding her hips, he thrust into her. She tipped her chin up, lost in the feeling of being filled for the first time in too long. Rather than thrust again, he held himself inside her and touched his finger to her bundle of nerves in slow, deliberate circles. "Is this the part where I stroke or where I caress? I can't remember. All that baking addled my brain."

She locked her ankles around his lower back and drew him deeper. "It's the part where you move. Doesn't matter how."

He rolled her flesh between his fingertips until she groaned. "Low standards?"

"You're driving me crazy."

"Okay, but do you feel ravaged?"

She let out a laugh. There was little else she appreciated as much as a sense of humor, and the mix of laughter and carnal pleasure took her to new heights of ecstasy. She needed release and she needed it bad. "Almost." She rotated her hips. "Are you trying to demonstrate your control?"

He pulled back. Unwrapping her legs from his waist, he pressed her knees to her stomach, then drove deep, thrusting hard as he worked his finger over her pleasure center, wringing sensation from her with ruthless focus.

"Yes. Is it working?"

"Yes," she answered breathlessly, her eyes closed as she felt the first stirrings of release building inside her.

She clenched, digging for it. It gathered force inside her, coming closer to the surface. "You win."

He pulled her hips off the table, tilting her in a new way that sent her over the edge. She tightened everywhere as the bliss of release rolled through her. Levi threw his head back, jaw clenched tight as he joined her.

He pulled her to sitting and wrapped his arms around her. Into her hair, he said, "That wasn't enough. I could never get enough of you."

She couldn't get enough of him, either, and therein lay the crux of her problem. She held tight around his shoulders, catching her breath, trying to clear her head. As lost as she'd been to her lust, now that she was sated, she couldn't ignore the voice inside her saying she'd made a grievous error. This, what they had done, wasn't scratching an itch. It was pure passion. It was forging a bond. It was falling in love.

She raised her head to the heavens, eyes squeezed closed. *What have I done?*

Mother Nature wielded an awesome, nasty power. Unpredictable and ruthless.

Over and over, Kate had felt its wrath. Today, as she stood amid swirling ash and blazing summer temperatures, she was keenly aware that she and the other citizens of Dead were nothing but ants at the mercy of a giant. The out-of-control feeling that had been triggered last night with Levi only compounded her anxiety.

The hard part was that Kate had no choice but to face her fear of Mother Nature head-on. The fire was headed their way, the power was out and there weren't nearly enough able-bodied hands to pitch in and prepare the ranch for the worst-case scenario. So instead of hiding in the house like her instincts screamed to, she was right in the thick of the danger.

It was enough to bring her to the brink of a panic attack. She tried to breathe through it as she crossed the ranch grounds, but the more she thought about breathing, the more she felt as if someone had a hand around her throat preventing her from inhaling a lungful of air.

She handed out the sack lunches and snacks she'd put together for those who'd decided to evacuate. Levi had offered her his car and his apartment. She'd be a fool not to take him up on it. The fire was coming and all that was left to do was run.

The time away would give her the space and solitude to think about what had happened the night before between her and Levi. She'd never made love like that, so profound that she was contemplating changing all her plans for the future to be with him. It was too overwhelming to think about at the moment, with the fire bearing down on them. Thankfully, he'd kept as busy today as she was, between caring for Jethro and helping round up the cattle, so she was spared from making any more snap decisions about her life.

Dylan had returned sometime during the night to pick up a second load of livestock. He looked worn to the bone, but she knew him well enough not to suggest he take a break. When there were animals' lives on the line, Dylan was all in. He saw Kate and offered her a grim smile, then wiped his palms on his jeans and took the sack lunch she offered.

"Hey there." His focus shot immediately to her hands, which were shaking uncontrollably. "You okay?"

There was nothing to be done but stretch the truth.

"Yes. Absolutely. The fire has me on edge is all. Which animals are you evacuating now?"

He scratched his head under his hat. "A second crop of sale calves, and Amanda's got the breed bulls."

"Are you going to try to evacuate all the animals on the ranch?"

"That'd be great, but if the fire's moving as fast as the news reporters think it is, then that's not realistic. We'll do what we can, then open the rest of the gates and fences so the remaining stock have a chance to flee if they need to. All we can do after that is hope for the best. What about you? Are you going to get out of the area until the danger passes?"

"Levi offered to let me stay at his apartment in Salt Lake City. I don't have anywhere else to go, so I'm considering taking him up on it."

Dylan nodded. Faye had been his only family and he'd grown up on the ranch, so she doubted he had anywhere to go, either. "He's a good guy. I've seen the way he looks at you. How do you feel about that? I've never known you to date, and I know you lost your husband."

How did she feel? It seemed to change with every passing minute. "I feel good about it. Surprisingly good. You're right about him being a stand-up guy."

"If he's offering you a place safe from the fire, I suggest you take it."

She hugged her middle, trying to stem the shaking.

"Hey, don't be scared. The fire's still far away. All this is precautionary. We bust our butts every year to maintain the firebreak around the ranch, and it's never been breached. Traveling on those crowded highways is probably more dangerous than staying put." He coughed. "This ash is what's killing me. I'm looking forward to being in my truck, out of this toxic air."

Then Kate had an idea. A way to help that would give her day purpose and get her mind off the fire and Levi and all the other troubles plaguing her. What the workers really needed were covers for their noses and mouths—and she had a fresh supply of cheesecloth sitting in her bedroom because there hadn't been a spot for it in the kitchen.

"I'll be right back," she told Dylan.

She ran to the house as fast as her legs would go, grabbing a flashlight on the way because the power had gone out again. The employee staircase was entirely void of light, but nothing was going to stop her now, especially not her fear of the dark. If Levi could come here, to a place loaded with his fears, if Faye could die to protect baby Avery, then Kate could do this.

She kept the flashlight near her shoulder to afford the widest beam of light. By the final leg of the stairs to the second-floor employee wing, she was jogging, her light bouncing with each quick step.

She opened the door to the second-floor landing, proud of herself. Faye would've been proud of her, too.

Then she was pushed, her flashlight jerked from her grasp.

She tumbled down the stairs, not sure if the noise was coming from her or someone else. She flailed, trying to break her fall, but hit the back of her head on a step. The grunt that rose up from her belly was the last sound she heard before the darkness seeped into her veins. Another thunk to the back of her head and she was out.

# *Chapter 14*

Any minute now, Levi expected his shield of self-preservation to kick in again. It had kept him safe for many years, but Kate had stripped him of his every defense. It hadn't been a temporary condition last night when his heart opened and he felt the power of his connection with Kate all the way to his core.

After they'd made love, it'd taken some time to get the kitchen put back together. He sensed Kate's panic at the feelings they'd stirred in each other and so had tried to keep his distance, giving her time to settle into the idea of being together as a couple. She'd rejected his offer to walk her to her room, and so he bid her good-night at the stairwell door even though every cell in his body wanted to toss her over his shoulder in a fireman carry and steal away with her to his suite.

He'd tried to catch her alone this morning while she

made coffee, but the rising sun, the fire threat and the endless list of ranch tasks that needed to be performed kept him from it. Jethro was due for a checkup and Levi planned to sit with him to give whichever sister was there a break, but he hadn't seen Kate in hours and worry was setting in.

No one had seen hide nor hair of her, and he'd been asking around for forty-five minutes. She'd been scared last night, but so much so that she'd run?

He rounded the corner to Jethro's bedroom and saw Gabriella sitting bedside. "How's he doing?"

"He's asleep. Hasn't stirred in hours."

Out of habit, Levi took Jethro's pulse at his wrist. His heartbeat was strong.

"Thank you," Gabriella said. "For being here and helping him. I never..." She swallowed, looking uncomfortable. "There wasn't anything I could do about the way Dad treated you. By the time I was old enough to understand the situation, it was too late."

Levi nodded. What could he say? He knew what she meant by it being too late. By the time they were teenagers, the die had been cast and the rift was too enormous to cross even if he'd been mature enough to want to.

For the entirety of his life, he'd reveled in hating the sisters. There was safety in the distance his bitterness created, and he recognized now how dysfunctional that had been. While he knew he'd never love Catherine, Amanda and Gabriella, he was beginning to like them, and that alone was game changing.

He could imagine how helpless they felt, watching their once-strong father's rapid decline. "I know what it feels like to watch your parent die. You're powerless to do anything but stand by and bear witness to the spiral. I went through it with my mom, and I'm sorry you have to go through it with your dad."

She took his hand. "He's your dad, too."

He wanted to pull away, but their fledgling truce meant more to him than reestablishing his personal space. "He's my father, but he's not my dad. And I'd rather we didn't pretend that he is. I'm actually okay. I'm making my peace with it."

"I understand where you're coming from. Our mother left us to run away with a rodeo cowboy, so I get it. If she came back today, I'm sure I'd feel the same as you."

He'd forgotten that piece of his half sisters' history, he'd been so wrapped up in his own pain. No longer, thanks to Kate.

"Do you hate me for dragging you into this?" Gabriella asked.

"Not at all. I know I didn't make it easy on you, and for that I'm sorry. The truth is I'm glad I came. This has given me the closure I needed, that I didn't get after my mom died. So I owe you my thanks for coming to see me about Jethro."

"Besides, by coming here, you met Kate."

Her name brought a smile to his lips. "I'm that obvious, eh?"

She pressed a finger over her lips, thoughtful. "I'm not sure I've ever seen you smile before. It suits you."

It did. He'd never felt so light, so at peace with himself. Now if he could only find Kate and convince her that what they had was worth taking a chance on.

"Speaking of Kate, have you seen her around? Nobody knows where she is, and I've been looking pretty good."

"No. I haven't seen her in at least a couple hours.

With the fire changing directions and Dad's collapse, everyone's in crisis mode. I've been so busy I hardly know what my own name is, much less keep track of anyone else's whereabouts. Have you checked the kitchen? That's where she usually hides out."

*Hides out.* That was a perfect expression for it. For as much as Levi had created distance between himself and others, Kate had manufactured a distance of her own, hiding in a kitchen in the middle of the Wyoming wilderness instead of giving her talent for baking the platform it deserved.

"Understood. Would you mind sitting with Jethro for a little while longer? I'd like to keep looking until I find her. If she shows up here, will you call my cell?"

"Of course. Take as much time as you need."

He descended the stairs. Despite the bustle of people both inside and beyond the windows, the dim light and lack of humming electronics lent an eerie vacancy to the place. Agnes was the only person in the kitchen. She stood in the shaft of hazy daylight that filtered through the windows on the far side of the room. Her back was to Levi as she bent over an enormous mixing bowl.

"Excuse me, Agnes. Is Kate around?"

With her eyes on her work, she said, "No, I haven't seen her lately, the fool girl. But she's going to hear a piece of my mind when she does see fit to—" She glanced in Levi's direction and dropped her wooden spoon in the bowl. Whirling to face him, she performed the same ridiculous curtsy as she did every time she addressed Levi. "Dr. Colton, please excuse my outburst. I'm not used to the family honoring me with a visit to the kitchen. Whatever you wanted with Kate, I'm sure I can help you."

It bothered him a lot that no one had seen Kate in the past couple of hours. Even if she'd decided to bolt from the ranch under the guise of evacuating, she wouldn't have done so without telling anyone. She was too honorable to shirk her job responsibilities like that, and besides, she didn't own a car. The more he looked for her, the more his need to see her built inside him.

"Thank you, but I had a question for her."

He let his gaze slide down the dark hall. "Kate's got to be around somewhere. I'll keep looking. If you see her, can you have her call my cell phone?" He took a business card from his wallet and set it on the island near where Agnes was working.

She dried her hands on a kitchen towel as she perused the card. "A business card. So professional. Thank you, Dr. Colton."

Levi was already moving toward the door.

Once outside, getting one of the ranch workers to slow down enough to hear his question about Kate was a frustrating exercise. The animals were being herded out of the stables and barns into pens and corrals, and everyone had too much on their mind to have given Kate a thought. He didn't blame them. They needed to have the next batch of livestock evacuees ready for a quick turnaround when Dylan and Amanda returned with the trailers.

Trevor stomped by, talking into a radio. Levi jogged in front of him to get his attention.

Once Trevor had finished with his radio message, Levi said, "I can't find Kate." At Trevor's lost look, he added, "Kate McCord, the pastry chef."

Trevor gave a little shake of his head. "Ah, of course.

Sorry. A lot on my mind. I haven't seen her. Maybe she evacuated already."

"I don't think so." Why did he have such a bad feeling in the pit of his stomach? Why the anxiety? "Could you ask over your radio for me?"

"Do you think something's happened?"

"I doubt it. Just a feeling. No one's seen her for hours."

Trevor nodded. "Instincts have saved me more than once. You're doing the right thing not to ignore them."

He got on the radio and a half-dozen responses came back. No one had seen her, and they couldn't remember the last time they had.

"I'll have a look around the grounds. You keep looking around the house," Trevor said.

"Thank you." Levi handed him a business card, grateful he kept a few on him. "My cell's on there if you find her first."

Levi's walk to the house turned into a jog as he deliberated the next logical place to look. Agnes was still near the kitchen window, still mixing.

"Agnes, where's Kate's bedroom?"

"Dr. Colton, this is highly irregular."

"I can't find her and I'm getting concerned."

Whether it was his words, tone or expression that did the job, she finally seemed to grasp the magnitude of his worry. She set her spoon down and leveled a serious look at him, her lips pursed. "Second-floor hallway, third door on the right."

He pivoted and headed for the employee stairs.

"Wait!" she called after him. He turned to see her reaching into a drawer. "Take this flashlight because, with the power outage, there's no light in the servant stairwell."

Nodding his thanks, he took the flashlight and headed for the stairs. Agnes was right. Without the light he would've been moving in complete darkness. The silence was unnerving enough.

Rounding the corner to the next set of stairs, he heard a noise. A faint sound like a whimper that could've been made by anything from a dog to a child to a gust of wind hitting the eaves just so. He stopped moving and swung the flashlight over the railing to look down. The employee stairwell included a basement. The flashlight range shone nearly to the bottom, but enough shadows remained that he couldn't be sure it was as empty as it looked.

Now that he was letting his senses take over, he recognized the unmistakable yet faint scent of vomit.

"Hello?" His voice didn't exactly echo but it hung in the air. The back of his neck prickled. His pulse pounded hard in his throat. "Kate?"

He stood completely still and held his breath, listening. Vacuous silence, and then somewhere above him he heard a shift, like the friction of a shoe sliding over the ground. He resumed his ascent, swinging his flashlight around the corner of what he assumed was the final set of stairs before the second-floor landing.

Bits of glass or clear plastic littered the stairs amid a broken flashlight. Then farther up, a lone, empty shoe. A black chef clog.

His throat constricting, he angled the beam of light higher and gasped.

# *Chapter 15*

Kate sat on a step, her knees pulled to her chest, one hand over her eyes and the other over her mouth. Her whole body quaked.

Levi couldn't get to her fast enough. "Kate, are you hurt?"

She didn't seem to register his voice. He dropped on his knees on the step below her. Frantic to assess her injuries, he fumbled with the flashlight, finally setting it on a step.

He touched her arm and she jolted. The hand over her eyes pressed more vehemently against her face. "Kate, I need you to answer me if you can." He barely recognized his voice for the strain in it. "It's Levi. Talk to me."

Bruises and abrasions dotted her hands. He pushed back the sleeve of the chef jacket. What he could see of her arm was pretty banged up. Her pulse was rapid and her skin clammy. Damn it. The shock was bad. He needed to get her out of the situation and treat her before the shock started shutting her organs down.

"Dark," she said in a muffled voice from between the fingers covering her mouth.

The noose of fear loosened at that single word. At least she was lucid enough to speak. "I know it was dark, but I'm here now and we have the flashlight."

"Don't leave me."

"I won't. I promise." To free up both his arms, he set the flashlight on the step above her, aiming the beam of light across her legs. He got his torso as close to her as he could without actually dragging her into an embrace and placed a hand on her shoulder near her neck so she could feel the skin-to-skin connection. "Can you look at me? Let me help you move your hand."

She allowed him to peel her fingers and palm away, but she still didn't look at him or focus her eyes. Not a good sign. This was the hardest thing he'd ever done, staying calm and keeping his wits about him. He wanted to scoop her up and run to the infirmary. He wanted to turn on the damn electricity so he could do a proper checkup of her and calm her nerves. He wanted to shout at her to snap out of it and turn back into his fearless Kate.

He ran a quick tactile inspection of her spine and ribs, then her scalp, where he found a baseball-sized knot. "Did you fall?"

"I hate the dark."

"I'm going to get you out of here. Do you think you could stand if I helped you?"

She shook her head and swallowed, her eyes glassing over with unshed tears. Her hand shuttered over her face again.

"Okay, new plan. Here, hold the flashlight." He peeled off the hand over her eyes and pressed the flashlight into it. He moved from kneeling to squatting and wormed his hands behind her back and the backs of her knees.

"S-s-so dark." She buried her face in his neck.

"I've got you now. I'm going to keep you safe. Got it?"

He calmed the moment her weight settled in his arms. Because now he was in control of the situation, and the most vibrant women he'd ever known wasn't trembling alone on a hard step in the darkness, in shock and fear and probably pain. He was going to restore her spirit by the force of his love and every ounce of doctoring skill he possessed.

Later, he would wonder how he'd safely traversed more than two sections of stairs in the near darkness while carrying Kate, but as he moved, he felt filled with a superhuman strength. Kate held tight around his neck and shoulders, still shaking, though not as violently as she had been.

When he stepped onto the ground floor, Agnes was standing in the hall, chatting with one of the workers. She made a noise of surprise at the sight of Kate.

"Out of my way," Levi growled.

"What happened?"

The worker hurried ahead and held the door as Levi passed sideways through it.

"Not sure yet," Levi said. "She was in the stairs, hurt. Call Gabriella in Jethro's room and have her bring the spare oxygen tank and my medical bag to the infirmary. Someone else can sit with Jethro."

There wasn't much light in the infirmary. The ranch worker had followed them out and held the door. Levi directed him to prop it open and eased Kate onto the examination table. She immediately curled in on herself, shivering.

"I'm cold." She looked too small, too fragile, to be the same woman whose vivacity had shaken his soul awake, but at least she was conscious and talking.

"You'll be warmer soon." He threw open bins and cabinets until he found a stack of white blankets, then bundled her from her neck to her feet. "Give your body time to figure out it's okay and regulate itself. I'm going to check you over now. Does anything hurt?"

"I have a headache."

Understandable, given the knot on her head. He wouldn't be surprised if she'd sustained a concussion. He grabbed an ear thermometer. Cupping the side of her face with his left hand to hold her head steady, he took her temperature.

Eyes closed, she turned her lips and nose into his palm. He wished for all the world that he could forgo the exam and simply hold her. Send all the onlookers away and gather her in his lap and whisper promises that he'd never let anything or anyone hurt her again. Some deep, primordial part of him knew that was what she needed more than anything—and what *he* needed more than anything, too.

Forcing his hand away from her cheek and his thoughts away from the impractical, he got back to the business of doctoring, checking her vitals, feeling her bones for possible breaks or sprains.

"Do you have any pain anywhere?"

"Only my head."

Gabriella arrived with oxygen and his tools. She stayed close after delivering them, finding Kate's hand beneath the blankets and radiating her quiet strength without asking questions. Levi could've hugged her for it.

The image he'd clung to throughout his life of his half sisters as spoiled, rich princesses was seeming more and more off the mark with every passing day he spent at the ranch. He'd never thought that blood ties counted for anything, but maybe he was wrong. Maybe blood mattered. Maybe it was time to let go of the pain that was holding him back from knowing his only family.

After he'd performed a whole body check and found no injuries save for the knot on Kate's head, he dosed her with a pain med. Time to get the straight story on what'd happened to her.

Standing near her head, he combed her hair with his fingers. "Kate, I need to ask you some questions."

She released a ragged breath and seemed to shrink even more beneath the blankets. The need to draw her close and wrap his arms around her reared up inside him, fierce in its demand. But Agnes, Mathilda and Gabriella were there, watching his every move. It frustrated the hell out of him that he still cared what they thought, even after all the changes Kate had wrought in him. He ought to give himself a break, though. Healing fully required time and patience and conscious effort.

Gabriella stood and offered Levi her chair. With a nod of gratitude, he took a bolstering breath, lifted Kate into his arms and sat, cradling her, giving them the connection they both needed. She rested the side of her head on his chest. He felt along her arm until he came to her hand and clutched it tight. "Tell me what happened today."

"I don't like the dark." A shudder skittered through her. "Not since William and Olive…"

He rubbed her back through the blanket. He wasn't sure he'd ever met an adult who was afraid of the dark. The information opened a whole new window to her soul and put her widowhood into perspective. It wasn't simply a painful piece of her past that she'd moved on from.

As if that were possible. Scars never really went away, did they? It seemed that the past was doomed to haunt, and there was nothing anybody could do about it. What an arrogant fool he'd been to think he could dismiss his history with this place. With Jethro and his mom. He'd tried so hard not to care. Not to let it touch him.

But the ghosts of his past couldn't not touch him. They *were* him. Like Kate's ghosts were her.

"Who's Olive?"

She screwed her face up as though she was battling against a sob.

He held her tighter. "You know what? Never mind about all that. When you were on the stairs, did you trip and fall?"

"I fell but I didn't trip. Someone pushed me."

Levi blinked. Whatever he'd expected her to say, it sure wasn't that. "You were pushed down the stairs? Are you sure?"

"Yes. No. I don't know. It was so dark."

He shot a look at Gabriella, Mathilda and Agnes,

all of whom wore stunned looks. To Gabriella, he said, "Find Trevor. He needs to hear this."

With a nod, she left.

Agnes rushed forward, wringing her hands. "Well, it's no surprise to me that it happened. What did I tell you about sticking your nose where it doesn't belong?"

"Agnes!" Abject horror stretched over Mathilda's features.

Agnes held her ground. "It's the truth, Mathilda. All this snooping and look what's it gotten her? She's lucky to only have a bump on the head. It could've been a lot worse. Hunting a murderer on her own. What did she expect would happen?"

Mathilda marched farther into the room. "That is enough."

"What are you talking about, hunting a murderer?" Levi asked Agnes.

"Oh, Miss Detective here hasn't told you about the letter?"

Kate raised her head and looked at Agnes and Mathilda. "I wanted justice for Faye. I thought I could help."

"Well, you haven't," Agnes snapped. "All you've done is gotten yourself hurt."

Levi's protective instincts took over. "That's enough. I know you're speaking out of fear for Kate, but if you can't dial it down then you'll have to leave. Kate's been through an ordeal, and I won't have you upsetting her more."

At least Agnes had the wherewithal to look contrite. Mathilda wrapped an arm across the other woman's shoulders and patted her arm.

"I don't have the letter anymore," Kate rasped. Her

eyes fluttered closed, as though the short burst of energy had exhausted her. "Jenny took it from me. She thinks she knows who wrote it. She's going to…" Her words drifted off.

She'd wanted justice for her friend, a noble thought, but far too dangerous for a civilian to undertake. Why hadn't she left it up to the police and Trevor? He looked to Mathilda and Agnes. "Is Kate talking about the kidnapping-for-hire letter? How did she get a copy of it?"

Mathilda set a hand on Agnes's arm in an unspoken "I've got this" gesture. "We don't know. Several days ago—the day you arrived, actually—the letter fell out of her jacket, and before long, it was common knowledge among the staff that she was working on her own to try to solve the identity of the letter writer. I tried to explain to Kate that the family and I are working closely with the police, and we're doing all we can to give peace and justice to Faye—God rest her soul. But Kate refused to sit idly by."

"I warned her, too," Agnes said. "There isn't any good that can come of snooping, especially in this cursed place." She made the sign of the cross on her chest.

Levi pressed his mouth to Kate's hair and closed his eyes, his heart swelling with relief that she hadn't been seriously injured. What had she been thinking, putting herself at risk to go after a murderer? When she was feeling better, they were going to have a long, stern talk.

Outside, a massive white diesel truck rumbled to a stop. Trevor hopped out of the driver's seat and hurried through the infirmary door. "What happened?"

Gabriella came around the truck to stand side by side

with Trevor. Levi did his best to explain how he'd found Kate, as well as Agnes's theory about someone coming after her for snooping into Faye's murder.

Trevor's brows knitted with concern. "She thinks she might've been pushed?"

"When I found her, she was fairly disoriented. She's not sure which way is up at the moment."

"There'll be time to question her more once she's rested," Trevor said.

Mathilda moved into Levi's line of sight. "We can move her to her room so she can sleep, if you think that'd be best. I can watch over her."

Levi had no intention of being separated from Kate, but fear clutched at him. The room was crowded with people. He could feel their eyes on him and Kate, taking in their intimate words and touches. It seemed that no matter how hard he tried, how vigilantly he worked at keeping his distance from the ranch and the people there, he couldn't help but lay himself bare—all his pain, all his desires, everything out in the open for all to see.

He gritted his teeth and pushed through it, tightening his arms around her. "No. I'll stay with her. Gabriella, we'll be in Kate's room if Jethro needs anything."

"I'll walk you there," Mathilda said.

"Thank you."

No one else spoke, and he didn't have the courage to look them in the eye and gauge their reactions. One step at a time. He roused Kate. "Can you walk or shall I carry you?"

She offered him a weak smile. "I think I can walk if we go slow."

He set her on her feet, took the blanket off her and

wrapped his arm around her ribs, holding her close to his side. He kissed the top of her head. "You're doing great. If you get tired, I'll carry you again."

Levi led her to the grand staircase. The power outage rendered the elevator useless, and she'd seen enough of the employee stairwell for one day. They took the steps with cautious slowness, Levi behind Kate in case she stumbled. On the second level, they were greeted by the tin drone of machine-gun fire from a video game. Trip and Tawny glanced at their procession from where they slouched in overstuffed chairs, handheld gaming devices in their laps. When Trip spotted them, he rose, as a nasty smirk spread over his face.

"Aw, now, Kate. Look at you." He sauntered into the hall. "What happened? Did you get clumsy again?"

Trip's taunting, compassionless tone set Levi's teeth on edge. Could Trip be the one who'd tried to hurt Kate, perhaps even be the mastermind behind Faye's death and baby Avery's kidnapping? One thing was certain—Trip had earned himself a place at the top of Levi's list of suspects. "Where have you been this past hour? And can anyone vouch for you?"

Laughing, Trip got up in Levi's face. "You think I pushed her? You got some nerve, getting on my bad side."

Mathilda skittered on light feet between the two men. "Mr. Trip, we appreciate your concern. But we must—"

Trip looked past Mathilda to Levi. "Unlike the rest of them, I see right through your *good doctor* act to the greedy bastard you are—literally."

What a pea-brained moron. Trip might have the physique of a beefy jock, but Levi had a good five or six years' experience over him and, at the very least, double the brainpower. If Trip was the person behind the kidnapping, murder and Kate's tumble, then everyone needed to stop referring to him as a mastermind. "Literally? Oh, you mean because I'm Jethro's illegitimate son? That's clever. Nice job."

Trip flinched and Levi could practically hear the wheels turning in his head as he processed the sarcasm.

Levi was done with this particular showdown. He'd talk to Trevor first chance he got about Trip's culpability, but for now, the sooner he got Kate out of sight of Trip, the better. "Come on, Kate. We're out of here. Mathilda. Lead the way."

As soon as they'd crossed through the door into the employee dormitory hall, Mathilda and Levi switched on their flashlights. The window at the far end of the hall offered a modicum of light, but he didn't want to trigger Kate's fear of the dark.

"My apologies about Mr. Trip," Mathilda said. "There's nothing to be done but grin and bear him."

"Why does Jethro let them stay here?"

Mathilda pursed her lips. It reminded Levi of Kate's reluctance to talk about Trip, Tawny and Darla. Maybe Levi should take his questions about Trip's family right to the source and see how Jethro responded.

Mathilda opened a nondescript door midway down the hall, then gasped and staggered back. Levi and Kate pressed forward. What he saw turned his blood to ice.

Kate's room was trashed. The drawers of the dresser were open, their contents strewn over the floor. The mattress had been pushed off the box spring, the stuffing spilling out of the half-dozen slices in the fabric. And written in a sloppy scrawl of red lipstick on the mirror were the words *BUTT OUT OR DIE*.

Before he could prevent it, Kate launched into the room. With a strangled cry, she fell to her knees before an overturned pastel-print box.

"Kate!" In an instant, he was next to her, but she didn't notice him.

She scooped up photographs and a pink crocheted blanket with manic purpose, chanting, "Oh, God."

Levi put his arm around her. "It's going to be okay. Let me help you."

He righted the box and lifted a handful of photographs from the floor. Below them was a man's gold wedding band. His stomach turned. This was a box of keepsakes, the memories of her marriage and William, and someone had desecrated them. No wonder she was hysterical.

When he'd first learned that she'd been married, he'd been utterly conflicted about how he should think or feel, but now the trials she'd gone through in her life only brought him the driving need to help her heal and give her new, happy memories to hold on to.

Desperate to snap her out of her spiraling panic, he cupped her cheeks and forced her to look at him. "Kate, listen to me. We're going to clean this up, but you've got to slow down and take a deep breath. Right now, do it with me."

Holding her gaze, he modeled an exaggerated inhalation through his nose. Kate tried her best, but her breath stuttered and her eyes filled with tears. "That's good. Just like that. The worst is over. Nothing's going to hurt you or your belongings anymore. It's only you and me, and we're going to fix this. Okay? Let's take it slow and do it right."

After another deep breath, he kissed her and let her

go. Moving with a detached numbness, she arranged the photographs and papers in the box. When she spied the pink blanket lying off to the side, she wrapped it around her neck and sat, trembling and watching Levi refill the box.

Levi finished gathering everything that looked as though it belonged inside. Then a flash of reflection under the edge of the bed frame caught his eye. He groped around and pulled out a dark photograph on thin, glossy paper. An ultrasound image of a fully formed fetus that had to be within weeks of its due date.

The image, the pink blanket—the pieces fell into place in Levi's mind. His heart squeezed, aching. He held out the paper. "Is this Olive?"

Kate's chin quivered. She took the paper and held it against her heart, then closed her eyes. He'd never seen a person look so wounded. Not even among his patients.

He set the box aside and pulled her into his arms. "I've got you. You're going to be okay."

She wept into his shirt. All his insecurities and fear of exposure fell away. Nothing mattered anymore except helping Kate find her way out of the dark place she'd gone to, protecting her from her past, from everything that was out to get her. He was a man with a single purpose now, and he felt that resolve course through him, fierce and absolute.

He got his feet under him and hauled them both to standing, holding her steady until she'd found her feet. She clung to him around the ribs, her neck wrapped in the baby blanket and her face buried in his chest. Tucking her head under his chin, he leveled his gaze at Mathilda, who stood in the doorway looking stricken. "Call Trevor. Get him up here to have a look at the room. If he has questions for Kate and me, tell him he's got until first morning's light to ask."

"Then what?"

"I'm going to try one last time to convince Jethro to go to a hospital. If he won't, then that's his problem. I'm not taking chances with Kate's safety for the sake of a dying man's stubbornness. I don't know what's going on in this house, but between all this and the fires, it's high time for me to get Kate the hell away from Dead River Ranch."

# *Chapter 16*

Kate's head was pounding and she was way too hot. She cracked her eyelids and found herself in a room aglow with light from the fireplace near the sofa she was lying on. Levi's suite. She pushed heavy blankets away and scanned the room for him. He stood at the window, hands in his pockets and his back to her, looking outside.

Knowing she wasn't alone, that he was the one who'd been watching over her, filled her with a kind of security she hadn't known for a long time. She'd forgotten what it was like to have someone to count on. She wasn't sure she was glad to have the reminder of what she'd been missing. Life could be so daunting sometimes.

Her memory was fuzzy about what had happened in the stairwell and afterward. She'd tumbled, but why? She had a vague awareness of being forced off balance, but it might have been nothing but her anxiety about the darkness getting the better of her. Or she could've tripped over an object that had been dropped on the ground or collided with another person darting through the darkness on their way somewhere. She'd had a flashlight but couldn't remember seeing anything except movement in the shadows. For all she knew, it'd been a play of the light.

What she did remember was Levi and the wash of relief she'd felt at the first sound of his commanding voice and the sensation of his arms coming around her. She swung her legs off the sofa and was grateful to note that the room didn't spin and her headache didn't get any worse.

Levi turned at the sound, his expression as intense and grave as ever.

It was some sort of miracle that she'd been able to make him smile on occasion. When he looked at her with that expression, as if the heavy gravity of the universe was pressing on him, she couldn't stem the wild urge to feed him and take care of him any way she could. A few bites of dessert worked like a charm to ease the intensity of his demeanor.

Tonight she'd have to settle for offering him a smile. "Hi."

He walked to her and knelt on the carpet before her. "How are you feeling?"

"Better. What time is it?"

"Nearly nine. I was about to wake you again to check for signs of a concussion."

"Believe it or not, I think I've finally gotten enough sleep."

He reached over to the end table for a water bottle that he set in her hand. "Time to hydrate."

She took a swig and was surprised at how thirsty she was. She drained most of the bottle while he settled on the sofa next to her and took her hand. "How's your head?"

The truth was that her head was throbbing so powerfully that she felt it all the way on the back sides of her eyeballs, but she wasn't about to let a little pain incapacitate her. "It's better. I've been through worse."

His expression grew more intense, if possible. As if he was ready to fight the world on her behalf. She wasn't sure anyone had ever before looked at her with such ferocity of purpose. "You ready to tell me about it yet?"

She shook her head, furious with herself for bringing up the past. It was as if her subconscious mind was working at odds with the rest of her, goading her into spilling the truth about her past with Levi despite her efforts to the contrary.

He nodded. "You scared me today. And I don't scare easily."

His admission slayed her resolve not to melt into him. She set the bottle aside and leaned her cheek against his shoulder. "I was scared, too. How did you find me?"

He took up the water bottle and tapped it on his thigh. "I was busy helping with the livestock when I started thinking that it'd been a while since I saw you. For whatever reason, I got a bad feeling about it, kind of like I'd had before Jethro's collapse. I was headed to your room to look for you when I found you in the stairwell."

"I'm so grateful you did."

He extricated his arm from between them and draped

it across her shoulders, pulling her against him. "That makes two of us."

She smiled her gratitude at him again, and though he met her gaze, he didn't smile back. As if he couldn't shake the negativity of the day. If only she had a cookie. Or a cupcake. She bet he'd love her Italian cream cheese cupcakes. She must be feeling better because she was already restless with desire to return to the kitchen and get busy creating.

"Do you feel up to talking about what happened?"

"The details are fuzzy. I was running to my room to get a new pack of cheesecloth I'd ordered for my baking so people could use them to cover their mouths against the ash in the air, and in the darkness I think I saw something or someone, but it could've been the shadows of my flashlight."

"You told me you were pushed."

She nodded. "That feels like the right answer, but I don't know why someone would do that. I don't want to start making accusations I can't back up with evidence."

"That doesn't seem out of line, not after Faye's murder and baby Avery's kidnapping. Agnes said you've been doing some detective work to figure out who wrote the kidnapping-for-hire letter. That worries me, Kate. You might've made yourself a target. I know Faye was important to you, but why would you take such a risk?"

"It's been a month and the person who orchestrated the kidnapping is still out there. I don't know what the police are doing, but whatever it is, it's not much. I thought with my position on the ranch, I could find out things that the police couldn't."

"So you still think the person works here?"

"Works or lives here, yes. I mean, I don't have any

proof but look at the facts—the person knew that nearly everyone on the ranch would be at the rodeo. And he knew the baby nabbed wasn't Cheyenne. Not even Duke, the kidnapper, realized the mistake right away, according to what he told the police. That's why the person who hired Duke didn't pay him the money or demand a ransom for Avery. He must've known that Mr. Colton wouldn't put out money for a baby who wasn't of his own blood. Whoever set it up knows the family intimately. I can feel it."

He sat back, rubbing his jaw. "Trip…"

"I thought that at first, too. But I'd bet you a million dollars that Trip's mother, Darla, already has something on Mr. Colton. Why else would they still be here at the ranch? I think it must be someone else here who wants to get at Mr. Colton's money. Like Jenny."

He shook his head. "It always comes down to greed with people, doesn't it?"

"Not with me."

He gave her a long look. Maybe, just maybe, she saw a hint of a smile dance across his lips. "Not with me, either."

She took his hand. "I know."

"You said Jenny stole your copy of the letter?" he asked.

"The night you arrived. Since then she's bragged to me and probably anyone who'll listen that she knows who the culprit is and that she's going to try to use the information to make some money. But she swears she's engaged to some superrich guy and has been flaunting a supposedly diamond ring. If that's true, then I don't see why she'd waste time with blackmail. Unless the blackmail excuse is a front, and she took that letter from me to destroy it."

"Maybe whoever she's engaged to is in on it with her."

"I hadn't considered that."

"You don't know who the guy is?" Levi asked.

"She won't say, but I bet it's Trip."

"All roads lead to him, don't they? I don't like the prospect of someone having it out for you."

"But nothing else bad has happened to me before today." Then she remembered. "There was one thing. A few days ago, someone planted a shrimp shell in the water kettle I use for coffee. I'm deathly allergic to shellfish."

His arm went rigid. "You didn't tell me that happened."

She wasn't used to having someone to share the details of her life with, and it didn't come naturally to her anymore. Funny how six years of loneliness shaped a person's habits. "I didn't think it was important. I confronted Jenny, and she swore it wasn't her."

"But if anyone could pull off a convincing lie, it'd be her, right?"

"Too true. I've worked with Jenny every day for a couple years. She's self-serving and manipulative, but I never took her as psychotic."

"Maybe the man she's engaged to is, and she's merely playing along. After what you went through today and with the shrimp-shell incident, I'm ready to get you out of here. You and I are leaving tomorrow morning. This place is too dangerous for you."

She agreed about the danger, but bristled at his command. "I know you're worried for me, but you don't get to boss me around. You have to understand—William and Olive died in vain, without the hope for justice. It doesn't have to be that way for Faye. I can't have any more what-ifs and unresolved wrongs haunting me. I can't, Levi. It's too much already. I need to find peace, and helping find the person responsible for Faye's death is the only way I know how to do it."

He pressed her hands between his. "Tell me about Olive. Please."

Damn, she'd said her baby's name aloud. Before today, she'd never slipped like that since she'd come to live at Dead River Ranch. It gave her solace that no one around her except Faye knew that most painful part of her past. It was one thing to be known as a widow and another thing entirely for people to think of her as a grieving mother. People got a different look in their eyes when they knew that. They treated her as if she might shatter at any moment. As she had over and over again during the first two years after William's and Olive's deaths. She'd shattered—completely, publicly and, she'd thought, permanently.

Leave it to Levi to coax the truth from her as no one else had. She stroked his cheek, telling him with her eyes what she couldn't say. He'd come to mean so much to her in such a short window of time that it terrified her. Nothing was as out of control in her life as her feelings for him.

She stood and walked to the window, looking out into the darkness. The night wasn't black outside, but a ghoulish charcoal-gray too dense with debris to make out the approaching fire. "I feel so helpless about this fire. I wish there was more I could do to help with the livestock evacuation."

"Me, too. But there's not much that anyone can do in the middle of the night while the power's out. I'm sure Gray, Jared and the other ranch workers will all be back to work at first morning's light, but it's more important to me, at this point, to get you out of here safely. And maybe Jethro, Amanda, Catherine and Gabriella, too."

She clutched the baby blanket tightly around her shoulders. "Mother Nature is so cruel."

Levi came up behind her and wrapped his arms around her, pulling her close. "Talk to me. Let me in to your life."

She turned in his arms and rested her forehead on his chest. If she couldn't tell Levi about her deepest, most precious secret, then what good was it even entertaining the idea of a future with him? She drew a calming breath and began. "Olive was my baby."

Levi's heart ached for Kate. He'd figured as much about Olive's identity. He kept quiet, stroking her back, waiting for her to gather her thoughts and tell him more.

"I was eight months pregnant. The doctors couldn't save her. I never even got to see her." She tightened the blanket around her shoulders.

A few short days ago, Levi hadn't been sure he was capable of loving another, and yet, with Kate, he couldn't hold her tight enough. He wanted nothing more than to ease her pain, to drop prostrate before her and offer himself as a sacrifice if only it would heal her. He was curious about the details of how Olive and William had died, but he knew from his own mother's death that the *how* hardly mattered. Only the loss. "I'm so sorry. Tell me what I can do to help you. Please, because I feel so helpless right now."

She looked at him through dewy eyes. "You're doing it. Can't you see, Levi? I didn't think anything was worth taking a chance on again. All these years since I lost William and Olive, and then my bakery, I've been living in hiding from the world, scared of what else it will take away from me. My family doesn't understand. Every time I look at my parents, I see the failure I was to keep my family safe reflected in their eyes. But you… you make me feel stronger and braver. You've made me believe in happiness again."

He brushed a tender kiss on her lips. "I never thought I was capable of being in love the way I saw it on television or in people I knew. I've tried my whole life not to feel—not pain or weakness or grief. I've worked harder on that singular goal than anything else I've ever done, even becoming a doctor. And I really thought I'd achieved it until I came to Dead River Ranch. I was hiding from feeling things I didn't want to, like you were, just in a different way. What if we were meant to meet and heal each other?"

Her trembling lips curved into a smile. She blinked wetness from her eyes. "I like that idea."

He kissed her, deeper this time and with more passion. "I've never been this close to someone, and I don't know how to act or what to do. I'm petrified that I'm going to mess things up, but you're worth taking a chance on. We're worth taking a chance on."

"You're afraid of messing things up? I'm the one that comes with all the baggage."

He tapped a finger to the tip of her nose. "And I don't?"

"Not just emotional baggage. Until earlier this year, I was in debt. Big debt. When my bakery closed, I filed for bankruptcy and that took care of some of the bills, but not all of them. I'm barely in the black, and my credit's shot to hell."

He scoffed good-naturedly. "I can trump you on that kind of baggage, too. My undergraduate and med-school loans are astronomical. And I've got three more years of residency before I can start my own practice and begin paying it back. Now, that's what I call debt."

Still grinning, she rested her cheek on his chest, and he contented himself with stroking her hair. "We're quite a pair, aren't we?"

"Perfect for each other, I'd say." There was one piece of himself he hadn't shared with her yet. She'd had the courage to tell him about her most profound hurt, and he needed to offer her his in return. "Could we sit down? There's something about myself, my past, I want you to know. Something I've never talked about with anyone before."

His heart slammed against his ribs as he led her to the sofa. They sat side by side, holding hands. Kate was quiet, waiting patiently, while Levi struggled to figure out where to begin. This was the scariest thing he'd ever done, the most vulnerable he'd ever made himself. But he wanted Kate to know everything about him, even the darkest parts.

"I was in a car accident." Saying the words felt like pouring dozens of spiders over his skin. He'd never spoken of this to a single soul except the police, insurance adjusters and hospital workers.

He tried to maintain eye contact with Kate, but his gaze slid away, lost in memory. All he could see was the darkness of that night so long ago. "After my mother's funeral, my grief came out as rage." He shook his head. "She was the only person I'd ever loved and she was gone. A drug overdose. I blamed myself for being away at college and not being there for her. She was lonely and I was off chasing a dream.

"Jethro didn't attend her funeral but Catherine, Amanda and Gabriella did. They tried to express their condolences to me afterward, but I couldn't take the gesture as the kindness it was because I was so wrapped up in my pain and anger. We argued in the parking lot of the funeral home and I left. I shouldn't have been driving because I was too upset to think rationally and there was a terrible storm going on. The worst storm of the decade, I learned later."

A look of pure horror crossed Kate's face. She let go of his hands. "How long ago?"

"Six years."

She backed up until she'd hit the arm of the sofa, putting space between them, as if he was a wild and dangerous animal. As if she was afraid of him. He didn't understand—he hadn't even gotten to the bad part yet. "Kate, I'm trying to tell you this, and I've never told anyone. I need you to..." He huffed and held out his hand for her. "Come sit with me, please."

But she'd gone completely pale, ghostly. Her eyes were wide with shock. "What month?"

He curled his fingers in. The emptiness of her denial to hold his hand was excruciating. "April."

She clamped a hand on her chin. "You were on Route Nine from Dead to Laramie?"

"Yes, and that's all I remember." He stared at the ground beyond his knees. "It was dark and rainy, and I couldn't stop the grief about my mom and the rage from the fight with my half sisters. I felt like I was drowning in feeling. I remember I was listening to music and this sad song came on and I cussed at the radio. That's the last thing I remember about that night.

"I woke up a week later in the hospital. My leg and ribs were broken and my lung was punctured. The doctors told me I'd been in a car accident but that was all they knew. I couldn't shake the idea that there was something they weren't telling me. I had this sinking feeling that I'd done something wrong. That's when the nightmares started. About the others."

She flattened her back against the arm of the sofa. "The others?" she whispered.

"In the dream it's dark and rainy. I see headlights coming at me, and I can hear a woman screaming, then everything turns red, and the body of a man slams onto my windshield. That's when I wake up."

He chanced a look at Kate. Tears streamed over her cheeks.

"I don't understand why you're so sad. I'm okay now. Will you please come sit close to me?" She shook her head. He swallowed and returned his gaze to his hands. If he was ever going to get it all out and come clean to her so they could move on together, he was going to have to plow straight through to the end. "Anyway, after I was released from the hospital and rehab center, I spent the next two years trying to piece together the details and find out if there'd actually been others involved in the crash or if that was only in my head.

"The police were vague and the insurance company wouldn't release any information. One time the claims investigator mentioned another car and I pressed for details, but he wouldn't say any more, telling me it was a matter of legalities about privacy. I finally convinced someone at the police precinct in Dead to give me a copy of the police report on the accident but it was missing.

"The trail went cold and all I had left was this nagging feeling that I'd messed up someone else's life and no one would tell me so I could make amends. That's why I chose to become a doctor. To help people and make peace with the parts of my life I can't remember. And it worked for the most part because the nightmares barely happened after I enrolled in med school."

He paused his story to study Kate. Her emotional state was deteriorating. Concerns about her possible concussion and the ordeal she'd suffered trumped any retelling about his past. He slid over to her. "Are you okay? Is the bump on your head bothering you?"

He reached for her, but she recoiled and shot to her feet. "Don't touch me."

He staggered back in shock, blinking. "What? How can you judge me like that? You know me. I would never have hurt someone on purpose. I've spent the last six years trying to make up for whatever happened that night."

She walked to the fireplace and stared vacantly into it, her lips contorted in the beginning of a sob that she choked back.

"Why are you reacting like this, Kate? Is there something I'm missing? Help me out here."

She turned to face him again. "Six years ago in April, I was driving out of Dead with William on Route Nine."

His stomach dropped. "I don't understand."

"A tree fell in the road and I swerved." Her cheeks were wet with tears, her voice tight and thin. She clutched the baby blanket like a lifeline. "I swerved and spun out and another car hit us. William was ejected. I was trapped and disoriented. Our car was on fire and I had to save Olive, so I found a way out and started to run, but I fell into the darkness off the side of the road."

That couldn't be right. It was too fantastical to believe. "William and Olive were killed in a car accident? Six years ago on the same highway my car accident was on?" Around him, the room started to spin. He cradled his head in his hands. "Wait—you think your car was the one I hit? That's impossible."

She was shaking from head to toe. "April seventeenth, eight miles east of Dead on Route Nine to Laramie. At seven-forty-five at night."

The room wouldn't slow down. He felt as if his spirit was drifting out of his body. "No. No way. It can't be." He dropped to his knees before her. "Please tell me it wasn't your car I hit. Tell me you weren't driving a red two-door, like in my nightmare?"

Nodding, she clamped a hand over her mouth and wilted against the wall near the door. Levi couldn't reach for her. He couldn't do anything but kneel in place, horrified at himself and at life. If he moved one millimeter, he was going to throw up.

"The emergency crews, they helped the other car first," she said. "They left William alone too long, and I couldn't climb the hill I'd fallen down because it was wet and dark and my body hurt so badly I couldn't breathe."

"I hit your car?" He fell forward to his hands and knees. "I can't… I don't… Help me understand how. You didn't live in Dead back then. What were you doing there?"

"We'd been in town for a church festival. I was sell-ing cupcakes and pastries, trying to drum up some business for my bakery."

He'd seen that festival down the street from his mother's funeral. He remembered it because at the time he'd thought, how could anyone celebrate on the worst day of Levi's life? How could the world go on while he stood there in pain with his only family gone?

Her face crumpled. "You killed my husband. My baby."

Bile rose in his throat. "Kate, please. I didn't know."

But she was already inching sideways to the door. "You got the only ambulance and all the attention of the paramedics, and we were left to wait for backup. You said you were nothing like the Coltons, and that you'd never used your name for power, but that's exactly what happened. You're no better than Jethro."

He jumped to his feet as she whirled and ran.

Levi felt the sickness coming up and stumbled to the bathroom, heaving violently until his stomach had no more to give. Bent over the toilet, he had only one thought—he'd ruined the life of the only woman he'd ever loved.

He washed his face and stood, numb. If he'd been given preferential treatment because he was a Colton, his worst fear would be realized. No matter what he did or how hard he tried, he couldn't escape the fate of having cursed blood running through his veins. Though it was too late to right the wrongs done to Kate or turn back time, she deserved to know the truth and so did he.

He strode from the bathroom and out of the suite, barreling through the house on a collision course with the only man capable and heartless enough to cover up an incident that big.

* * *

Kate's car had collided with a Colton. It all made sense now. No wonder she and William hadn't been given first shot at the ambulance and why no one had ever been made to pay for the crime. Worse, she'd gone and fallen in love with the person who had a hand in destroying everything she held dear.

Blindly, she ran through the house toward the front door, not knowing where she was headed, paying no mind to the darkness of the house. But the farther she ran, the less she believed the words she'd spoken to Levi in anger. The more she considered the details, the less convinced she was about his guilt. How could she be angry with him if he hadn't known what he'd done? He'd been in the throes of his own grief when he crashed into her car, and she knew firsthand how devastating and all-consuming grief could be.

She froze. Maybe the crash and cover-up weren't as cut-and-dried as she'd initially thought. Her car had been nearer to the tree. If not for the buffer it had provided, would Levi have plowed into the tree and died? That would have been as awful a tragedy as William's death.

She looked around. She was standing in the foyer, alone. The clock read half-past midnight. The only sound was the grandfather clock ticking the seconds away in the hall. Regret flooded through her. Levi had opened his heart to her with his darkest secret, and she'd treated him like a monster for it. She owed him an apology along with her forgiveness about his role in the car crash. But how could she forgive him for his role when she'd never really forgiven herself for hers?

Looking at it now, it was tough to feel an overabundance of anger, even toward Mr. Colton. He hadn't caused the accident, and though Levi had been given preferential treatment by the paramedics, she had no way of knowing if William had died instantaneously or if medical treatment could have saved him. She could waste the rest of her life on what-ifs and vengeance and justice.

She leaned a shoulder against the closed front door. Perhaps the better perspective was this—did she really want to waste one more day caught up in blame and bitterness, hating an old man who lay dying? After all, Jethro Colton would answer to a higher power for his crimes soon enough.

Her gaze traveled to the grand staircase. Upstairs was a man who loved her, and he was one of the best, most decent men she'd ever met. He wanted to build a life with her, and, more importantly, he made her the happiest she'd ever been. She'd be a fool not to grab hold of his hand and hang on forever, but to do so, she needed to forgive herself for being at the wheel during the accident and put the past behind her. There was only one way she could think to do it.

With a deep breath, she straightened and opened the door to the darkness. It was time to look her greatest nemesis in the face—not Mother Nature and not darkness, but her fear of all the many things that were out of her control.

On sure legs, she strode into the night. The wind whipped the ashes around her face. On a nearby ridge, the flames of the wildfire were visible. She walked over the grounds, toward the forest and the unknown.

She wanted to stand in absolute darkness for a minute with the knowledge that she was okay. It was folly to believe sinister things were lurking in every shadow, waiting to get her. And even if there were, she was done fearing them. Bad things happened to good people all the time, but rather than be paralyzed by possibilities, she wanted to have the strength to live her life out loud.

She fixed a picture of Levi in her head and looked at the fire that danced in the distance beyond the firebreak, but still close enough that she could make out individual fingers of flame licking the sky.

Her heart pounded, but her hands were steady and her mind was calm. She'd never felt so alive.

"You're not going to hold me back anymore," she shouted at Mother Nature. "Living isn't about money, and it's not about a job. It's about love. You stole it from me." With every word she felt stronger, braver. "You took everything that mattered to me, and I've been hiding here waiting to stop being afraid of you and afraid of myself. I'm done with that. I'm in love with Levi Colton, and you're not going to hold me back. I'm not afraid of you anymore."

She fell forward, bracing her hands on her knees, and let loose with a cathartic laugh-cry.

Eventually, her tears and laughter subsided, making her aware that the knot on her head throbbed, which was weird because the incident in the stairwell felt like ancient history.

Hands on hips, she took stock of her surroundings. The stable was to her left. Horses had always been good at clearing her mind, and she knew a few workhorses had yet to be evacuated. She snagged a lantern from a nail on the stable wall and pushed the door open. It gave way with a creak. In the soft glow of the lantern, she counted only two horses poking their heads over the tops of their stalls, curious about the midnight visitor.

She walked to the nearest horse and held her hand out for it to sniff. Behind her, the stable door creaked again. If that was Levi, she'd tell him how sorry she was for what she'd said. She'd beg forgiveness and fight for their future together.

Smiling, she pivoted toward the door. "Levi, I…" But it wasn't Levi. "Agnes, what are you doing here?"

# *Chapter 17*

Levi flung the door open to Jethro's suite, not caring in the least that it was the middle of the night and he was probably waking up half the house. The magnitude of his fury was too profound to temper.

Catherine bolted to a seated position on a coat in the sitting room. "Levi? Is that you?" She rubbed her eyes. "Are you here to check on Dad? He's had a rough night with coughing. That ash really got in his lungs."

Levi barely slowed down as he passed by her on his way to Jethro's room. He punched the light switch on the wall, and it took a second to register that the electricity hadn't yet been restored to the house. He flung the curtains wide to the night. The moon was shrouded by clouds dense with fire pollutants, but afforded enough light for him to find the lantern on the dresser and turn it on.

"What's going on?" Jethro rasped.

Levi rounded on him. "I'm here to get some answers."

"Now?" Catherine asked, rushing into the room. "It's the middle of the night. What's gotten into you?"

"Answers about what?" Jethro grunted. He scooted his head higher against the headboard.

"About your crimes, old man."

Jethro gave a wheezy laugh. "Which ones?"

Catherine bullied her way between Levi and the bed, shielding Jethro from view. "I don't know what's happened, but now's not the time for this. Dad's worn-out. Let him rest."

"Catherine, I appreciate what you're trying to do, but I'm not waiting until it's convenient for Jethro to get the answers I need. How about you give us some privacy? This is between me and my father."

Catherine crossed her arms over her chest. "Not a chance."

"Fine. Listen in. You might as well know the whole story." He walked to the other side of the bed.

Jethro pushed the rest of the way to a seated position, scowling. "Out with it, then. I don't have all night."

Levi drew a deep breath. "Six years ago, the night of my mother's funeral, I was in a car accident."

"You were?" Catherine said.

Levi ignored her and continued. "I don't remember any of it, but I woke up a week later in the hospital, and nobody could tell me the details about what had happened. Ever since, I've had nightmares."

"Sounds to me like you're a sissy."

"Shut up and let me finish. I had nightmares about hitting another car and killing the people inside. When

I went to the Dead Police Department to read the accident report, nobody could find it. Guess why?"

"I'm all ears."

Levi's hands curled into fists. The sarcasm was getting old. "You're going to play dumb?"

Jethro's scowl morphed into a hard smile. "I've been accused of a lot of misdeeds in my life, but playing dumb isn't one of them."

On that, Levi had to agree. "I couldn't find anything about the accident because you arranged for the records to be destroyed, didn't you? You're the one responsible for covering up the details of the crash. How soon were you tipped off that I was in an accident? That night, later that week?"

"I was called about the accident the minute it came over the police wire. Of course I did everything I could to keep you out of trouble. I was trying to protect the Colton name. You would've dragged it through the mud."

A chill washed over Levi. "What did I do that night that made you think you needed to protect the Colton name? Was the crash my fault?"

"I figured you'd been drinking."

"I hadn't."

"I know that now. At the time, the pictures looked like they had *drunk driver* written all over them, especially since it happened the night of Eileen's funeral. I figured you were out of control."

He had been, but not with liquor or drugs—those were his mother's crutches, not his. "You saw pictures?"

"Of course I saw pictures. Read the report, too. I paid good money to get all the copies destroyed. You ought to be thanking me for getting you the best medical care my money could by and keeping your driving record clear."

Levi's fury surged anew. From behind gritted teeth, he said, "I never asked you to do any of that."

"You didn't have to. I took it on myself."

"Other people's lives were involved. Didn't you care about the other car, about the people I hit? I never got the chance to make amends."

"Don't be a sissy. Family comes first."

Levi couldn't believe what he was hearing. "Family?" he growled. "You're not my family. You're a monster."

"Don't talk to him that way," Catherine said. "He's sick and he's weak. I know you're angry, but can't you see this isn't helping?"

Jethro patted the bed near her. "It's all right, Cath. I can speak for myself." He returned his attention to Levi. "Am I a monster? Maybe so. But I stand by the choices I've made. I refuse to die with regrets."

Pacing to the window and back, Levi plunged his fingers into his hair, getting a grip before he lost control. "You said you read the police report. Do you remember the names of the people I hit?"

"Not a chance."

Levi drilled him with a glare. "It was Kate, Jethro. I hit Kate's car."

"My God." Catherine dropped onto a chair. "That's how Kate's husband died? I can't believe it."

"That's not all," Levi said, holding Jethro's hard stare. "She was eight months pregnant and lost the baby as a result."

That got Jethro's attention. He jerked his face away and looked at the floor. "I didn't know that."

"I was ready to try for a relationship with her. Something that mattered." Echoing Kate's words made the pain of the truth howl in his heart. "Then, come to find out, I killed her husband and unborn baby when I slammed into their car. I can never fix that for her, and I can't take it back. I ruined her life. You ruined her life, too. A father/son one-two punch. It's like I can't escape your evil no matter how hard I try."

"I did what I thought was right." Jethro's facade of arrogant sarcasm was gone, replaced by a voice thick with emotion.

Levi fisted his hands on the side of the bed and sank into them, drained and defeated. "It's the damnedest thing, too, because I had forgiven you. I'd made my peace with being the son you didn't want. And now this? Where do we go from here, Jethro? How can I be your doctor when I hate you all over again?"

Somewhere in the house, someone or something made a sound like a scream.

Levi stood, cocking an ear to the open door. "Did you hear that?"

"What was it?" Catherine said. "One of Trip's video games?"

A second scream came, a woman's voice, shrill and scared.

*Kate.*

Before he could react, an explosion reverberated through the house. Then another.

Jethro threw his covers off and swung his feet over the side of the bed. "That was a…"

But Levi already knew what it was and had taken off running. For a man who grew up in the Wyoming backcountry, there was no mistaking the sound of gunshots.

Levi ran the length of the third-level hallway, listening. Behind him, Jethro and Catherine quarreled about him staying in bed. A floor below, a door opened. No more gunfire or screams rang out.

He ran through the list of possible places Kate would've gone when she left his room. The kitchen came to mind first. As Gabriella had pointed out, it was the place she liked to hide. He doubted she would've returned to her bedroom, as trashed as it was.

The third possibility filled him with a mixture of hope and fear. What if she'd left? What if she'd taken one of the ranch trucks and blasted out of town? The roads were dangerous, and if that was the case then he had no way to contact her. Then again, if she'd left, then she was out of danger of whoever had fired that gun.

He refused to entertain the possibility that she had been the woman who screamed.

*Please, don't let it be her.*

He flung open the door to the employee stairwell. In his haste, he hadn't grabbed a flashlight, so he groped through the darkness until he felt the knob of the second-level door. He opened it a crack, listening. Somewhere in the house was a person with a gun, and he'd be no good to Kate if he was ambushed.

He heard women's voices in the hall talking frantically and stepped out of the stairwell, breaking into a jog toward Kate's room. One of the maids shrieked, and Mathilda clutched her chest. "It's me, Levi. Have you seen Kate?"

"No. What was that noise? It sounded like a gun," Mathilda said, shining a flashlight in his direction.

"I think it was. Go back to your rooms and lock the doors. But let me have that flashlight first, will you?"

She handed it over and continued with a litany of questions, but Levi was firm in his purpose and kept moving. The door to Kate's room was closed. No lights glowed under the door. With Kate afraid of the dark, he knew immediately she wasn't inside. He opened the door anyway to be sure. "Kate?"

He scanned the disastrous space with the flashlight and hovered for a moment on the message on the mirror. *BUTT OUT OR DIE.*

Choking on a fresh surge of panic, he pedaled back and sprinted for the stairs, past Mathilda, who looked to be gathering the female staff members in a single room.

He loped down the stairs, moving far faster than before with the benefit of the flashlight. He skidded to a halt at the first-floor landing and shone the light down the stairs toward the basement. The idea that Kate might be down there, trapped or hurt or hiding in fear, sent a chill up his spine.

He raced to the bottom and threw open the single door, shining the flashlight into a vacant laundry room. "Kate, it's me. Are you down here?"

He paused, listening, and was answered only by yawning silence. Back on the first level, he crept forward into the employee dining room.

The muted whir of a machine was the only sound. Levi assumed it was the generator he'd helped Gray set up the day before to power the kitchen appliances. A small green desk lamp glowed brightly in the empty room, indicating that this room shared a circuit with the kitchen. Rather than turn any other lights on and potentially alert the gunman to his presence, Levi lurked through the hallway to the kitchen, which remained shrouded in darkness.

The kitchen was deserted and Levi was losing his patience. Where the hell was Kate? Or the woman who'd screamed. Where was the person wielding the gun? He jogged through the kitchen to the swinging door leading to the formal dining room and skidded on a slick spot in front of the pantry.

Arms flailing, he went down hard on his side. The flashlight clattered out of reach. Cursing, he flipped to his knees and pressed his hands into the goop-covered floor. The liquid was thick, tacky. Cooking oil? He pulled himself up on the center island, wiped his hands on his pants and punched the overhead light on. The red-brown smear left on the light switch had him doing a double take.

He looked at his hands. He was covered in blood.

His ribs seemed to tighten around his lungs. His gaze rocketed to the floor and the pool of blood stretching from the pantry out. A woman's bare feet lay prone on the pantry floor. As a doctor, he knew blood loss as significant as this didn't indicate more than the slimmest odds of survival, but if that was Kate, if there was a chance she was still alive…

Working on autopilot, he lurched into action, sloshing through the blood pool. A woman's body lay on the pantry floor, her arms and legs at odd angles and straight, brown hair covering her face.

Clamping his molars together, he hung his head and exhaled a ragged breath. It wasn't Kate. While it remained a tragedy of the worst magnitude that someone had died, he couldn't stem the relief that it wasn't the woman he loved.

He squatted near the victim's head and checked for a pulse at her neck. Nothing. Damn it.

A killer was loose in the house and Kate could be anywhere. There was no time for fear or hesitancy. Leaving the victim, he went straight for the knife block on the counter and withdrew the largest knife he saw.

A clatter of movement sounded behind him. He whirled, wielding the knife.

A man slammed into him from the side and tackled him to the ground on his stomach. Levi's mind raced. He jabbed with his elbows and tried to get the knife into a stabbing position. Whoever had a hold on him, though, knew his way around a brawl.

In a flash, a hand clamped around the wrist of Levi's knife-wielding hand. Levi fought to buck the man off as his hand was slammed repeatedly into the ground until the pain forced his fingers open. The knife clattered to the tile.

Fists it would have to be, then, because someone lay dead in the pantry, and there was no way Levi was letting the assailant kill him, too. He twisted, creating a pocket of space to get his knees under him. Grunting, he shoved up with all his might. He nearly had the man's weight off him enough to reach for the knife when hard metal pressed into his back.

"Don't touch that knife, Levi, or I swear to God I'm going to shoot a hole through your gut."

Levi froze. He knew that voice. "Trevor?"

"Yeah, I know who I am—now put the palms of your hands on the floor."

Levi complied. Trevor was no murderer. That meant the real killer was still somewhere in the house. "Trevor, listen. Everyone in the house is in danger. A woman was killed in the pantry. I don't know who it is. Whoever killed her is still somewhere nearby."

Trevor pushed away from him and stood. “Stay on the ground,” he commanded.

He hadn’t realized until that moment that Trevor thought he was the one who’d killed the woman. “Come on, Trevor. You can’t think I killed her. I don’t have a gun. I’m a doctor, goddamn it.”

“Jethro has guns all over this place. There’s nothing sayin’ a man has to own a gun to know how to operate one. How did you get here so fast? I came as soon as I heard, but you were already down here, a knife in your hand and covered in blood.”

“I know what it looks like. I heard the shot, came running and slipped on the blood in the dark. You’ve got to believe me.”

A stream of people rushed past him into the kitchen. Levi was facing the cupboards and couldn’t see who it was. “Let me up, Trevor. Come on. We’re wasting time.”

A woman’s yelp sounded. “It’s Jenny. She’s dead.”

Levi was lifted up by the scruff of his shirt. “Up. Now.” The gun was shoved back into his kidney.

He looked at each and every one of the crowd of faces staring at him, some disgusted, others scared. “I’m telling you, I didn’t do it—”

“Let him go, you idiot. He was with me when we heard the shot. He just moves a bit faster than I do.” Jethro stood in the doorway, bracing his forearm on the threshold as if the trek to the kitchen had used up the last of his reserve strength.

Trevor’s gun dropped immediately.

“What are you doing out of bed?” Levi asked.

Jethro’s eyes narrowed. “I’m not dead yet, and this is still my house. What’s going on? Whose blood is that?”

“Jenny’s,” one of the maids said.

"I don't see why we're all still standing here," Levi said. "Someone shot Jenny and I'm not him, which means the killer's still in the house or on the grounds. Gather everyone in the dining room and figure out who's not here. Anyone seen Kate?"

"Mathilda's gathered the women in her room," Catherine said, coming up behind Jethro. "She called my cell phone to let me know she has all the housemaids with her except Agnes and Kate."

Jethro and he exchanged a look. Jethro's jaw rippled and Levi could tell he understood the fear Levi was feeling for her safety.

With a subtle, private nod to Levi, he said, "Levi's right. We're wasting time. There's a killer on my property and a dead body in the pantry. Who's called the police? Anyone have any sense left?"

"I'll call the police," Catherine said.

"Everyone else in the dining room like Levi said. It's time for roll call."

The ring of the house phone cut through the murmur of voices that ensued as people filed to the dining room. Levi and at least a half-dozen others flinched at the unexpected sound. Trevor picked up the line. His expression turned stony as he listened.

He hung up and stroked the handle of his gun. "That was a reverse 9-1-1 auto call that everyone needs to evacuate immediately. The fire's coming."

# Chapter 18

People poured outside by the dozens. According to Gray, every vehicle on the premises was accounted for, which meant Kate, Agnes and Trip—the only residents of the house who hadn't checked in for the dining-room roll call—hadn't left the grounds.

The fire line was visible in the nearest valley and inching closer by the minute. Concern shifted from finding the murderer lurking in their midst to locating the three missing persons before the fire reached the property line and cut off access to the two roads leading in and out of the ranch.

While trucks were filled with evacuees or driven off by one of the handful of men and women staying behind to notify those ranch workers living on the outskirts of the property of the evacuation code red, Levi congregated in the driveway with Jethro, Gray and Trevor to form a search party.

Levi was out of his mind with fear. Only the hope of finding Kate kept him upright and moving. He fought for numbness, fought to stop feeling so intensely, so he could concentrate on bringing her into his arms once more. The alternative was inconceivable.

"The fastest way to search the grounds is on horseback," Jethro said. Life had returned to Jethro's pallor, but being up and about was nothing compared to riding a horse through the ash-thick air in the middle of the night. "We leave no building left unsearched, sweeping west to east."

"Sounds good to me," Levi said. "But are you sure you're up for this?"

Jethro scoffed. "What's it going to do, kill me?"

They jogged across the grounds toward the stable and were halfway there when the shadow of a man darted across the yard.

"Over there. Nine o'clock," Levi shouted. He and Gray sprinted ahead, eating up the ground between themselves and the fleeing man. Gray tackled him by the legs before he cleared the driveway. Levi leaped on top of him, pinning him down. He straddled the man and shoved his chin up with his palm.

"Let go of me," the man shouted. "What's wrong with you?"

"It's Trip," Gray said.

Levi didn't ease up on his chin hold. "Where have you been?"

"Out."

"Wrong answer," Gray said. "Get him up so we can pat him down for a gun."

Levi rocked off his torso. Gray grabbed him by the shirt and hauled him to standing.

"Why would I have a gun? I don't get it," Trip whined.

While Trevor searched for a gun on Trip, Levi asked, "Do you know where Kate is?"

Trip looked more baffled by the second. "What? No." He smacked at Gray's hand. "Get off me."

Jethro, Catherine and the others had gathered around.

"Shut your hole, boy, unless you have an alibi for where you've been the past hour," Jethro said.

Trip shrank a little. "I'm going to tell my mom about this."

"Check this out," Gray said, pulling a gallon-sized plastic bag from the waistband of Trip's pants. It was stuffed with green, fresh marijuana leaves. "There's something in his pocket, too." He dug deep, ignoring Trip's sniveling protests, and held up a diamond ring.

Catherine said, "That's Jenny's ring. Oh, my God, Trip, what have you done?"

"Huh? Jenny gave it back to me."

Levi was losing his patience. He glanced at the fire line. He'd support Gray and Trevor with Trip for another minute, and then he was getting on with his search for Kate. They were running out of time.

"Jenny did, huh? When?" Trevor asked.

"Tonight."

Trevor got up in his face. "Nice try. Jenny's dead."

Trip's mouth hung open. "Is this some kind of joke?"

Gray waved the ring in his face. "How do you explain this if you didn't kill her?"

"Aw, man. Is she really dead?"

Trevor shook Trip's shirt. "Stop whining and tell us how you got this ring."

"I was with Jenny in my room a couple hours ago and we had a fight. She told me she was done with me because she had something else in the works and was going to make a lot of money. She was going to keep the ring but that wasn't fair. I was so pissed, I took it back anyway. Dude, I'm telling you, I would never hurt her. I was going to marry her."

"Then explain to us why you were out here running in the dark," Catherine said.

"I was checking my stash. The pot, man. I didn't want my whole crop to go up in flames, so I was out there harvesting what I could. Check out the bag."

"This clown didn't kill Jenny," Gray said.

"I'm with you on that," Trevor said. "I'll take him up to the house and see if anyone's found Agnes yet. Keep me updated on your search for Agnes and Kate."

Levi nudged Jethro. "I've got to keep moving to the stable, guys. I'm going crazy not knowing where Kate is."

"I'm right behind you," Jethro told Levi. "My body's working a little slower than yours right now."

"Then you need to take a break," Levi told him.

"Hell, no. Your woman's missing. Let's get out there and find her."

With a nod, Levi took off for the stable. He should have never let Kate out of his sight, not after her push down the stairs and her ransacked room. He'd been so mired in regret and anger about the past that he'd failed to protect the woman he wanted to be his future.

If she was alive, then somehow he had to get her to see that he wasn't the same man who'd crashed into her car. He'd spent every day since the accident trying to atone for that night, as well as the temper he once had. He'd beg for her to give him a second chance. Never again would he let his past cloud his judgment.

The lights were off in the stable. Levi yanked a lantern off a nail by the door and barreled in. "Kate?"

Rather than Kate, he saw Agnes. She lay on the floor, blinking and groggy.

"Agnes, what happened?"

He rushed to her side and checked her over. She sported a hematoma on her head the size of a grapefruit. Footsteps sounded behind him. Through the door, Jethro, Gray and Catherine piled into the stable.

"It was a man," Agnes told them. "But I couldn't see who. Too dark. He's got her. He's got Kate."

Jethro brought a handgun out of his pants pocket and flipped off the safety. "No time to lose. Let's saddle these horses and get this rescue going. I don't like the way the odds are stacking up against your pastry girl."

"I'll get Agnes up to the house," Catherine said.

Levi, Jethro and Gray worked at lightning speed, gearing up the two horses in minutes flat.

"Jethro, you go back to the house," Gray said. "You're in no shape for this."

"Not on your life," Jethro said. "This is something I've got to do."

There was no time to waste with arguing. With a nod, Gray acquiesced.

Outside, Levi and Jethro swung into the saddles. "Which way should we start?" Jethro asked.

A wall of flames was coming from the west, and to the east was absolute darkness. Levi couldn't imagine the killer taking Kate toward the fire, but that was also the direction of the most immediate danger. It made the most logical sense to start there and sweep their way east. As he debated, a high-pitched sound drifted over the wind. A scream.

"Did you hear that?" Gray asked.

For the second time that night, Levi felt like throwing up. "Sure did. Let's go."

They sped off toward the valley that was engulfed in flames, in the direction of the scream that continued to drift intermittently over the wind. Levi rode in the lead. The air was almost too thick to breathe. His eyes stung and his lungs burned. How could anyone survive these conditions?

He glanced beside him at Jethro, whose shoulders slumped. Whatever was compelling Jethro to help Levi, he was grateful, even if he wasn't sure he could ever forgive his father for what he'd done to Kate.

On the edge of his vision, barely visible in the ghastly, putrid air, Levi spied movement. A horse and rider. "Look left," he called. "You see that?"

"Sure do."

They spurred their mounts faster, gaining ground on the mystery rider.

"There's a second person on the horse," Jethro said.

Levi wiped debris and water from his eyes and took a harder look. Jethro was right. Someone had been flung sideways over the saddle, stomach down, if Levi's eyes were seeing it right. It had to be Kate.

He was a man possessed now. Urging his horse on, he and Jethro pushed their mounts to their limit, riding straight at the fire.

The other rider seemed to finally notice them and swerved, dropping onto the dirt-road firebreak around the ranch's perimeter, parallel to the wall of flames that was so close, Levi could've hit it with a rock.

"I'm going to squeeze off a warning shot," Jethro called. "Let's see if we can scare him into making a mistake."

The crack of the gun was absorbed by the roar of the fire, but it did the trick. The rider vaulted from the horse, leaving Kate on. She stayed on her belly as if she was tied in place.

The man scrambled down the hill toward the flames. Jethro squeezed off a succession of shots in the man's direction, but Levi didn't take the time to see if he hit his target. His sole concern was Kate, still trapped on the runaway horse.

Levi stayed the course to Kate, never letting his gaze waver lest he lose sight of her horse in the dense smoke and darkness. After what seemed like an eternity, Levi's steed bridged the distance to Kate's horse.

"Levi!"

"I'm here, Kate. I'm going to get you off of there." He nudged his horse's flanks until the two mounts were galloping neck and neck.

"I'm tied on," Kate said, squirming. "I can't break free."

Ahead of them, flames fanned over the dirt path, threatening to breach. As their horses careened toward the fire, Jethro's horse appeared on the other side of Kate's. Over his head he swung a rope. A lasso.

Ingenious.

"Hang on, Kate. Jethro's got an idea."

Levi held his breath as the lasso soared through the air. If Jethro missed this toss, there was a chance he wouldn't have time to try again before the fire was upon them.

Jethro didn't miss. The rope settled around the horse's neck. He pulled, putting all his weight into it. Levi turned his horse in, crowding Kate's mount, pressuring it to slow. With the force of the lasso and Levi's efforts, the runaway horse dropped its speed.

"Whoa, there," Jethro hollered. "Easy, boy."

Finally, the horse came to a halt.

Levi vaulted from his horse while Jethro continued to keep pressure on the rope from astride his mount.

Kate was crying and shaking. Levi tore the bindings from her wrists and waist, then pulled her into his arms. Relief had never felt so sweet. "I've got you."

"We have to keep moving," Jethro said in a weary voice. "This fire is itching to do some damage, and I don't know how much longer I'm good for."

Levi looked at Jethro. He'd caved over his saddle, looking gaunt and exhausted, as if he was barely able to stay upright.

"Are you okay to ride double with me?" Levi asked Kate.

"Yes. Let's get out of here."

Levi took the lasso from Jethro. "Are you going to make it home okay on that horse?"

"Midnight and I will make it just fine. You take care of the pastry girl and let me worry about myself."

Levi helped Kate into the saddle, then swung up behind her. With his arms around her, he took hold of the reins and nudged his mount's flank. The three horses lit off toward the sanctuary of the ranch. For the first time since Kate had stormed from his room, Levi felt a glimmer of hope that tomorrow would be a brighter day.

# *Chapter 19*

Jenny's memorial service had been a well-attended but quiet affair, reminiscent of Faye's. Jenny would've preferred flowers and opulence, Kate imagined, but in the wake of the fires, a grand display hadn't been possible.

The ranch chapel sat on a hill to the south of the main estate, affording views of both the fire-ravaged hillsides and vast stretches of still-pristine wilderness that had escaped the flames. Somewhere out there lay the body of the man who'd abducted her and killed Jenny. Now that the winds had died and the fire was near complete containment, police expected to send investigators and cadaver dogs looking for the body within the next few days.

As for Dead River Ranch, the firebreak that Dylan, Gray and the other ranch workers had created around the property had held, thank goodness, with only two outlying sheds destroyed. Slowly but surely life on the ranch was returning to normal.

Kate stood in the grass surrounding the chapel and closed her eyes, soaking in the sun's warmth. The past few days had flown by in a blur. Immediately following her rescue, Levi had tended to her cuts and bumps and had told her about confronting his father about the accident and that Mr. Colton had confessed to demanding preferential treatment by the paramedics for Levi, then covering up Levi's role in the crash.

The news hadn't surprised her, and it hadn't renewed her outrage at Jethro. What she'd learned since Levi had come to the ranch was that forgiveness wasn't so much about the person she granted it to, but about herself. About letting go of what hurt her and giving herself permission to move on.

Even though what Jethro did was wretched, his help in rescuing her went a long way toward fueling her compassion, as did the sharp downturn in his health that followed on the heels of that fateful night.

Though the revelations about the accident hadn't incited her anger, they had brought with them a fresh wave of grief. She'd asked Levi for solitude to think, and he'd granted it to her, not that he would've had much time to spend with her given how busy he'd been caring for his father, patching up the people around the ranch who'd sustained injuries during the fire and working with the police conducting the investigation into Jenny's murder.

The time apart from him had been good for her. She'd needed it to process all that had happened and everything she'd learned. But today, she'd woken feeling revitalized, her strength regained. It was a new day and a new beginning, at least in her heart. Jenny's memorial service had brought it home to her that it was time to let it all go—the burning need for justice, her fear and her anger about events that had happened six years ago.

It was time to tell Levi the truth about her feelings.

She turned her face up to the sun, took a deep breath, then opened her eyes. Levi was standing before her, as if conjured by her thoughts.

"Hi," she ventured, adding a small smile.

His jaw was tight, his eyes nervous. "I know you asked for space, but I'm on my way to do something that's long overdue, and I'd like you to be there."

Her pulse sped. "Of course. I was about to go looking for you anyway."

On their way to the house, he took her hand. She twined her fingers with his. Such a simple pleasure, holding hands, one she'd taken for granted when she was married. No more.

"How are you feeling?" he asked.

"Better. I haven't slept well, but that's okay because it's given me time to process everything that's happened."

"I haven't slept well, either, truth be told." The shadow of a smile crossed his face. "I'm trying to get used to the bed in the guest suite—or my suite now, I suppose—and it's too comfortable to be comfortable, if that makes any sense. And while I'm lying there tossing and turning, all I can think about is you and the time we joked about ignominious furniture. You're the first person I've met with a crossword-puzzle vocabulary."

She swung their joined hands. "I'll take that as a compliment. Maybe you should move the sofa from the employee dining room up to the suite so you can get some rest."

"I like the way you think, even if Mathilda and the rest of the staff would look at me like I was nuts."

They shared a smile. "I'd defend you."

"I know you would." He tugged her near and kissed her temple. "Jenny's service was nice. It was the first one I'd attended since my mom's, and it wasn't as hard as I thought it would be."

This wasn't how or when she'd planned on having this conversation, but one of the many lessons she'd had to figure out was to not take any opportunity for granted. "Not for me, either. After all I've been through, I think it's finally sunk in that sometimes, for no reason at all, bad things happen to good people. But being afraid of what might happen and all the millions of things out of our control is no way to live.

"Since William and Olive died, I thought I was doomed to a lifetime of being haunted by the memories of people I'd loved and lost. But I know now that's not true. Their memories aren't a burden—they're a gift. A reminder to hold tight to the people we care about and not waste a single moment of our time with them."

He squeezed her hand. "I know exactly what you mean."

She had a hunch where they were headed when they entered the house, and it turned out she was right. They walked up the grand staircase to the third level in comfortable silence and through the double doors of Jethro's suite still hand in hand.

Catherine, Amanda and Gabriella had beat Levi and Kate to Jethro's bedside after the memorial and stood near his head, describing the service to him. They offered Kate and Levi solemn smiles when they entered, then exchanged hugs with Kate while Levi took up his medical bag and began the comforting ritual of taking Jethro's vitals.

Jethro was stable, but it wouldn't be long until his final day came, something he and his half sisters had discussed at length since the night of Kate's abduction and rescue. Catherine, Amanda and Gabriella accepted the news with heavy hearts and admirable grace.

When Levi was finished with the checkup, he pulled a chair close to the bed. "I talked to Mia this morning," he said. "She's on her way back to the ranch. She said the fire's ninety percent contained with full containment expected by tonight or tomorrow."

"Thank goodness," Jethro said. "This place has withstood one danger after another since I built it thirty years ago. It'll take a lot more than some backwoods fire to shut it down."

"Agreed." Levi smoothed the edge of Jethro's blanket, then touched his shoulder. "Your vitals are stable. How are you feeling?"

"Like all the people who've told me to go to hell are finally getting their way." Jethro grinned before succumbing to a round of rattling coughs.

Levi helped him sit and braced an arm on his back. All his hatred for Jethro had evaporated, replaced by pity for the shell of the powerful force of nature Jethro Colton once was.

For the past few days, Levi had had a lot of time to contemplate his return to Wyoming and what he wanted from his life moving forward. The more he reflected on his mom and his meeting with Luella, the clearer his choice came into focus. On the surface, it didn't seem fair that his mom had died while Luella, equally weighed down by drugs and inner demons, lived on. But the truth was that the drugs were only partially to blame for his mom's death. The real culprits that killed her were bitterness and pining for a person who'd rejected her.

He'd been on the same path, poisoning himself with bitterness. It was time to break the cycle. After all the years and energy he'd wasted hating his father, Levi had finally figured out that breaking the curse of his Colton identity was entirely within his control. To free his heart and spirit to love Kate like she deserved, this was what he needed to do. It was time to forgive Jethro, not because he deserved it, but because Levi did.

He set a hand on Jethro's arm. "I couldn't have saved Kate without your help. Thank you."

Jethro turned his weary eyes on Levi. "Let's just say I owed it to her."

"There's something else, and it probably doesn't matter for you to hear, but it matters to me to say. We may never see eye-to-eye on much, and I don't understand most of the choices you've made, but for the first time in my life, I'm at peace with my past and having you as my father." In his heart and all around him, he could feel his mom's presence, not haunting him, but giving him courage to take this final step. "What I'm trying to say is that I forgive you. For everything."

A hand touched Levi's shoulder and he turned to see his three half sisters behind him, smiling and teary-eyed. Kate entwined her fingers with his and held on tight. Their support lightened him as much as the forgiveness he'd granted. It was the sensation not of a weight being lifted from his shoulders, but of a weight shifting so that the burden was shared. He knew unequivocally that he'd never again walk this world alone.

Jethro's bloodshot eyes met Levi's. He slipped his arm out from under Levi's hand and patted Levi's forearm. "I wished Eileen would've taken you away from this town, away from me. Being a Colton man is a curse. We're born with a fire in our hearts and stubborn independence in our blood. Turns us into hardened men if we let it. I didn't want that for you. I know you don't think I did anything for you all these years, but I kept you away from me, and that's got to count for something."

Levi cleared his throat, fighting the lump that had settled there. "It counts for a lot."

"My girls, they think they're doing me a favor by going behind my back and hiring a private investigator to look for Cole, but they're not doing anybody any favors. If Cole's alive, he's better off not being dragged into this. Besides, I want to spend my final days in peace, not digging up old feelings I've put to rest. Girls, swear to me you'll stop looking for Cole."

Amanda took hold of Jethro's hand. "Okay, Daddy. We swear. The P.I. we tried to hire fell through anyway, so you don't have to worry."

Jethro grunted, clearly having reached the limits of his sentimentality. "Good, because I don't need any more people making plays for my money after I die. I'm just relieved that's not what this one came here after."

The declaration was said with a hearty measure of affection, as though Jethro was remembering Levi's first day on the ranch, their first run-in, and was offering Levi the closest thing to an apology that he was capable of for the insulting assumptions he'd made. "You're finally coming around about that?"

Jethro snorted, then smiled. "I've gotten a few things wrong over my lifetime, and that was one of them."

"You were right about one point, though."

"What's that?"

Levi swallowed. This was it—the moment he'd waited all day for. "As you pointed out last week, I am, indeed, in love with the pastry girl." Kate's hand stiffened within his. He turned and met her look of surprise. "I'm in love with you."

He didn't care that his half sisters were there and who knew how many mousy maids listening from the corners or in the hall. No more self-protecting shields, no more distance or bitterness. If he was going to be a man worthy of her, he had no choice but to give up everything that was holding him back.

"I've been falling in love with you since the minute I heard you arguing with Jethro about bread pudding. You breathe life into this house, into me. You've shaken me awake, and there's no going back. I feel freer and more alive than I ever have, thanks to you. I don't know how to win you over after all that's passed between us, but I know that I love you. More than I've ever loved anyone.

"You're the brightest light I've ever known. I'll never eat crème brûlée or bread pudding or peaches without thinking about you. I want to do the Sunday crossword together and teach you how to ride horseback. I crave talking with you and touching you like nothing else I've ever longed for, like a hunger that won't go away. And I know now that I'll never be satisfied until I wake up next to you every morning for the rest of my life."

She pulled back to look at him. Her eyes were glassy with unshed tears.

His breath caught in his throat. "Say something, Kate."

She looked at their joined hands. "When I was on that horse and I could feel the heat of the flames, I thought I was going to die, and all I could think about was you and how I'd never get the chance to tell you how wrong I was about what I said and how much I love you. I can't imagine a future without you in it. Please say you'll let me take care of you forever."

His gaze locking with hers, his heart filled with happiness beyond anything he'd dreamed was possible. "It would be an honor, Kate McCord. The greatest honor of my life."

Catherine, Amanda and Gabriella clapped.

"Kiss her already," Jethro said.

Levi took her face in his hands and ran his thumb over her trembling lower lip. "Don't rush me, old man. This is the good part."

Then, in the presence of his family, right there in the room where his love awakening had begun, he pressed his lips to those of the most magnificent, beautiful woman he'd ever met and kissed her for all he was worth.

* * * * *

# *Join the Mills & Boon Book Club*

Want to read more **Intrigue** books?
We're offering you **2 more** absolutely **FREE!**

We'll also treat you to these fabulous extras:

- **Exclusive offers and much more!**
- **FREE home delivery**
- **FREE books and gifts with our special rewards scheme**

***Get your free books now!***

**visit www.millsandboon.co.uk/bookclub**
**or call Customer Relations on 020 8288 2888**

**FREE BOOK OFFER TERMS & CONDITIONS**

Accepting your free books places you under no obligation to buy anything and you may cancel at any time. If we do not hear from you we will send 5 stories a month which you may purchase or return to us—the choice is yours. Offer valid in the UK only and is not available to current Mills & Boon subscribers to this series. We reserve the right to refuse an application and applicants must be aged 18 years or over. Only one application per household. Terms and prices are subject to change without notice. As a result of this application you may receive further offers from other carefully selected companies. If you do not wish to share in this opportunity please write to the Data Manager at PO BOX 676, Richmond, TW9 1WU.

BS/ONLINE/I1

# *The World of Mills & Boon®*

There's a Mills & Boon® series that's perfect for you. We publish ten series and, with new titles every month, you never have to wait long for your favourite to come along.

---

**Blaze®**

*Scorching hot, sexy reads*
4 new stories every month

**By Request**

*Relive the romance with the best of the best*
9 new stories every month

**Cherish™**

*Romance to melt the heart every time*
12 new stories every month

**Desire™**

*Passionate and dramatic love stories*
8 new stories every month

*Visit us Online*

Try something new with our Book Club offer
**www.millsandboon.co.uk/freebookoffer**

M&B/WORLD2